Dr Gillian Polack is a writer, editor, historian and teacher, with doctorates in both history and creative writing. Several of her books have been short-listed for awards. She is a member of Book View Café and also blogs for the History Girls and for Medievalists.net. In her copious spare time she practises sarcasm, cooking, reading and narrative analysis.

From her very first novel readers told her that her fiction reflected her life, when it really didn't. To make up for this, she generally includes at least one real episode in each of her novels. She vows to stop doing this after *The Year of Fruit Cake*.

The Year of the Fruit Cake

OR

Aliens With Irony

BY

Gillian Polack

The Year of the Fruit Cake

All Rights Reserved

ISBN-13: 978-1-925759-91-4

Copyright ©2019 Gillian Polack

V1.0

Printed in Palatino Linotype and Arno Pro.
Cover art and design, Luke Spooner.

IFWG Publishing International
Melbourne

www.ifwgpublishing.com

To Vonda

The Observer's Notes

I AM OTHER

My experiences as a Human, for the most part in Canberra around the Year 2016, chronicled in a bastard form of the English language.

These are my personal observations, made for private purposes only, and should not be taken as part of the official documentation of my work on the species. They reflect nothing more than my passing responses to my circumstances.

The Observer's Notes

I try.
Every day, I try.
Some days I like this planet. Some days I despair.
Every day, I try.
Some days I am trying. Some days the human race is trying.
Every day, I try.
I'm more grateful than I can say that I'm not human, though every day, I try.

Notes towards an Understanding of the Problem

*D*on't stop me now!
It was a *Queen* kind of night. The bright, forever-in-the-moment Queen. So different to the quality of their friendship. Yet it brought them together.

That was the moment of wonder. Not the joys and terrors of life. Not even meeting an alien. Having a great time out, as if they were entitled to joy. Normal stuff wins, hands down, always.

Normal stuff is way harder than meeting aliens. It's also something we try for, every day. Meeting aliens is a *meh*! kind of thing. We might be kinda-sorta interested, but we hardly spend our whole lives striving for it. Not unless we're astrophysicists, really. And astrophysicists don't tend to *meet* aliens. Aliens *try* to meet aliens from time to time. I speak from experience. Life is more ironic than it ought to be.

It comes down to who the alien is, really, and what they're trying to achieve.

An astrophysicist once tried to meet me. I refused. End of story.

Also, it's not this story, and not this planet. The Research Branch and normal human culture were neither of them involved. It was, in fact, not related to human culture at all. The problem is that human culture and my own, when we meet in the middle, provoke digression.

Humans claim there are many human cultures, but I only know this single one. The one represents the many. We always focus on knowing something well by drilling deep down into it, rather than by general understanding. It's who we are. It's also easier to represent mathematically.

Enough wittering. Back to middle-aged women. They're important. Another thing that ought not be ironic at all and yet is pretty ironic. Given the cultural contexts of middle-aged women, and given the circumstances I'm writing about, irony is unavoidable. Given the language I'm composing in, wittering is also unavoidable. Its vocabulary and structural potential encourage enhanced wittering. Let me say now, before I go any further, that this language is not the strangest I've worked with, but it comes close.

Middle-aged women often remind themselves that they're permitted happiness. They could remind themselves that they're normal, too, but that's harder.

"Normal" is what appears in ads and in focus groups. "Normal" isn't a woman over 45, however successful and however interesting and however precisely she reflects demographics or belongs to an average family. It's easier to be permitted happiness. That's why normal stuff wins, hands down—it's so damned difficult.

I've been struggling with this subject for years, and it never gets easier. I don't know how they get through life, myself. I possibly should find out, but it's not essential. All this learning is to address a far bigger question.

Today's set of notes covers how they bonded. Five women who, for their own reasons, had developed a broken record of "*I'm allowed to be happy*" and who, one night, one cold night when the wind was off the snow and the golden wattle lined the streets, all decided "I am doing this thing called happiness, now, with a group of people I've never met in my life."

If they'd met the Devil that night, he would've been included in the group. A bit more reluctantly, mind you, because it's harder to relax in a group that's not all women, but he would still have been welcomed. Unless he was a jerk, of course. That would have prevented the hunt for happiness even before it properly got started.

These women became each other's good luck trinkets. When things went too bad, they met and distracted each other, supported each other, talked it out.

All the crises. All the time. Because nothing was going to stop them. Not now.

How they met is almost irrelevant. The mood that the meeting carried with it, that's what transformed their lives. Nevertheless, how they met possibly needs to be chronicled. In case it's important.

Even the smallest things can change worlds, after all, and at the very least, this evening on the town changed five lives. Maybe it changed the human world. Maybe it changed a lot more than that. And if this moment had a backing tape, it was Queen, being unstoppable.

This voice echoing my ideas in someone else's words is also unstoppable. You'll just have to accept it for now. I'm immersed in my subject.

Humans tell story and music, and the story *is* music and the music *is* story. They seldom understand the purity of music but then, only a few of them have an inkling that purity is even possible. This intrusion by music, then, is one of the large differences between them and us. Music is not a social activity. And narrative is not at the core of our being. I'm writing about aliens, in their own language, using their own constructs. And, sometimes, those constructs are exceedingly alien indeed.

The city's pub scene isn't that friendly to middle-aged women. Trina was fine there, most of the time, for her makeup and hair and clothes demonstrated that she was really twenty. Inside and outside matching. The body-age itself lying. Her makeup suggested borderline vampire, and her outfit suggested Rocky Horror. Her hair was coloured into submission, and those dark blue and purple streaks also suggested that she wasn't forty-nine. This is where her unstoppability came from that night. She knew she rocked her outfit and she was determined to do so in town, along with the teens. Only the teens were drunk and didn't care.

It didn't dampen the mood that they didn't care. She had been hit upon three times, so of course it didn't matter. She'd made her point.

Trina looked up and down the pub segment of London Circuit and decided that pubs were more her scene than clubs, in any case. A better class of hitting upon, especially as she was old enough to be the last youth's mother. *American Horror* she was happy to be. *Mrs Robinson*, not so much.

Then she decided that chocolate was essential to her existence. Better to be alone at a table with good chocolate than getting drunk with a group of out-of-control teens. *It's odd,* she thought, *that being drunk seemed so much better when I was putting on my makeup than it feels now.* It was the look of the pavement that had convinced her. She didn't want to spend her evening sidestepping human mess.

She wanted to retain her inner sound track. Unstoppable.

Chocolate made women unstoppable, and so chocolate it was.

Trina wasn't the only person who had eschewed the club circuit in favour of chocolate. The second-best chocolate shop in Canberra was more than full.

Trina was still unstoppable. Instead of being decorous, she shouted at the room: "Is there anyone willing to share a table?"

A sedate-looking woman her own age (or maybe a bit older, who cared?), alone at a small table, raised her hand, and not only did Trina join her, but three other women from the queue also extracted themselves and sat down. One of them had a handful of bright yellow daisies and handed them to each woman at the table. One polite woman and four unstoppables, now with personal blossoms, crowded around a tiny table, drinking hot chocolate and sharing stories of their favourite flavours. It was the safest of safe environments. The polar opposite of the one Trina had sought an hour ago. And Trina was happy.

She looked around the table. "I'm Trina," she said. "We didn't get round to names."

"Names had to wait until we ordered. Priorities. Chocolate first, life details after," the very tall woman said. She could have been an athlete. She shone with robustness. "I'm Leanne."

"Diana," said the woman whose table it had been, briefly.

"Janet," the fourth supplied, she of the daisies, "And I'm sorry we've ruined your nice quiet evening by descending upon you."

Diana blinked twice, as if she'd heard something unexpected. "Don't worry about it," she said. "I was merely people-watching. I'd rather have company. I didn't want to be alone at home."

"Me neither. That's why I came in search of chocolate. I'm Antoinette." Antoinette was as round as Leanne was tall. Her face, however, was divided into triangles. It was all lines and geometry. Elegant and convincing.

And that was the five of them. From that day on, when life became a trial, they found chocolate as a team. When they needed to meet, they always met somewhere that sold good hot chocolate and they crowded round a tiny table. Touching elbows and stepping on each other's toes brought back the soundtrack of that first Saturday night. Unstoppable.

The Observer's Notes

"The doctor is ready to see you now" is only ever said twenty minutes after a complete sense of futility has set in.
—said in a conversation among friends

I picked up a stray piece of paper because it offended my sense of order. I hadn't written it. It had escaped from my folder of scraps. Ideas picked up, or odd words written down and left by others at libraries. This scrap was from the hospital library.

After I'd been in hospital three days, a woman came round with books and offered me some reading. I found the paper in its pages and used it as a bookmark, then absent-mindedly slipped it into my bag when I went home. I'd dealt with the rest of the folder two weeks before, when my husband nagged me about the mess, so this was an outrider in more than one way. By itself. So much alone.

In the interest of understanding humankind, I read it before I recycled it. It said:

"He loathes me and loves me, staring at my face from a distance, as if I only half-belong in his life. I look to the right of his face so that I'm not caught staring at him the way I caught him staring at me, so that my face doesn't betray my feelings the way his betrayed his feelings towards me. His terrible pursed mouth tells me everything."

Sometimes I feel as if I understand humans. Sometimes I look at words and wonder if anyone can. Sometimes I look at words and wonder if they could be my words, and the thoughts could be mine too. My husband's mouth doesn't purse, ever. It pouts from time to time, like when I forget to put my rings on. He knows I forget things, and is scared I'll lose my rings. Especially the engagement ring. These words had my patterns, then, but not my thoughts. The English language presses patterns upon us. Styles of narrative. Thank goodness these ones were written by someone else.

I don't want to know a man with a pursed mouth. Pursed mouths indicate greed and meanness and judgement. Of these three things, the worst is judgement. My husband sulks, but he never judges.

The woman's slow voice...

was counting again

One, two, three, four, five. I started school. It was a bold day. Bright and hot. I wanted to wear my yellow hat.

"You don't wear your yellow hat to school," Mummy said. "You might lose it."

I always wear my yellow hat on sunny days. Always. School, home, playground—I wore my yellow hat if it was a sunny day. I didn't want to go to school without it. I hated school if it meant not wearing my hat. I wanted to stay home and play in the sunshine, wearing my yellow hat.

After that day, I liked school. I made friends and played and ate playlunch with my friends and had a small bag of chips with my sandwich. "Your special treat," said Mummy.

It was still wrong. Yellow hats and sunny days belonged together. I still knew this. A small segment of my heart had been cut out and put aside, but I only noticed when I had to go to school on a sunny day.

I didn't understand. I still don't understand.

Yellow hats and sunny days.

It's important. I know deep down that it's very important. More important than my schoolbag. More important than holding Mummy's hand when I crossed the road. And the frills are inside the hat, not outside. The outside of the hat is bright as the sun and reflects it back. I know this. Deep inside, I know it. I hated being five. I have to remember it, because that was when I lost my hat.

Notes towards an
Understanding of the Problem

"God, it's a fucker of a day." Trina used language cheerfully, as if the day would fly away if she didn't swear. Leanne gave her one of those looks and Trina laughed. "Sorry. I always forget that you're our polite Queenslander. Next time I'll be less forcibly offensive."

"Thanks," said Leanne. "It feels wrong that I'm Ms Prunes, but…"

"But you are," Trina agreed. "You're CWA and respectable, and you keep me in line. You'd keep my girlfriend in line, too, if she were still here."

"Any news?"

It hurt Trina to even consider the absence of her loved one. Before she was forced into making an answer, Antoinette joined them.

"I'm not late, then?" She was surprised.

"Not only are you not late," said Trina, "but you saved me from bawling my eyes out." Diana had sat there, quietly, throughout, but at this she looked puzzled. "A letter," Trina admitted. "I got a letter from her." Diana still looked puzzled and this time, so did Antoinette. "My other, my heart, my soul," clarified Trina.

There was a supportive silence and, luckily for Trina, someone came round to take orders. Leanne ordered a coffee for Janet. "Janet texted me. She'll be along soon. She wanted to wrestle a son into submission. Which reminds me…" She hauled some slightly crushed flowers from her handbag. "She asked if I could give you these. They're not the regular variety. I found them on the way here, so they're entirely illegal."

"Thanks for the illegal petals. Janet'll need her coffee soon and strong, I fear me," said Trina, calm restored. "Thank Go…odness I don't have sons."

This was the pattern of their meetings. Big matters were touched on, gently. Never pushed. Never explored beyond comfort. Until the occasion was right. Much of their conversation was subtly determining whether a topic was safe or not.

Diana commented on their habit of care from time to time, and whenever she did, someone always pointed out that there was quite enough harshness in daily existence. This was the safe place. This was the place where they each worked to limit the hurt of the other. Important discussion happened; it was essential to all of them, however, that matters were touched on gently, and a sounding was taken before anyone explored with any fervour. On a bad day, they might talk only about the weather and chocolate. On a good day, the depths of the world were dissected, from their own lives to the major politics of the day. Conversation was never no holds barred.

Every meeting was different. Except that it contained them. And it contained chocolate. And flowers, generally yellow. Sometimes they met several times a week. Then they wouldn't see each other for a month. Sometimes family came first. Last meeting had been cancelled because Diana's husband wanted to see a film with his wife, and everyone respected that their time together was sacrosanct. Working relationships were to be supported, at every turn. Since it was just a get-together, they didn't feel the need to change the time. They simply cancelled it.

Today, however, was not a simple get-together.

This meeting had been called for Trina. The love of her life had sent her something from a distant city. That was all the other women knew. All she would say. That, and that Trina wanted to marry her.

Trina was torn between the rule of law forbidding their marriage, and the fact that her love wasn't quite certain about a permanent relationship in any case. They shared lifegoals and were a very political couple, and Trina's love was always travelling to persuade this person or the other that marriage rights were not something that could be delayed. That equal rights counted for all.

"I'm not quite ready," was her excuse when asked about her own marriage. Trina's excuse was that this didn't stop her being in love or having a relationship. Trina found this exceptionally ironic.

Diana found it puzzling. Diana found a lot puzzling. The others found themselves forever explaining their actions to her until they had wiped the confused look off her face. It was a hobby. They had descended on her table, and that carried with it a burden of explanation ever after. Just as she was most likely to find a table and hold it for the others, they were prone to explaining. Their tiny set of specialisations.

Diana understood a lot of things in a general kind of way, but didn't find it easy to apply her knowledge with any kind of understanding. She didn't understand why Trina put on makeup and went on the town like a young thing. Having a good time wasn't something she'd done when she was young, she explained, with slight diffidence.

"Your voice is too gentle," Antoinette said, that night. "I fear as if the wrath of heaven will rain down on me."

"I know what you mean," agreed Janet, who had finally arrived. She put down her bag and other accessories and slumped into the vacant chair with a sigh. "Just like it's raining down on me now, outside." The water rose from her in a faint breath. "My favourite teacher in school was just like that. Sweet and soft, and gave us all detention. So much detention."

"I bet it was the best subject in the universe," said Trina.

"Of course it was. If it weren't for the detention."

"Teenager wrestled?"

"For now. I'll have to reinforce the edict later."

"How long later?"

"An hour, I'm afraid."

"Just enough time for a chat," said Diana.

"Just," agreed Janet. "And to get a bit dry before it rains on me again. Even the wood I carry is soggy."

I still can't believe that these conversations were consequential. Honestly. Look at them. Take your time.

Nothing important was said. Even if you count these intimate lives of small people as world-shaking (which, for the most part, intimate lives of small people aren't), nothing important was said. And yet, we know the outcome of these ordinary conversations between five very dull people.

We know the outcome, but we're not sure it was the conversations. That's what I'm here for.

I want to write about super-technologies. About drama and the moment before death. About cliffs and people hanging from them. I want to write action and suspense and thrills and... *murder*. I'd love to write about murder. Also, mayhem. Mayhem would be entertaining to write about. All this story stuff is exciting. Alien and cool and rather fun. Why don't I have exciting things to write about?

Instead of mayhem, murder, thrills, chills or spills, I have been given an assignment so important that I can't see where the interest is. It's not that I'm bored (or maybe I am, just a little bored), it's that I'm writing down the actual real-life conversations of five middle-aged women. I've travelled across a galaxy-and-a-half to obtain them. I've learned their native language in order to write precisely. I'm embedded in their culture. Doesn't make me less bored. I'm like Janet's half-wrestled teenager.

Pivotal moments should not rest upon mugs of steaming chocolate and glasses of café latte and small pools of water turning a walking stick into a bridge across unplumbed depths. Except that, in this instance, one seems to. That moment was epochal. I know this for a fact. The numbers prove it.

I don't doubt the decision, I just wish I could see something interesting in the moment. And I've been deputed to write it. "With human style," I was told. "As fits the story. Before you do your analysis. Or maybe as an aspect of your analysis. We need to *understand*. It'll be easy, since you're researching in a human language."

That's how important this is. It's become a story. Something so change-inducing that we have to narrate it in a friendly and approachable and alien manner, lest we scare ourselves and everyone else. When did stories become acceptable? Sixty-one years ago they were unknown.

It happened sixty-one Earth years ago. Still sending shockwaves today. And so we research and we write and I compose chatty notes for the English version, in the hope that it's not too worrying. In the hope we find answers. In fact, I've been told to find answers. Make recommendations. Fix things. The tale is but a tool. Most of the records so far have bogged down in analysis, or in entertainment. They want results this time. We *need* results.

We've reached a changepoint: we're in trouble if we can't find out how and why this thing happened. Terrifying trouble.

Conversations about chocolate and children and lovers and the small details of ordinary lives. They can't turn six civilisations upside down. Except they did, and I must tell you of them.

Maybe we'll understand this time. It's what I'm here for, and I'll keep myself out of the story as much as I can (except when I forget), and I'll use narratives from the files when I can, but I'm not promising excitement. I'm also not promising that I'll keep myself out of the story, since I'm here, anyway, and I'm expected to develop opinions.

It would still be more fun if there were mayhem.

The Observer's Notes

To be natural is such a very difficult pose to keep up.
  —Oscar Wilde, read online (quotation not verified)

Hair. I hate it. I want to depilate forever and never have to get it cut, or walk the aisles in search of shampoo, or comb it down after sleeping, after a breeze, after sitting in a tall chair: I want it gone.

Today, someone stupid suggested I get the colour changed. Purple streaks would be nice, she said. Make me look younger, she said. Make me less intimidating, she said. Once you reach a certain age, she said, it's better if you look approachable.

When I told my husband, he half-agreed. Thought it might be nice. I wondered if colouring my hair would turn me into the wife of his heart rather than the wife of his preference. If hair-colour changes something as profound as that, we shouldn't be married. And yet we're happy, in our way. This means he's wrong. He does that from time to time. Says wrong things because he thinks they're what I need to hear.

That woman is even more wrong. Why would I want to look less intimidating? It's possible to be both civilised and feral, and my face should show this. Not always. Just when it counts. Like in that moment when a young woman suggested that looking less intimidating was a path one should travel. This one should not travel that path. Ever. It's important my face be able to communicate, since the other parts of my body have limited capacity to politely express disagreement.

I hate that woman. She has a name, but I do not deign to use it.

She is many years junior to me and she knows everything. Her life is easy, so of course she knows everything. It's easy to know everything when one lacks experience. The kinder life is the less one knows and the more judgements one makes.

She made many judgements about me. We talked for a whole evening, and she never stopped judging and judging and judging. Expecting me to act on her judgements. All of them. She left no room for me to negotiate or discuss or reason. All she left me was outright refusal.

It wasn't only the hair. It was the career. The marriage. The other marriage. The loss of a child. The illnesses. My child would still be alive if *my* child were *her* child, she implied. This makes me wonder whose child it was. It also makes me wonder how anyone can live with so much judgement inside them. How they can hate so easily while being so very friendly?

I got the feeling that everything would have been well between us if I only made a bit more of an effort to look the way she expected. Less like one of the crowd. Except that she also wanted me to look *more* like one of the crowd. Less like *A Woman with Issues and Almost at Menopause*. Less intimidating. More rebellious. Less my own age. More hers. She judged my life by how I look. Such a shallow young lady. So condemnatory.

I don't want to look different.

Even if I wanted to, I'm not allowed to. I'm stuck with shoulder-length hair because women my age have hair this length and in this style if they have faces the same shape as mine. I have to go into the hairdresser and tell the young lady to "keep it simple." And she does. Simple and within the tenets of normaldom. When she tells me I should change, it just makes me hate her as well as my hair. It doesn't give me permission to draw attention to myself.

Right now I wonder what I had before I had hair, why my hair is such a damned nuisance now. Fur? Scales? Bone ridges? Something *other*, that's inconceivably alien to me as a human?

I know there was something, because half a memory breaks through from time to time. Half a memory. The bad half. The half that tells me: "This bit of life was easier back home. You could change colour and you had those limbs to communicate with." What colours was I changing? What limbs did I use to help me be rude to fools? How were they articulated? There's a joke in there, about articulation enabling articulate and polite put-downs. There's no hair in that memory of mine.

It lets me remember just enough to know that I didn't need a bloody hairdryer. Nuisance memory.

My life was easier when the memory had been completely effaced and I lived in this body as if it were natural. I wasn't less angry then. I didn't know where the anger came from. That was the only difference. Now I know where it comes from, I have options. I don't need to feel guilty at looking ordinary: I can plan revenge.

I'm going to pretend I had spikes once upon a time. Long ones. Sharp ones. Golden ones. *Attack* spikes.

And we're back to humans I hate. It would be so much easier to not hate, to just be left alone. Except being left alone is what causes the isolation, the despair, the hate. I bet I had attack spikes and I bet I knew how to use them. I am a unicorn among women.

Notes towards an
Understanding of the Problem

"What do you hate today?" This was Trina's favourite question. She began conversations with it, given a chance. It had become a bit of a ritual, like Janet bringing daisies. When neither of these happened, the rest of the group felt that their luck was out. Superstitions are, I think, bits of fragmented culture that have lost their ancestral links and not yet found a home in the new order. Stray integers without an equation. Some are fading and will soon be lost. Some attach themselves elsewhere and confuse the cultural streams. Story is problematic in this way—it produces superstition. Stray integers are safer, to my mind.

Trina didn't hate much at all, as a rule. She just liked the question and its answers. "I express myself so forcefully that there's no room in me let for hate," she'd explained once. "It's all in the clothes."

"But you hate the Federal Government." Leanne was bewildered, for Trina had spent almost the whole of their previous meet-up being angry at a vast array of current political decisions.

"That's different," Trina said. "How could I even come close to approving of what's being done to people in our name on Manus?"

Diana nodded and said, "Sometimes, we have to be clear."

"Totally," said Trina. And so began the *What do you hate today?* conversation, which became a tradition very quickly. Trina's normal opening gambit became everyone's.

Today the first hate was Donald Trump, followed narrowly by the suffering the Syrians were still enduring.

"There are some times in our lives when something evil trumps even our personal issues," said Antoinette.

"You and your puns," Janet smiled across, complicitly.

"Personal hurts are important, though," said Leanne.

"I only talk about them when I'm ready," Antoinette shot in a reply before anyone else, as if she were staking a claim or avoiding being put on trial. More the latter, I think. Although one can never be quite sure, when one is reliant on human faces and body language. It tells as many lies as truth. Or as many truths as lies, for that matter. Maybe she meant what she said literally? "I can tell you now my parents disowned me, but..."

"Not ready to tell us why," said Leanne, wryly.

"May never be ready to tell you why. There are too many uncertainties."

"Friends can be counted on for this sort of thing. Even when family can't." Leanne wanted to pursue the thought. The moment when personal hurts had to be talked about because they were important.

"Just proves," said Trina, "that all of your hurts are things that you feel safe talking about. I have a friend who can't talk about his childhood. He can't talk with anyone. I only know about it because we were at school together. I saw him beaten up and ostracised by everyone but me, and he has scars on top of his scars. The beating-up was because of his ancestry, but the thing from his childhood is abuse. I'd never ask him to talk about it. His trust has eroded."

"He's Catholic," said Diana, almost tentatively.

"Well, he is, but that's not the point. He didn't have to be. Just because we're talking about those paedophile priests now doesn't mean that there isn't abuse elsewhere. And he ought never be pushed on it."

"Surely nothing like that applies here." Leanne was confident for her friends.

"Other people hurt. Other people were endangered. Not people you know?" Diana turned to face Leanne directly. It was obvious to the others that she was hiding her own hurt and that she was trying to make this clear without admitting anything.

Trina replied for everyone. "It doesn't matter whether we do or we don't. It's wrong to push a person into talking about it. I'm volunteering to talk about my hurt, but I'll never, ever make someone else talk about theirs. How do we know—" she said, her hands beginning to speak in the same key as her voice—"How do we KNOW that our friends aren't on the edge of suicide?"

"We can help them." Leanne's voice echoed vast confidence in her ability to solve the world's problems.

"Only if they'll let us," said Janet, quietly. "Pushing help on someone is taking advantage of their defencelessness. It's another form of abuse. I've been there and will fight it, every time, even if it means I act like a disobliging bitch."

"Only if they'll let us, yes. And only if they're ready. That's why you always, always wait."

"I don't get it," said Leanne, stubbornly. "Why shouldn't we help whenever we can?"

"Manus Island is what the government thinks of as help," said Diana, unexpectedly. "It's cruel and...and..."

"Inhuman," Antoinette provided.

"Yes, inhuman." Diana took up this word with relief. "But it's being done to help Australia, and to help other refugees by preventing them from coming here. And it's a complete failure on all grounds. The 'help' hurts.'"

"While this is all very nice and ethical," Leanne abruptly changed her tone, "I didn't come here to be lectured. I came for chocolate and light conversation."

"Light," said Janet. "Not like the bread I made on Sunday, then."

"Tell us about that bread," said Trina.

This is another problem with the human record. I can't know what they would have said if the conversation had not been turned aside. All I know is that one of them has secrets, and that these might be the secrets that damned the human race. If Antoinette had spoken honestly, at that moment, would there be no problem now? And what was Janet referring to?

Maybe not. Perhaps what was too big for these women to talk about was nothing at all in the reality of what was happening around them. Humans are like that.

My problem with writing about humans is that, in order to write about one, I virtually have to become one. Alien studies require changing, chameleon-like, the way our neighbours change their genders. It's supposed to be effortless and natural. God, I wish it were. Sometimes I'd exchange my few difficult gender shifts for their many, easy ones, and the way they turn each into a lifestyle with new body parts and different coloration.

Humans judging other humans for the hurt they've inflicted would be very useful for my needs, thank you. This whole project ought to be about all the damage inflicted by humans on themselves and on each other. Like the *Hitler* study. That presented us with our approach to humanity—the need to interpret from inside in order to understand. It was a neat and classic study of an obvious evil.

The classic study was wrong. Humans don't see themselves the way the Scholars did when they were bringing it together. They don't act that way for the most part. The Hitler study points to something so nasty that a whole species was easily condemned by its outcome, but it also might point to something that's an aberration for the species. It translated into mathematics easily enough, but I'm not convinced we understood that humans don't use mathematics the way we do. I'm worried we went astray by making that translation at that point.

The study was completed well before the twenty-first human century, and was one of the major reasons humans were listed as potentially in need of Judgement. Would everything have been such a mess if the Hitler study had been the great success everyone claims? Would I be evaluating an event that's technically dead and gone if we'd had any idea how that event actually unrolled?

This is one of those cases where all the knowledge in the universe doesn't necessarily lead to wisdom.

"I know," said Leanne.

"What?" Janet was quick to want that change of topic.

"I'll bring you all scones next time. Scones will help."

"Help us trust?"

"Well, maybe. I was thinking more that we can talk about food if things go funny. We did until now, only—"

"Only," said Diana, "we've exhausted the menu here. And their hot chocolate's not as good as it used to be."

"We could also try other places. They won't be as friendly," said Trina, "but it gives us something safe to fall back on if one of us has a bad day. You don't have to make scones, but the fallback is a really terrific idea."

"I like making scones." Leanne was obdurate. "I do it to support friends. And it doesn't have to be scones. I make a mean slice, and there's no-one at home who'll eat them anymore. I need an excuse to make them."

"And we need something to talk about, as backup. You're entirely right," said Antoinette. "I'll bring something too, from time to time, but it won't be food. I'm OK at cooking, but it doesn't give me any joy."

"And I'll keep bringing flowers," suggested Janet.

"Yes, to flowers. And food settles me right down. Cooking for a mob is calming."

"And we're definitely a mob," admitted Trina. "Although, if you want a different focus just today, we could talk about my amazing new footwear. Have you ever seen a heel as nice as this one?"

The next time they met up, Leanne brought an almond cake. "I've always wanted to try one of these," she explained, "and it's gluten-free, Antoinette."

Antoinette seemed surprised that Leanne had remembered. Diana seemed surprised that Antoinette was surprised. The whole group bought takeaway coffee and then they found two park benches and sat in the sun, munching on cake.

"At this moment," Antoinette declared, "I am Marie-Antoinette."

"I've always thought it was brioche they were told to eat," suggested Janet.

"Doesn't matter," said Trina. "It's cake now. In this moment, we have the Queen of France among us. I could enjoy getting fat this way."

"I get fat any way," admitted the newly-discovered late Queen of France. "It doesn't worry me."

"You're not fat, though," said Leanne as she squizzed her friend closely. "Just round in a really feminine way. I always wanted to be like that. I'm all bones and lines and sharp elbows"

A smile emerged from deep within Antoinette. A silence engulfed the group, as they sat enjoying their solidarity.

"I brought you something," said Janet, to change the subject. She handed out files, to the puzzlement of the others. "You don't have to give comments or anything. I just thought you'd like to see them."

"They're stories," said Diana, first to open the folders.

"I'm no good at cooking, and I can't do all the crafts and things, but I write a little. I thought you'd like to read a little." There was a silence. Janet was obviously used to the eventual next question and didn't wait for it. "I've had two of my stories published. There are copies of them at the back. Don't worry, I'm not plaguing you with horrendously illiterate garbage."

There was another silence. While each of the women had wondered what secrets the others held, they hadn't expected this. Janet looked far too ordinary to be a writer.

Trina found a way of saying this. "You don't look sufficiently Bohemian," she said. "And you have a day job and a husband and three children."

"Are you saying I'm too ordinary to write?" Janet wasn't at all offended. In fact, she repressed a grin.

"You camouflage," Trina responded, her dignity intact.

"It's my second-biggest secret," admitted Janet. "I don't write under my own name. I don't generally talk about my writing. It just seemed proper to share it with you, now. I don't really want to talk about it at all, but I thought you'd like to know."

"This is a great honour," said Diana, very seriously. "I've never had a writer for a friend before."

"I'm still the same person, you know." Janet's voice sounded almost edgy. "It's just part of who I am. If it makes you uncomfortable, don't read it. And I'd rather you didn't give me literary analysis—it feels really wrong from my end. I wrote it; I don't need to hear a dissection."

The angles on Antoinette's face broke up and met in wholly different angles, as her smile overtook them. "That makes it all a lot easier. I'd love to read your writing, but I really don't feel confident about making an opinion aloud."

"It suits both of us, then," said Janet, finishing the subject by snapping the last words out. "You've no idea how much courage it took me to show you my work. There are people who can talk all day about their writing, and there are writers who create email addresses that say "Billisawriter", but me, I'd rather not talk about my writing."

"Interesting," said Diana, "and perfectly fair. Thank you."

That was the highlight of the meeting. After that, conversation descended into current events, and there was no joy in the world. The only brightness came from the flowers Janet had brought.

"Thank goodness we found each other," said Leanne. "Or rather, thank goodness Diana found a table and Trina screamed until Diana heard her."

"That's not quite how it happened," said Trina. "I never screamed.

You don't want to ever hear me scream, either. I merely spoke at a reasonable volume."

"Effectively," said Antoinette, "and in a *join-me-I-am-fun* tone. You're right, Leanne, it makes everything much more able to be dealt with. I would still rather that innocents weren't murdered in gun battles in the US, and that we didn't have explosions in Oz, but if the world must come to an end, at least we have the very best people to end it with."

They toasted their very-bestness with coffee and tea. Solidarity twice in an afternoon wasn't a bad thing at all.

The Observer's Notes

The children sang and chased each other.
"Round and round the mulberry bush, the monkey chased the weasel. The
monkey stopped to pull up his socks. 'Pop!' goes the weasel."
—overheard in a park

My friend writes two kinds of stories. Only two. Her published stories all appear to be these two kinds of stories perfected. When my friend showed us her first two published stories, she showed us one of each. Will I ever get used to saying "my friend" with this kind of pride in the term? Ever since the memory started coming back, I've doubted this and that and the other, but some friendships are not to be doubted.

The first (for I am being rational and non-emotional today, and quite capable of creating a simple list) is about ghost children. These children trap other children and carry them off to somewhere mysterious. Happy lives end suddenly. They're not cruel stories. Dark, and nasty, but not cruel. The bad dreams they give me are not malicious.

She writes this tale in twenty different ways but the results are always the same. The story is always the same. Evil children create lost children.

The other type of story is not dissimilar. Dark, but not cruel.

She writes so many stories about a child who has been shunned. Every child has a different personality. Some are nice, some are noble, some are warped, and some are woeful. Society gives each and every child a set of promises. The child might read stories that promise that Cinderella will find her prince and the Ugly Duckling will become a swan. They are presented stories on film that promise great futures. Their dreams are developed through these stories and they plan many plans and live complex lives. They always end up alone. Always. Alone.

I wonder why she lets me read them. They give me nightmares.

I don't dare tell her. Thankfully, she doesn't want to hear my opinion.

Notes towards an
Understanding of the Problem

I'm damned if I know how it all went wrong. I'm going to have to go back through the whole thing, chronologically, with all the identified moments and all the interpretations and just try to work it out. Not working it out isn't an option, given that the effects are still piling up. To put it in simple terms, *how the fuck did it happen?"*

That single event changed everything, and it stymies me. I've spent years researching it just to get where I am now, being chief handler of the critical project that will help us understand and that will allow us to move on. I ought to have an answer already, given those years. What's the problem? Why am I stuck having to start yet again?

I need to make this moment a fixed point. A constant. Not a variable. Right now there are too many variables.

I need a name.

There's no term in English that comes close to summarising what happened. No formal term, and no informal one. It's a change, but calling it "the change" or even "the great change" makes the whole thing sound menopausal and whatever-deity-these-people-trust knows, I get enough of that in my source material. I can't keep calling it *it*. "Armageddon" is too long and ugly. "Collapse of all we hold dear" is too depressing and too long and not quite right. "Damn humans" is accurate, but doesn't really describe an event in English, which is a strangely limited language. I might call it "fruitcake".

This time round, I have full access to all the archives. Yay, me. The perks of power.

This is a good language for sarcasm. I should stop noting things like this so that my account is interpretable literally. So that all human studies are misinterpreted in different ways, with mine being misinterpreted subtly and the Hitler study misinterpreted coarsely. That wouldn't solve a thing, but it would cheer me up. Today I need cheering up. *Fruitcake*, even with full access, is depressing.

This full access thing isn't full access at all, to be truthful.

I get to see what happens in the vicinity of the critical incidents. It's very full access in that sense. I can see the emotional reactions in faces and the physical reactions through the bodies. I can hear the speech. I can even rebuild the feel of the table the drinks sit on when the group sits down to coffee. Mood is extrapolated, but I have a lot of material to base the extrapolation on.

The technology behind it all is extraordinary. If all I wanted to do was browse through private lives in the year of fruitcake, it would be perfect. That's what the tech was designed for: entertainment back home. What one of my subjects might describe as "porn for aliens".

There is a different issue with that, I think, and it emerges from the technology used in the interactions with Earth. It wasn't an important place—the newest and greatest technology wasn't ever bought to bear in the study of it, just the tech from which we could get the most…ah…*interesting*…results. There was a time when the anthropologists downloaded all their sensations, and those downloads were mined for profit of various kinds.

This issue isn't that. It's related, but it's less ethically dubious.

There were poor choices by those who recorded, and those who selected the equipment for recording and so on, back to the discovery of the planet and its population. Some of those choices were guided by the desire for titillation.

This means that the types of data to which I have access are limited. The amounts of material are wonderful, but it's primarily of the style we used to call "alien observer in a strange land", and doesn't look into the peoples and cultures outside small circles.

We have amazing information on several branches of English language culture, for instance, some information on other branches of English language culture, secondary information on those linked to English language culture and bugger all on the rest. This has been the case since the beginning. Even the Hitler study was mainly undertaken through the English language. If Hitler were a god in

Kurdistan (which I seriously doubt, but bear with me on this), we wouldn't know. English ignores any views that the Kurds might have on Hitler.

Why English? Because of English language distribution as either primary or alternate language in our location of choice. Why Australia? Because we like the neatness of an island continent. An underpopulated island continent without too many human buildings messing it up. Because the ground and the climate are suitable for our homes, which are always considerations when we examine a species, because it means that we can settle in a place for which we already have an affinity. We don't like inhabiting cultural wastelands or adjusting terrain to suit us.

I'm quibbling. All the work of these last years points to this group at this time in this place. The equations point to critical moments and causation, and these are them. It's the Earthlike justificatory narratives that are so damned messy, and I only fall into them in places like this, where I'm using English.

I trust the earlier work, for I've already been through it and inquisitioned it rigorously. *Fruitcake* happened because of this place and these people.

But...I feel very uncertain about the project. On top of all my doubts, it has such great importance that it could make or break my career, and that makes me want to walk delicately in the world of these far-too-dead humans.

I will call *it* "irksome fruitcake".

Now I have a clear term, I want to go back to the language issue. Spelling everything out, as if I were thinking it for the first time, is how I understand within the language. This means there is a lot of repetition here, but I need it if I'm to push past the obvious.

Earlier studies were imperfect. We knew what happened from them, but not *how*. The maths is wonderful, but it's not the story, and I think, for this, that the human reliance on stories might give enlightenment. I would have anyway, to be honest. Normally I don't write this many notes, and normally I am not so explanatory. Embedding is not a luxury this time round: it's critical.

We are trained to work in the language of the people we're studying because we need to be able to interpret nuances. Translation happens after conclusions are drawn. Old hat. Worth documenting here that I'm doing it according to these standards. This means that there'll be a lot of stuff that won't be in the final report. And, as I just said, I'm pushing the traditional right to the edge. This is partly because I have to: no-one has made sense of it at all. Maybe human language will work when a real language fails? Maybe the solution is at the interface between the two?

Just because I can, however, I translate back into *Standard*, I make my report a thing of beauty. Not only standard practice, but it means I can play silly buggers with content and get the daftness of this culture and language out of my system. This is one reason why it's standard practice, of course, but if I'm stating the obvious, I might as well state that.

This particular note, then, is for those that encounter my notes after it's all done and want to know why I wander off on tangents so often. It's because I am old-fashioned to the core, and these wanderings are part of process. They do not enter my final report. They are a way of keeping tabs on my feelings, so that my feelings won't bias the report. And they're a way of finding my way out of the mess I've been left.

Sixty-one years without a solution. Sixty-one years of suspended policy on planetary settlement. Sixty-one years of public humiliation for our species.

For irksome fruitcake, right now, I need to think like a human being. Specifically, an Australian, preferably female, in the approach to life. Preferably a *mature* female. No worries. No problems at all with this, in fact. Except that I'm not talking like just any human being. I'm talking like one particular person (initially, it will fade in and out), and that's intentional, but it's also worrying. The idea is that it will help me unravel what happened. How everything irksome fruitcakeish changed all of our lives.

It's ironic that getting into heads helps us explain a crazy culture where everyone is individual, where no-one communicates fully. Not once in their lives. Never. It's terrifying.

It's changing me, this level of individualism, and being alone. Already. Maybe humanity corrupts. That's one of the theories out there. I don't think so, however. What I think is that I'm missing something critical.

I know why the decision to send a Judge was made. Of course I do.

Humanity was on the brink of sending people into space. Had been for years, but something in the technology made it look imminent. Our test messages had been seen and we did the tally of the lives of those on Earth, and found they were destroying the planet. We did the Hitler study and that reinforced everything concerning our early ideas about Earth and its humans. One can't Judge a species on environmental destruction or on a short period of historical madness, but one can certainly use this material as a basis to send a Judge in to do a fair evaluation. We Observed and analysed and generally tried to make sense of one of the messiest species I've ever encountered. Also one of the loneliest. We did this for sixty years before we sent the Judge in.

It wasn't as if we went, "They saw us, oops, better kill them all." We don't do that.

I say this defensively, don't I? This is because one of my teachers suggests there might have been an instance where this actually happened. A long time ago. I'm certain we don't do that any more. It's only happened once, anyhow (and that's only if my teacher's right—it hasn't ever been verified or examined or definitely proven), and it's not my problem. Someone else can handle that possible, putative, previous ethical breach. Someone else can find a way of not talking about it when it has to be referred to, also. I'll just leave this note here for that someone else to handle, shall I? Thank you, someone else.

Me, my problem is why the heck things went the way they went on Earth.

If we go by what humans did and said to each other in that single year, then everything should have followed perfectly ordinary paths. They would have been Judged and either gone forever into the dust and debris of their solar system and their world freed for normal colonisation, or joined us as members of a colleague world. A very junior colleague world, given the evidence.

Instead, the whole system is adrift and there are inquiries into forty-six different situations of which this was the first. The pivotal one that led to all the others, but merely one of forty-six. Forty-six irksome fruitcakes. In a surprisingly short time period.

Incredible.

If I were to list the main news items on Earth in a single day, then the whole subject looks cut and dried. You'll be able to see our quandary more easily, perhaps. There's both a problem and no problem at all.

Before I make my little list, let me be frank about its contents: it doesn't help. It's part of my traditional approach, and this examination of main news headlines has to be shown not to work in this instance. Irksome fruitcake is still entirely inexplicable, and the situation is still a foul-smelling mess. Or maybe a chocolate-smelling mess. There's certainly chocolate in this fruitcake. (I need to ponder upon the prevalence of chocolate.)

Moreover, I can see nothing in a group of five middle-aged women that would cause our system to come crashing down. Nothing. And I can see everything in the shape of the Earth in that year that would cause a rational Judge to choose death. The continuation of whatever was happening on Earth just then wasn't even an option. Humanity at that time was spiralling downwards, and no-one sane would think it had anything redeemable about itself. It's that simple.

Except, in reality, it wasn't. Reality ignored all the equations and all the considered outcomes. We got irksome fruitcake.

Yes, I like typing "irksome fruitcake"—right now I have very few small joys, so permit me this one. If there were a word in English for this phenomenon, I'd probably still have used "irksome fruitcake", for it's the best description of this situation I've ever seen.

One single day. Let me take that one single day. Using random function is not a problem, as long as the time period I focus on comes from within the confines of the research period. So it's a random date within a non-random context. This date will show you why I'm annoyed. Or maybe it won't.

That day is (drumroll, please): 3 November 2016

The viewpoint is Australia, because that's where everything went to pieces. All this means is that my list is derived from a composite of the Australian news headlines that day from various news sources, as compiled…by humans. What a surprise. I've quickly compared headlines from other countries' viewpoints (with equal sarcasm, of course) and they're no saner. In fact, the US is completely bonkers both in that year and on that day. If the Judgement had been made in the US…

Thinking about alternate series of examinations that never happen-ed would be diverting, but it's not going to help. It's the sort of thing that humans consider, and humans are trouble. With a capital T. And besides, there's always the (distant, but less distant than before) possibility that the fruitcake was not actually caused by the perversions of humanity.

These are the top ten news stories in numerical order from a randomly selected Australian news compilation website.

1. A man is found guilty of murdering his wife
2. Someone retires
3. A TV show will be continued in 2017, even though no-one watched it in 2016
4. Someone apologises for causing a lot of trouble after he ignored safety proceedings and got lost in the bush
5. Famous sportsman on trial for child sex
6. Someone lost in another place ate wild greens to stay alive
7. A senator resigns and the government loses the balance of power, just before critical legislation is put to the Senate.
8. The fate of the world is at stake if Trump wins the election
9. Rebels reject the latest offer from Russia, and Syria is still at war
10. United Nations special rapporteur to investigate Australian immigration laws

Ten is such a very human number. Sixes and tens make up so many of their counting systems. Personally, I'd rather have ninety-eight, but in this case, ninety-eight won't be any more illuminating than ten. It's more fun arithmetically, however. And more satisfying emotionally.

Do you know how few humans spend their leisure time playing advanced arithmetic games? Almost none. Humans are depressing. They're the flour in the fruitcake, if I want to take the metaphor too far. Which of course I do. In which case lions are the raisins. I like lions. I would eat one if I were given the opportunity.

The headlines are listed in order of importance to the compiler of the stories. I erased the drama out of them and leeched all the shock from them. This is why they make such little sense. The sense is given to them in the way they're written and the way they're presented. Headlines help. One can't judge a society on headlines, however. Well, one can, but one would get into trouble from the Ethics Board.

I wonder why I'm bothering, even for completeness-sake. Except that they do show how warped humanity was in the year it was being judged. How it was very, very fortunate that we don't judge species using this kind of material. Humanity had a chance. Several chances more than it deserved, in fact. I learned that from my early research.

I hate human politics. I hate the way humans hate people. And it doesn't help that now I'm using a human language and that my emotions are somewhat human. I hate the way humans hate people, and my hate is a very human hate.

The fact that humans murder wives, damage children, ignore guidelines and rules, go to war, treat other humans harshly, is enough, isn't it? Then one adds the human who was surprised he could stay alive by eating food that occurred naturally in the region he was walking, and the fact that entertainment need not be entertaining, and one wonders about the intelligence of the species.

Except that when I learned the language, my perspective changed. The hate came into it, of course, as the emotions link more closely with one's own as one enters the depths of language. From my new perspective, humans did all the bad things and all the stupid things and all the random things, and yet they still gave meaning to their lives and they hadn't (mostly) destroyed themselves or the planet by the time we explored their world.

And I can see why, however much I hate humans, their complexity and capacity to learn means they couldn't simply be disposed of by a superficial decision based on the Hitler report. We had to do more than go through the motions of Judging back then, and we have to do more than go through the motions of sorting this mess out now.

We once deleted a species because they were capable of doing to us what humanity has already done to itself. This is why Judgement was established. Power is something that should never be wielded without due care. And once a species is dust, all we have are records. There's a deep lack of ethics.

I'll be honest and admit that the only reason humanity had a second chance is because that first time was so catastrophic. We've changed (most of the time), but not that much, really.

I don't like the process. I also don't like the fact that I've been delegated to find explanations. There's no rule or guideline that says I have to be kind to humans. If I'm stuck seeing the close, small lives of the five women, and am solely reliant on sources they had ready access to for everything else, then so be it, but I don't have to be polite or kind or gentle or nice. Humans aren't nice, and I'm doing this study in a human language. If you want backup and evidence and so forth for this decision, look again at my list of ten. Examine it. Admire it. And accept that it forces me to be sarcastic. In someone else's voice.

The woman's slow voice...

was counting again

One, two, three, four, five, six, seven, eight, nine, ten, eleven, twelve. I was twelve in 1975. I say it often so that I can remember. Twelve in 1975.

I went to high school. I wore a uniform and I caught a bus. There was a lot more to high school than this, but every school day began and ended the same way: with a bus.

I remember getting off the bus with my friend. Every day. I never remember catching the bus.

I don't know where the bus left from anymore.

I ought to know. I caught it every day. Every school day for all those years. Six.

I can count them. I can count the steps going down, one two three four. I cannot count them going up for I cannot remember going up any stairs into a bus at all. There was a vertiginous quality to descending the steps: it was personal. My feet were at war with the metal. Why can't I remember ascending, then?

I need help with my memory. There's something wrong with it. I need to start counting again. Maybe if I count again, I can remember getting onto the bus. Counting is supposed to reinforce my human memory. That's what the techs say. Every time they say it. I ask every time, as if it were the first.

Every school morning. I remember sitting on the bus. My favourite seat was halfway down, where I could hear the boys at the back and see what was happening at the front. I can remember walking to the front and getting off. I can't remember getting on the bus. I need to remember. It's become important to me. A hole in the memory of a critical year of my life.

43

Let me try again.

One, two, three, four, five, six, seven, eight, nine, ten, eleven, twelve. I was twelve in 1975. I say it often so that I can remember. Twelve in 1975. But I never got on that bus. I must have. But I never did.

Let me try again.

One, two, three, four, five, six, seven, eight, nine, ten…

Notes towards an
Understanding of the Problem

"I really need my hot chocolate today," said Trina. "I'm so full of PMT that fire will emanate from my eyes and smoke from my ears if anyone so much as looks my way ironically."

"I'm exceptionally thankful that I'm past that," said Leanne, twiddling with the flower Janet had just given her.

"I don't get it as badly as you, for obvious reasons." Antoinette's daisy was sitting in her hair, its brightness providing counterpoint to the seriousness of her tone. "Sometimes I wish I could, then I see what my friends go through and I'm grateful. I would have loved to be able to become pregnant and bear my own children. But the full evil of overwhelming hormones? My teen years were more than enough," Antoinette sounded yearning, despite the firmness of her statement. She recognised her mixed emotions and immediately qualified what she'd just said. "Mind you, I'd rather have had the capacity and a hysterectomy than to go the route I did."

Diana was the only one in the group who looked puzzled. "Hysterectomies are big operations, though," she said. "It's not the easy option."

"Nor is…whatever they call it these days. Gender confirmation?" said Janet.

"I'm missing something, I believe," said Diana. "A hop or a skip. My PMT is so bad that it feels as if I'm trying to break out of my own body, but that's not what I'm missing, is it? It's not having PMT at all."

"I have PMT," Antoinette said. "HRT can't actually give me periods, but I have cycles. I just don't get PMT as impossibly as either of you, and I've never actually bled, obviously. And what you're missing,

Diana, is that I was assigned male at birth—I'm a transgender woman."

"Now it makes sense," said Diana, "Thanks. I think this means we need chocolate all round, to support those who need it more."

"Yes! I like being supported in my time of woe." Trina's enthusiasm illuminated her woe. It was more marked than usual, and her voice was a little on edge. It sounded perhaps a trifle sharp. "And chocolate is our saviour."

Whenever any of them had any kind of hormonal fluttering from then on, it became an excuse for chocolate. Leanne complained, occasionally, that it wasn't fair, leaving the menopausal woman out of things.

"You're having chocolate for all the years that went before," said Janet. "You don't need to earn it again."

The Observer's Notes

Instead of seeking new landscapes, develop new eyes.
  —Marcel Proust, read online (quotation not verified)

Today I'm obsessed with hands. When I stop thinking about hands, I worry about my husband. He didn't come home last night and he can't remember why.

Hands are safer. I always watch hands, anyhow. If I look at them long enough, I can see so much about a person. Their age is easy. It's the first thing I decide on, as a rule. Classify the easy aspects of a person first, then move on to the more difficult. Analysis depends on collection and the amount one understands, after all. And age is a straightforward datum.

The man on my left right now is my current theoretical age (or thereabouts). His hands are still a little plump with adulthood but already a little stained with age. The woman on my right is younger—the stains are from outdoors and her skin shines from the sun.

Data collection isn't the only use I have for hands. I can tell so much about a person by their hands. I befriended someone once, because her hands were exquisite and graceful and reliable and trustworthy. Rare, rare hands. They reflected some of her inner self, which was sufficient. My husband's hands reflect his inner self, too. Pragmatic. Solid. Mostly honest. Honest enough so that I know he was telling the truth when he couldn't remember. We were both worried. All we could do was move on. Pretend it hadn't happened. My memory is enough of a burden.

I need to think of hands and to escape, but now, though, I'm tired of hands. Even the word is ugly to me. "Hands." Too short a word. Too open a word. I dislike it.

My obsession is not with staring at them and analysing them. I've done that. Duty has filled my soul and exhausted me.

I'm tired of hands. Tired of grasping human digits. Tired of the curves and kinks. Tired of sun-stained and age stained. Tired of nail polish and stickers and cuticles and knuckles and tattoos. I gave my report yesterday and I'm already forgetting the reason for the obsession.

My memory funks make a nonsense of my observations. Yesterday I knew hands. I had a vast array of data that I fed into our ever-hungry system. Today I'm a frail human being with slender paws that are just beginning to look old, and tomorrow all I'll know is that I was obsessed with hands for a while and that I'm suddenly quite over that obsession.

Hands will be annoying. Not just the word, but everything to do with them will frustrate me because they'll point to things I knew and no longer remember. I'll start learning my humanity another way, and I'll take that into the next report. I'll see humans afresh.

I fail to achieve a deep or broad understanding by this method. What good is it to anyone? Why do they make me forget? And does this have anything to do with my husband going missing overnight?

The woman's slow voice...

was counting again

One, two, three, four, five, six, seven, eight, nine, ten, eleven, twelve, thirteen, fourteen, fifteen, sixteen, seventeen, eighteen.

University. A place for lost people like me. Lost people who have reached drinking age. For some people it's a bad thing that the two coincide, but for me it was most excellent. University and drinking were such a powerful combination. I learned how to blend. I learned how to belong. I argued and spat fire about politics. I laughed at anyone who took student politics seriously. I joined clubs for their social events, and especially for the wine and cheese parties. I sat on park benches and talked and talked and talked. My eighteenth year was the year of wine and cheese. And pizza. And coffee. And words. So many words.

Money was a mystery. I could afford things, I know, for I remember them so clearly, but I don't remember holiday jobs. Holiday jobs weren't important, anyhow. What was important was finding friends. People like me. Sharing pizzas. Drinking coffee until three in the morning. Bringing my intellect and emotions to bear on everything as if no-one had ever done this before.

Becoming an adult.

The Observer's Notes

"Go away."
—said by me, everywhere, all the time

Why can't I just find my burrow and squirrel into it and sleep out this cold? It comes from inside me, and nothing I do will help with it. Nothing. Not medication. Not rest. Not anything.

Most certainly not this man who tells me thing after thing after thing as if I can pay attention. This man who asks me thing after thing after thing as if I can do each of them for him at once. This man who wants thing after thing after thing, as if his needs ought to be my universe. This man who can't even find his socks.

I can't find my burrow because humans don't have burrows. That's why. They live together. Such a stupid, stupid thing to do.

Stupid humans.

Stupid virus.

Notes towards an
Understanding of the Problem

"This isn't our usual place," Leanne said, stating the obvious with much satisfaction.

"We plan something for weeks, and all you can say is 'this isn't our usual place.'" Diana was annoyed. "Any moment you'll say 'and these aren't our usual flowers.'"

"Well, they aren't. Roses are not daisies. Not even in my imagination. Even yellow ones. And I'm a very amusing woman. I amuse myself all day long." This was one of Leanne's favourite sayings when she felt witty.

"Are you going to make amazing jokes all day?" asked Trina.

"I can and I shall, for there will be enough chocolate to cover your misery."

I've never tasted chocolate. I had the opportunity to do all kinds of things when I was pulling information together, but I didn't see the use in tasting strange foodstuffs that were no doubt only suited to humans. Potentially dangerous. I still need to examine this subject. This note can be considered the beginning of my examination.

One of the things that I least understand about humans is their obsession with certain foods and drinks. On this charming occasion, the women would be spending the whole day tasting different types of chocolate and making different types of chocolate and even, if I understand it properly, drinking different kinds of chocolate. I've seen mentions of drinking many times before, so this must be correct. It's one of those things about a culture that can happen, but feels so very wrong when placed against one's own culture that they are rejected out of hand, time after time. We should have been alerted when the drinking of an edible substance came up as an action any of our people observed on Earth. Native instincts were undermined.

Even they themselves didn't quite understand a whole day of chocolate, I suspect, and perhaps weren't looking forward to so much addictive substance in so short a time period. I say this because they showed clear signs of discomfort.

The first hour was a big meeting in a large room, and everyone present was given samples and ate samples while being given information. I have the words in front of me, but I can't re-create the experience from the words. I can't even do it from the additional data. They don't mean anything to me. They're just words and material surroundings. Humans have more senses than we record (as we do, but that's not relevant) and this is, today, a problem. It is at this point in my study that I realise that reconstruction is not sufficient. I have called from the archives all the things I thought were important. I was very proud of myself for finding the texture of the table and the level of background noise. Five senses humans have, and I knew this and called up sensual material.

This was hubris. I'm faced with a day that proved to be one of the six critical occasions, and all I can technically say is that it was possibly because the women spent more time together.

If they bonded in any special way, it was over something I can't call forward. Something that means nothing to me, emotionally.

At this moment, I'm further from understanding than I've ever been.

Since I made that last note, I've spoken to the supervisors. They can't approve another trawl for information that covers a wider range of senses. Given the current state of Earth, it costs far too much and would, in any case, be unreliable. They indicated their disappointment in me not seeing that this was a possibility when the initial material was obtained.

To the supervisors, reading my notes, it's obvious that chocolate is already clearly a substance of critical importance. It doesn't need verifying. Possibly the actual substance that lured the Judge into doing the impossible. Did I say "irksome chocolate fruitcake", or was it "chocolate irksome fruitcake"? Or did I merely imply the chocolate? The supervisors think it was chocolate cake the whole time. Probably literally. They have no idea what cake is, and fail to understand metaphors.

Ironic that English has the word "hubris" when it doesn't have descriptors for the foodstuff these women were testing. Not specific descriptors that make sense to someone like me. One can describe cream with the words used for chocolate, or mousse, or ice cream. Anything fatty and mellifluent. The colour descriptions, likewise, refer to so many other substances.

I am tripped up by an oddity of human culture. Obviously there isn't a clear link between the specificity of vocabulary and the importance of something, for how could I possibly have ascertained the importance of chocolate from the limited vocabulary directly associated with the substance? Not even my five women have specific vocabulary for this substance that would occupy their entire day. And how can something be important without clear vocabulary to indicate this? Maybe my own vocabulary is not up to the task?

Retrospectively, this makes sense. There are jokes on social media around the time of a Mad Max movie. A Mad Max movie—this is precise. It's of clear cultural import. And yet the jokes relied on the word "girl" used atypically. "Girl" is a very common word.

Human linguistics isn't as simple as it should be, given their single brain. They have layers and levels of variants from the personal to the language, from one person to millions of millions. And my capacity to learn the language through immersion has obscured some of the distinctive features, for it has brought me into an idiolect, directly, without sufficient context.

I shall take a break from this study. I will only return when I have determined how chocolate caused our simple and rational decision lines to fall apart so completely.

I am so much more human than I was when I began this project. In no way at all is this a good thing. I understand now that chocolate is no more important to humans than sports or the place where one grows up. These all have changing importance according to the person and their lives.

A simple description. Unfortunately, it makes no sense at all.

I still have to examine chocolate because I've been told to, because

I identified it as a potential trigger, and we're still lacking potential triggers. That identification was quite real, even though I'm now ambivalent about how it could be so. I have confused myself.

There are two possibilities as I see it.

The first is that the chocolate has damnable effects. The powers think this is the issue, now that I've alerted them to the existence of the substance. I was depressed by this possibility a moment ago, but I suddenly find it inexpressibly amusing.

The second is that it isn't chocolate at all that is to blame. If it's not chocolate, it has to be something else concerning that group of women.

If it isn't chocolate, what the hell is it? I hope it's chocolate. Both the first and second critical events are focussed on chocolate. (It's such a good thing that I have never tasted it, and will never have the opportunity to. Obviously, chocolate is a very destructive substance.)

There is nervousness about spending the whole day in the company of chocolate. Chocolate has physical effects on bodies. The women know this. They didn't talk about it as much as they talk about their hormones or their shopping, so it's deep knowledge.

If, at a later stage, it appears that I have misinterpreted, I shall return to this day and analyse it again. Yes, I shall leave it here at this time. I do not have to explore the chocolate-making, nor the indecorous moment in the women's toilets. I have my tentative answer. The file will be just open enough to admit new ideas, for my supervisors said that when the situation is this obvious, one needs a potential second explanation to meet the briefing requirements, but mostly what I'll do is find evidence to demonstrate that chocolate is the culprit.

This will be a satisfactory outcome. All we will have to do in future is ascertain if the race under Judgement has an equivalent to chocolate. If it has, I can recommend we pull out immediately and put them on the no-go list. If it has not, we can proceed with advanced anthropological surveys leading to possible Judgement.

A very satisfactory outcome, I feel. I still have to prove it, but chocolate has appeared in every single critical incident, so it won't be difficult to demonstrate.

Even if I don't believe it myself.

The Observer's Notes

"Human life is more about waiting for Godot than it is about waiting for God."
—overheard on a bus

So few simple models fit this society. I use one, and then modify it and modify it until it digs its heels in and refuses to explain what I see. When it becomes stubborn, I reject it.

I wish I'd studied human anthropology. 'Anthropology' is the wrong word, but it's the closest speakers of this language have. It might have helped. I also wish I was permitted to talk to my colleagues. Then maybe I'd understand what to do. They seem to have innate knowledge, regardless of the state of their memories: I lack this knowledge.

My deficiency in knowing how I should go about my tasks is not our only difference. The longer I'm here, the more I realise how much of a failure I am. Yesterday I tasted my failure, when my husband gently pointed out that he was unable to eat dinner. He forgave me, he said. This was not the first time I'd forgotten his allergy. I don't even know how to work within a human marriage, much less the tasks I am formally assigned.

The point is, of course, that I consider these matters outside tech sessions, whereas everyone else seems to operate entirely as humans most of the time, and only know who and what they really are during those tech sessions. They don't know they know, but I know I don't know.

Right now, it's a waiting game.

I need to develop systems to understand what's happening

around here, and I need to make interpretations, otherwise I am a waste of time and space. I don't know if this is the right thing to do, but I'm scared to ask. It may be that others fail the way I have and that they've lost their essential personality. That they're aliens masquerading as humans, but hollow at the core.

This is my biggest fear. This is why I can't ask. That there'll be nothing left of me.

I make up a system, and apply that system to everything I possibly can until the system fails because it's too complicated and too heavy and cannot sustain the data. My husband helps, for both our lives are easier when I remember the everyday and fail to poison him by mistake. When it becomes too complicated, my memory becomes more erratic and he warns me. I have notes that he gives me so that he doesn't have to explain. Then I start all over again.

It's becoming easier now. I cause less damage. This is why he was upset with me when I nearly killed him by mistake. I think it was easier when I was needy, and it's easier when I'm competent, but in-between is difficult for both of us.

He doesn't love me as much as he did (the look in his eyes when he gave me my engagement ring is long gone), but he's there for me. He is scared for me, I think, if he leaves.

My models help me forget this, most of the time. That's something I want to forget. Or grow beyond. It's lonely to be unloved but to occupy so much of a person's waking life.

I need to move on now. Be safer.

I make descriptions of this culture. My new one is in terms of privilege and not-privilege, in terms of white and male. Fragments of the culture in which I currently reside. My memory takes longer to break down when I do this: the system is reinforced in my every day.

My descriptions don't look at Earth people, but Australians (and possibly other parts of the English-speaking world) at this time. It looks at those with advantage and those without. Those who are blessed and those who hurt. It's very oppositional. And I am not one of those insiders who are blessed. There is some tension in this that I'm beginning to acknowledge. I suspect I wasn't in a beta group back home. Alpha into beta does not go.

Thus endeth the lesson.

I cannot like this system. I cannot.
Today is a day when I'm very pleased not to be human.

The woman's slow voice...

was counting again

One, two, three, four, five, six, seven, eight, nine, ten, eleven, twelve, thirteen, fourteen, fifteen, sixteen, seventeen, eighteen, nineteen.

Summer holidays. That time between one university year and the next, where one replenishes one's funds and rests one's brain. This is the perfect theory of the summer holiday. It reflects an imperfect world.

There were no jobs. The economy resembled the undead and so did most of the people in my vicinity. I walked into a dress shop, however, obviously not one of the walking dead produced by this undead economy. I asked if there was any work going, and was instantly employed. It was like something out of a teen novel. I sold semi-luxury clothes to strangers from just before Christmas until I was twenty-one.

I learned so much about artificial skins, about hang and drape and feel and colour and texture and how to be politely off-putting to anyone who the boss thought would not give the shop the desired sense of fashion. If a woman had a poor complexion, was overweight, dressed down, and if I didn't give her the polite rebuttal, then she would be faced with a much more direct and nasty one from the boss.

Everything was to do with style. Nothing was to do with kindness unless style and shape and income were already present. Even the unkindness, however, was done with style.

This is where I learned that cruelty could be soft and even sweet. The tool I acquired was the capacity to watch the slump of shoulders or the defiant intake of breath, the angry mouth or the cheeky "this doesn't affect me" tilt to the head. There are so many methods women have of dealing with the gentle rebuff. There are so many ways of administering the rebuff. The fact that we used so many methods in the shop was the worst of all, however, for it taught these women that they were unacceptably large or sloppy or poor, and that the gates of heaven would be forever denied them.

I spent my quiet time watching women walk past the shop, defiantly not looking in the window, or looking wistful and then resolutely turning their head away, or busying their body language with something else or... These were the women the shop had rebuffed so very much that they couldn't bear to come in. No matter how successful their lives were, they had the memory of being hurt when innocently buying clothes.

Working in a dress shop was quite possibly the cruellest and most educative job I could find. If anything hardened me and caused me to hate in my university years, it was this experience. Being cruel to others blunted my sensitivity, it lost me access to my gentle soul. I don't know if I've ever found it again.

The Observer's Notes

"It is impossible to eat elephants," stated the boy to his father.
"I told you, you eat it one bite at a time."
"The skin's too thick."
    —overheard on a bus

I ought to be in a US sitcom. My life ought to be *Third Rock from the Sun*. And that ought to be an aphorism.

Say it. "My life ought to be Third Rock from the Sun."

Look at it one more time. "My life ought to be Third Rock from the Sun."

Leave it to admire another day. "My life ought to be Third Rock from the Sun."

Real life doesn't work like US sitcoms and it most certainly doesn't work like aphorisms. It's impossible to leave a situation static to return to and to admire another day. It's almost impossible to admire even the first time. It's too intimate. I'm pretty certain humans do these things as a giant pretence that their lives are under control. That everything can be explained, or laughed at, or both.

Me, I'm making up my own techniques from this. A year ago I was lost. I was petrified. I latched onto anything that would give me answers. Including popular song.

You can hear echoes of my music in my speech from time to time. I sing the songs sometimes, and my husband sings along. It's one of the things that binds us. It helps a bit. I started chronicling my experiences in order to diminish the sense of vastness and impossibility the outside world gave me. Humanity was too much.

Then I remembered that I'm here as an observer. That there are others. That I'm one of many, but I am the only one in this place at this moment watching humanity from whatever direction appeals. I feel alone and overwhelmed, but I'm neither. It's like the male voice joining in when I sing. I've always been solitary, but I've never been alone. It's the nature of the job. Maybe it's the nature of me.

I tried joining a self-help group, attending the theatre, doing Renaissance dancing. All these activities taught me is that humanity distrusts difference. Even polite humanity. Very nice people othered me in a series of very charming ways.

My answer is generally *science fiction*. Also Flanders and Swann. Always Gloria Gaynor. Today's theme is Flanders and Swann, for I yearn to stay in an elephant's nursing home until I get my memory back. Flanders and Swann fit my internal self-understanding far, far better than Third Rock from the Sun.

I like my cultural echoes. I like my jail, too. I don't want my memory back. I especially like walking down the street of my jail and looking for weeds in the gaps in the pavement. Sometimes the weeds contain the prettiest flowers. I think that this is a symbol somewhere and sometime. For me it's a good experience. Once, the pavement split and gave way to a miniature iris. Profoundly purple and exquisite. It really ought to be a symbol. Without most of my memory, would I even know?

Gloria Gaynor, science fiction and Flanders and Swann, and, on a miserable day when I'm glad I'm not human and am tempted to poison pigeons in the park, Tom Lehrer. It wouldn't harm for my old alien overlords to sing rousing Lehreric choruses.

Science fiction always starts my list, for it means that whenever I feel particularly alone I can decide on a particular trope to apply to my situation. I can live the dream of the solitary alien on the planet Earth.

Am I an ironic observer?

Am I a judge who will decide the fate of humanity?

Am I a bloody anthropologist observing everything and getting involved despite themselves?

Am I a time-traveller, documenting the dead?

Do I represent collectors, come to identify and steal the best humankind can offer?

Do I represent a race of invaders, with the goal of destroying humanity and taking its place?

Or am I simply barking mad, and are the days like today when I remember things actually the days when I've lost my connection to reality?

Who am I? What am I? Why am I here?

Combine not-quite-complete mindwipe with science fiction (and just a touch of Tom Lehrer), and the possibilities are delightful. Even if I know, not very deep down, that I am an anthropologist and a failure at my job. I shall delight in the possibilities, even the ones I will never explore.

The woman's slow voice...

was counting again

One, two, three, four, five, six, seven, eight, nine, ten, eleven, twelve, thirteen, fourteen, fifteen, sixteen, seventeen, eighteen, nineteen, twenty.

I completed university only because I'm right-handed and he's left. It was a pass degree because honours would have kept me away from him for a full year. This is where I'm different. I heard *Someone Eminent* explain once that he dropped out of Medicine because of holding hands with his girlfriend. I didn't drop out. Unlike the *Eminent Person*, I didn't get a career, either. Not much of one, anyhow. For a long, long time. Like the Eminent Person, I married the person whose hand I held.

We took notes together: me with my right hand and he with his left. What our other hands were doing was…holding hands. If we did anything else, we'll never tell.

He was marking time in those lectures, he said. He had completed everything except one simple subject, due to illness, he said, but it was probably because he'd failed something and instead of repeating, he chose a new subject. He lied all the time, about everything, did my sweet amour.

The love of my youth. My true love. My always-love. I gave up everything for him.

He finished his Law-Arts, and I finished my Arts. I kept him until he was able to earn a living. It was all very modern and just. Just as we were very modern, being each other's right and left hand. Modern, but fairytale nonetheless.

Notes towards an
Understanding of the Problem

Today I'm going finish writing up some detailed notes about shoes. I've already taken notes on many other potentially shared items in the target group's lives. Daisies were ill-advised, as were the other flowers. Salt was a curious one to study. So was hair. Hair proved to be a diversion, but a fascinating one. The note on shoes has been attached to those other notes, rather than included in this main account.

As you can see from the file heading, I discount them either as the source of the problem or as a major contributing factor. Shoes demonstrate much about the culture in which they are worn and the socio-economic status and personality of the wearer, and in one case indicates the source of back pain, but do not appear to indicate anything that could help explain the fate of Earth.

Chocolate is still the most likely common factor between the women in question. They came together in a chocolate shop and consumed chocolate at all critical meetings and most non-critical ones.

I had assumed that a physical human factor was more likely, until I examined their physical characteristics in depth. They are all women, but apart from that they display significantly different characteristics. Despite a limited age range (about fifteen years from oldest to youngest), not all share the trait of having menstrual cycles currently, and they have significantly varied levels of physical well-being. All have roughly the same level of income. Level of income is highly unlikely to be the critical factor.

Culturally, they are all female and English-speaking. Although two do not possess English as their first language, they are all native speakers of English. They are all Australian. They all have Australian accents, some broader than others. These are such obvious shared characteristics that every other researcher has focussed upon them and demonstrated clearly that, while their gender and nationality may be minor factors, they are not what caused the fruitcake.

The previously-studied items that the women shared in all their meetings include (but are not limited to) trace chemicals, beverages, air, various parts of their bodies, physical movement (divided into walking, sitting, standing, and the connections between these different states), ingredients in comestibles, content of bags, bags and other accessories, clothes and other accessories. I have not yet completed my extensive study of hormonal fluctuations in these women, as I had not realised its importance until recently. The earlier studies didn't take account of it at all. It's a concern that it was neglected. The fact of those cycles is not a point of data, therefore, but material arising from them might be.

I have a theory about this. Our studies are biased to reflect the cultures we are studying. Or samples of them. One country from a planet. We then either bring them together for an intense and immense overview, or we dissolve into specific studies to check out specific problems. The prevailing trend on Earth in almost all subjects is to bias towards the male. I cite (as most others do when this subject is raised) the local Earthian thalidomide controversy.

Testing a substance on males and then using it on females has distinct and occasionally very nasty ramifications, but humans still do it. And we copy what humans do, for this is how we enter into other cultures: we use their terms.

Female hormones and life cycles were not included in the earlier studies because they might impede the simplicity and elegance of our approach, because it didn't fit our method of analysis and it certainly didn't fit theirs. We were looking at Earth as if it were mostly male, because human studies themselves are so heavily weighted towards the male, and it's inelegant to not use existing studies. Resting results on mathematical elegance has thus proven to be a research flaw. We still need to preference a culture's own self-view, but we need to not fall into their native bias.

I have created this list and implemented the connecting research from my own analysis, and also from previous analyses. At this stage, none of them suggest that they are important to outcomes. This is why only an overview is included here. The details are attached to this overview, however, in case they become important later in the study. The study of hormonal fluctuations will be attached to the list if it proves of little importance, and otherwise will obviously become a subject of major discussion in its own right. I am not in a position to know which is the case as yet.

It is also possible that all of the women ingest certain substances in a way that does not manifest in an obvious way when they socialise together, and that this substance is mind-altering and has affected outcomes from that direction. No previous studies have been able to ascertain if this is the case, and it was the first possible factor to be examined. It has, in fact, been examined more times than any other single potential factor, for if the Judge was affected by mind-altering chemicals, then the Judgement was flawed.

Discovering a flawed Judgement doesn't change what happened, but it means we understand how to avoid it next time. This has many ramifications, some of them extraordinarily broad in impact. I have not, however, been able to determine if anything other than the usual food ingested and drink were taken. I see no evidence of this.

I am checking various analyses and assessments of chocolate and coffee, for they are the most likely means of mind-altering chemical ingestion, and members of the group themselves discuss how these substances make them feel. And because I've painted myself into a corner with the damned chocolate thing. However, they are not specific to this situation and thus ought to have been identified by earlier anthropological studies. Due to the importance of the subject, I cannot leave this unchecked.

I do not, however, believe that it is the case. The chief addiction I've determined so far is not chemical, it's cultural: the tendency to create situations that favour human males.

The Observer's Notes

"I am a lawyer. I buy my son so many books." Said to a mother who was taking her son to visit the library.
—overheard in a library

Why am I here?
I'm here under cover. Under more cover than usual. I'm moonlighting for someone from my purported workplace, in the Parliamentary Triangle. Work sent them to a dull day of lectures and they wimped out and so it's me here instead. The irony doesn't escape me. Irony seldom does. Some days I can't remember my name for more than an hour, but I always know irony. Today is such a day. Fortunately, I have a name tag.

I'm in the Main Committee Room in Parliament House, listening to speakers talk about the Magna Carta. I'm writing so that I can reread, and not forget. My husband gave me a note to remind myself of this, over breakfast. He looked worried. That, at least, I remember, though I'd rather forget it. It hurt both of us, him looking so concerned.

"I'm working on it," I told him. "It's not as bad as it was."

"I know," he said, softly. "And one day I'll stop worrying. Until then, keep the note where you can see it, and let me pick you up afterwards."

Today I'm observing (for my alternate self, which appears more of the time than it used to—I feel less bereft of identity than I was even a few weeks ago) how modern specialists react to the Magna Carta. What values do they attribute to it? How far are their emotions engaged? What does this say about humanity, past and present?

For my paid work self, I'm merely appearing because we needed a representative and I didn't flee quickly enough.

These people presenting to this public assume so much about their own importance to the culture and to the rule of law. One of my big questions (which I really need to address before things get too far out of hand) is: "Are they right?" Or are they minor eruptions of whatever-they-think on the face of humanity? Sparkles or boils? Boils or sparkles?

These people, who are mostly lawyers in various categories of public service, may be irrelevant. These people may be precisely what I'm here for. I don't know yet.

I won't find out today. Today is about gleaning information to be pulled together later. It's also about sitting (by mistake, if anyone asks, lest I be accused of irony) on a modern calligraphy copy of a later original of a copy of the Magna Carta. *Sic transit gloria mundi.* My briefing in human cultures stuck, but it didn't bring respect. I can type Latin without respecting humans. This is what advanced minds do.

Some thoughts. They are not coherent. This is probably a good thing.

Not so good is my mind, which wants to use a different kind of narrative to the human one. I feel it creeping through when I don't monitor my thoughts closely enough. Today is more difficult than most.

#1 The Attorney-General (whose name is Brandis and lends itself to bad jokes—this is not ironic) did not feel that it was necessary to be here. Thus this major event reflecting a major moment in human history isn't major in any way that counts. It isn't critical to the government to understand modern Australians and their reaction to past documents. Officially, he sent a senator in his stead: someone not too old and not too male. Someone not too important. Possibly reflecting the Government's view of the Magna Carta, and maybe of the rule of law. In fact, *probably* reflecting the Government's view of the rule of law.

This latter view is me thinking as humanly as possible. Also sarcastically. It should not be mistaken for truth. Or maybe it should not be mistaken for fact, but is indeed true. I love it that I can hold contradictory thoughts in my mind like this. It's like... I can't think of an analogy that doesn't involve things I can't remember.

I need to accumulate data if I want to prove that the government's view of the rule of law is what I say it is. I don't know if I want to prove this. Let me note to myself, then, that we need more data on the level of respect this Government has for the rule of law. Let me leave this matter with the techs, so that they can programme someone else to obtain the data. Let the techs think it's something they thought up, in their cleverness. As long as I'm self-aware before I enter, I can access the machinery and make this happen. I probably won't. Won't be self-aware. Won't make this happen. But I enjoy imagining it.

#2 Inherited history can prevail over common sense. It can also be worshipped with undue fervour. By "can", I mean to imply that it prevailed today and was worshipped today. They told the story over and over, gradually shaping it into something holy through their attitude and through their stylised language. This is Australia's numinous. If we (the hidden "we", not the Australian women "we") did academic studies, there'd be a study in it. Since we don't, there is merely a note about this society. That note becomes part of a mathematical argument when the collection is written up, for we tell everything mathematically, from the collection of data to its final presentation. Mathematics lies at the heart of my real people.

I'm pretty sure the maths is how we tell *story*, even though I've only this moment remembered. We think we don't tell stories, that our maths makes us different from humans. But our maths is not bereft of tales, because we write the story into it, through notes and through structure. We think we don't, because the entertainment element isn't there. We entertain with the material that then gets processed. Raw stuff.

I don't know if we're stranger than humans, or if humans are stranger than we are. I wish I could remember other species to compare. I wish I could remember everything I once knew.

Today is all about irony. When I forget again, that will also be ironic. There is at least as much forgetting in the history discussed today as there is remembering.

#3 my first two points appear to contradict each other, but they do not.

#4 Things that make sense: high-minded tosh isn't the same thing as low-minded tosh. One speaker used one, and another used the other, and the first was very entertaining in all the right ways and the second was entertaining in all the wrong ways and required much use of my sarcasm-coloured pen. For the purposes of this seminar, my sarcasm-coloured pen is puce.

Also, lawyers manufacture the truth. Or truths. If I had to trust lawyers with the future of mankind, I would have to consider this more thoroughly. Fortunately, I'm an observer and I only have to consider lawyers when they force themselves upon me. Like today.

That reminds me, I need to uplift my material immediately after this event is finished. Sounds so noble but is so demeaning—I always need to take time for shopping or coffee-shopping afterwards, just to return my self-respect to its proper place.

I should uplift in an hour, according to my rule book (which is not a book in the human sense and whose rules I only remember sometimes, but which nonetheless exists), but alien mind stuff might not quite be acceptable in a parliamentary committee room. It's fine on the streets at night, on the rare occasions when I do it remotely (doing it remotely sucks and produces bad results—it's only useful in between the three-monthly major sessions, when life demands. Download may be painful, but it produces better results, I think—not that I know for certain).

Last time I uplifted in a public place, the police ignored me. They arrested someone a few metres away, however, for drunk and disorderly behaviour.

Today I'll do it in the proper room, with the techs monitoring. Technically, this is closer to Download than Uplift, but…really, it falls somewhere between the two. I need to see if cutting down how much I try to fit into a day will help diminish the pain. If it doesn't, I need to see a doctor, even though we're discouraged from doing this. Still, my human body is authentic enough unless they test my DNA. If this human suit is damaged, I trust a doctor more than techs. I trust lawyers more than I trust techs. This is because I only remember the techs on good days, I think, and I never forget lawyers.

Writing my notes now will save energy (hence the notes "in class"), and getting Download/Uplift straight afterwards will then give me an early night. That will help keep the human suit from breaking down, perhaps. One can only hope. Whoever designed my human suit did a bad job.

Also, going tonight will explain the time lapse between my memory returning and me uplifting, since I can't be there until after work finishes. At that point, I'll probably lose my puce pen. I should enjoy being sarcastic with it while I can. All my most interesting pens are stolen by techs. Only they don't call it stealing. Techs have no sense of what belongs to me.

It's bad enough that they copy some of my memories. They're supposed to copy memories, but it's still intrusive. I always feel that they know me too well—that they pry when they copy. This they're not supposed to do. But the things they say…

They don't just copy my physical possessions; they say: "This is nice", and when they say that, I don't get the original back. There's a black market in these things. It's more active when a planet is submitted for Judgement, of course. Normally I'd leave something as interesting as a puce pen at home, or I'd uplift in private, but I didn't have a choice today. I'll take the fake Magna Carta I sat on, and see what happens. Maybe they'll acquire that instead of my pen. Or as well as. One time they acquired my shoes and undergarments and bus card. Getting home was uncomfortable and very slow. I hope they got lots of credit for them on the black market.

From the way they talk, I'm pretty sure I'm not supposed to remember what they say. I learn a lot by pretending I don't.

Right now, the learning is important. This is personal. I hate the stranded feeling I carry with me everywhere and want to understand for myself why I have it. And this is something I've written down so that I won't uplift it. Self, hold yourself to it. And hold yourself to that nice supper your husband promised you when you lied about going back to the office after this seminar.

#5 There's a lot of history bandied around today. Historical examples of all the kings of England and none of the queens make James I sound remarkably educated. If the speaker had only added in the education of the queens, James I would have appeared less impossibly brilliant. Queens and their education, however, don't count for this group. It's full of privilege, this group is.

Whoever is the Judge would have to see this as a sign of decadence. More and more, humanity ought to be grateful that Judgements are not being made by me, in this place and in this time.

If there is a Judge. I've not heard that Earth has been submitted for Judgement yet. The techs certainly haven't mentioned it. It all depends on how like us these people are, for they're too lacking in technology to be considered a threat. Or I've forgotten. I don't think I'm forgetting that sort of thing any more, though. There is beginning to be a small constancy in my mind.

Historical examples of all the kings of England and none of the queens, making James I astonishingly educated...because the queens and their education don't count. I need to say this thing twice, for it astonishes me so very much. How can genders not be equal? Maybe the lack of gender shifting damages humans' capacity to see each other as equal. Maybe they're just obnoxious and pig-headed. Puce pens are very useful to write words such as "pig-headed". I think it's a side effect of most humans being so very static in their genders. Understanding others is a personal quality, and demonstrates insight and maturity. It ought to be a natural function of the species. Stupid species.

Generations of lawyers know these things, things like knowing that the one who is speaking now counts even Queen Anne as "invasion by the Dutch". How can women count if only men's names and distinctions are given? How can humans understand gender if they shape their society through the privileges of one gender? If they only see two genders?

Humans may not shift genders with any aptitude (I do believe a few shift, but hide it—if I were human, I'd have to prove this, but I'm not, so it's true enough for my purposes), but they could at least see that there are more than two genders. And they don't. Women are a secondary gender, which must hurt. All other genders are nearly invisible. This is damaging.

How can humans understand themselves if they're gender-blind?

If women are an inferior gender and other genders are not visible, where does this leave me? How do I view these humans from a position of ongoing inferiority?

Oh, this speaker liked James I. That's why he quoted him. How can any human male like James I? Fortunately for me, I'm neither human nor male. I can judge him for his rule of witches and the number of lives he destroyed. I can judge him for the callous experiments he did on children with the aim of discovering God's language.

Not only can I judge him—I *will* judge him. I *have* judged him. He is a turd. His turdishness adds to the measure of humankind. It will be part of my judgement. Thank goodness that my judgement is only on my own behalf. I can judge all I like with no consequences. I am a mere anthropologist. Right now, that's a very good thing, because otherwise my puce pen would be recording the possibility of blood baths and species destruction. As it is, it records sarcasm.

Generations of lawyers have known these things that lawyers are telling us today. The story of the rule of law. It is a lawyer who cites even Queen Anne as an "invasion by the Dutch". How can women count if only men's names and distinctions are given? And if half the species is of no importance, why should humanity expect to live?

I say things twice and thrice and over again because I cannot make sense of them otherwise. I resort to the proper way of thinking, because the improper one is full of holes. That's another problem that humans have: they expect life to be lineal and they do not repeat themselves enough for comfort, much less enough for understanding.

It's very hard to act like a human today.

How do I hide today's level of self-awareness from the tech? I shall obscure it by being so very hormonal and emotional that they will be fascinated and record me as a cultural curiosity (and sell my feelings to the highest bidder) — James is thus useful, after all. I shall secrete myself behind the emotions he invokes.

Let me wallow, therefore. Let me not, however, repeat the same thought a fourth time. There's wallowing and there's floundering.

If women don't count, where does that leave the Judge? How does the Judge tally cultures that can't tally themselves? There are minorities who count even less than women, that make it even more difficult to excuse humanity and argue for the species' continuation. How does the Judge handle the view that I'm being presented with so forcefully today, that humanity must be seen as continually inferior?

Yes, I am thankful that I am an anthropologist. Again. Always thankful. I would not want to Judge these people.

The speaker just liked James I, again. He quoted him at length. I need to say this again and again after all, for it leaves me aghast (and besides, I'm wallowing). How can any human male (apart from the man's lovers, of course) like James I and VI? The man who killed infants and persecuted those he thought might be witches? Fortunately for me, I'm neither human nor male. If I were Judge, I would be angry with the lawyer who likes James as much as with James himself.

James destroyed fewer than the number of lives the Judge will destroy if humanity fails. There are contradictions wherever I look. Contradictions in human kind, contradictions in my own kind. Right now, I'm both human and other, so I'm a walking, talking, puce-pen-writing contradiction.

I can judge him for the callous experiment James did to children in the name of discovering God's language. But who judges me for judging him? James I was a turd. There, I have judged him again. Twice in five minutes. And no one dies.

I shouldn't have come today. It's good data, but I am filled with an overwhelming desire to go to the Prime Minister's staff and announce: "Take me to your leader".

If I had known so much memory would return today, I'd have pleaded sick. And of course, I couldn't know my memory would return, for I forget because I'm brainwashed.

I can't admit to humans I'm not one of them. I'm not what I used to be, either. I fear, today, that I am just an embarrassment. Too human. Far, far, far too human. Techs constructed my body and fitted me into it far, far, far too effectively. Even though I sometimes feel my body yearning for its proper gender, it never actually changes. It merely yearns.

If the calculations of passing time that I made during this morning's shower are correct, I've missed a whole gender by being here. I've lost a unique sector of my life. My body is changing without me, for without change it would die. It goes through the change clinically, without any of the functions or social relations that make a gender real.

I should be gone from here. I don't know why I remain, half-defunct and each day further from reality. No wonder I'm dreaming of Judgement.

I remember a story of a Judge who decided on the Death of a World, but who had become so very much One with that world that it (for this was not a gendered world) decided that it must die along with the world. It had taken on all the problems, and there was not enough glory to redeem anyone. Not even the Judge.

It is not good that I remember this story.

Why do we have anthropologists and a Judge? Why not simply

anthropologise? I wish I remembered reasons for this. It worries me that I can't remember something this big.

The woman's slow voice...

was counting again

One, two, three, four, five, six, seven, eight, nine, ten, eleven, twelve, thirteen, fourteen, fifteen, sixteen, seventeen, eighteen, nineteen, twenty, twenty-one, twenty-two, twenty-three, twenty-four.

We finally married in 1987. University was already a thousand years ago.

We were saving for our home. We were about to start a family.

We knew what our future would be. We'd predicted it based on our dreams and our friends and the state of Australia. We told each other that we were prepared for anything. Of course we did. All our friends shared that mixture of hopeless optimism and dark feeling about the future. We didn't believe in either, but we pretended to act on both. We were an archetypal couple, and the way we held our heads and walked to the shops together demonstrated this to the world.

We were a café couple, in the Carlton set. Our regular haunts were trendier than the ones next door, where the university students hung out. They were drunken yobbos. We were young sophisticates. I read the jackets of books and the titles, and I talked about them as if the author were my best friend. We all did. More domestic couples talked about gardening. We aired views on literature and wine and the latest Melbourne Theatre Company production.

1987 was our charmed year. We were a perfect couple, and had a perfect wedding. The Botanic Gardens, of course, with the swans in the background, offering their black grace to the proceedings. It was very picture-postcard. We, too, were very picture-postcard.

Notes towards an
Understanding of the Problem

Artisanal
Assortment
Beans
Bittersweet
Blend
Block
Butterfat
Cacao
Chocoholic
Cocoa Endorphin
Fat content
Flavanols
Ganache
Melt
Milk chocolate
Nibs
Powder
Praline
Serotonin
Truffles

That's 10% of the vocabulary I examined and established at the request of idiots who listened to my daft comment about chocolate and who are reading this despite the fact that it's my set of personal notes and only my immediate staff are supposed to read it. Humans do that, you know, make obvious jokes.

I realise that chocolate is a drug, but it's not the kind of drug you think. "Specialist" knowledge is precisely that. So, in fact, is "team leader". Anyhow, to get you out of my hair this once, I've done a list.

Please note that this is a one-off. How very much is this a one-off? Well, next time I will give a standard response, and that will include notes about your trying to run the project and interfering with both project management and process and thus delaying outcomes, and this note will be appended to the file. "Next time" includes requests for information about words of any kind, as you've made it patently obvious that your English is now sufficient to undertake such tasks yourself. You know what these notes will mean to your career, so don't test me. And I expect to see all of you in Advanced English next session.

There are just three words in the selection above that could be useful in my research: endorphin, flavanol and serotonin. Just those three. They encapsulate the physical reaction to the substance, to my mind. The human body's reaction to the chocolate could have completely changed the temperament of the Judge and caused everything to fall apart. It's possible.

I was doubtful about chocolate as anything more than a distraction initially, then I thought it was the only possibility, and now I'm doubtful again. Also cynical. Also feeling that I'm following false leads.

To add insult to injury, the studies of the substance are in and they entirely back human assumptions. Chocolate is, in fact, good for one's mood, and hormones, and health, and waistline, without having any noticeable effect on the state of the universe. There's nothing that could cause extreme reaction in terms of personality change. Mild reactions, yes, but nothing as extraordinary as what happened.

Just because something appears frequently in accounts, doesn't make it critical.

We've spent a long time chasing a substance that may be important but has never been important in the critical sense that you lot are assuming. Go back and think about what else has appeared that chocolate has distracted you from. Now. While you do this, I shall finish my note.

For completeness' sake, I shall finish this task. The key words from my vocabulary listing will be sent back to the scientists, and they can match them up against the human body (female variety), and we'll have the closest possible to a definitive ruling. My gut feeling (*ha!* Another joke! English is a language that tempts one into disrespect) is that the chocolate plays a role. I kept returning to it because it's there time after time after time. This cannot be chance. It plays a role: just not the simplistic, "substance changes all" role you want it to play. That you informed me about three times recently. I try to forget this latter because I have great difficulty accepting my superiors as being that very imbecilic. I'm not happy with my inferiors right now, either.

For my next task, I shall list all the other common elements in the women's meetings. They sat down, every time, for instance. I shall check out the possibility of tables being part of the equation that led to implosion and wreck. This should please my superiors. Solid, thoughtful research.

Right now, my job feels very, very stupid. Tables appear a lot. Air was a common factor, too. And words.

This is going nowhere.

Less and less does this feel like serious research into one of the great problems of our era, and more and more does this feel like a waste of time. Wrong method, for one thing, and possibly wrong researcher. This researcher is still currently using the voice of one of us implanted into a human body and that person used a puce-coloured pen.

This puce pen was recently sold for a notorious fortune, because she referred to it in a part of her analysis. Every time she referred to something, it mysteriously disappeared when she went in for testing, and the prices these things go for right now are astronomical. Pun entirely intended. We (as a species) Judge and yet we (as a species) lack simple ethics.

I'm going to have to go back into the record another time. I do not enjoy doing this. It's invading private lives. We can do that with each other, for we have etiquette and limits and rules about when to stop, but to do this with other species? Who can't do it back? Who have no phrases that indicate "*Enough!*" and no awareness that it's even happening? When did we decide that this was ethical?

It feels creepy, anyhow. Everyone's dead and I've studied the past before, but this is different. The women are real to me. I'm eavesdropping. And some of the things they said to each other should never have been recorded. But they were part of the record made prior to Judgement. Standard procedure to ensure that the Judge has not been bribed or threatened or otherwise tampered with.

In this instance it's beyond important to check that standard procedure was followed once everything was in place, especially given that it was most certainly not followed at two prior key points.

I'm telling myself things I know because I don't want to state the obvious: right now, it looks as if fruitcake was caused by the improper actions of a group of technicians. I would rather it were chocolate or air. Bringing the Tech Institute to trial will be a resolution, but it won't be a good resolution. Our interplanetary work will still be affected, and maybe other things as well. Techs are too powerful to be reprimanded and reformed without changes to our systems, and even to our culture. In other words, the very political becomes the terrifyingly political.

The big issue (and why I have taken so long to state what is quite possibly the reason, and why no-one else has stated it at all?) is that almost none of the changes in this scenario will work to our benefit. No doubt our colleague worlds will agree with most of them. Yet so much of our lives rests on our approach to aliens. It's at the heart of our civilisation in many ways.

I shall be so careful. I shall make so many glossaries for everything that is present at the six critical moments, and even at the ones that seem less critical. I shall rule them out, clearly, or let them in clearly. I shall be impossibly thorough.

I suspect humans would have appreciated it if their fate rested on chocolate. I suspect this is not the case. I can't be certain, but I do suspect it. The fruitcake is still irksome, but I doubt it's chocolate.

The Observer's Notes

"I had my womb removed, not my brain. They're not connected."
—overheard in a meeting

I can tell what ought to be happening. I can also tell that it's not behaving as intended. My body is listening to my profound wishes. It's trying so very hard to change and to become who I am.

It can't change. It remains female, despite its very best struggles to move from parent to pre-adult. My cleverest inventions don't even begin to reflect the simple concept of respectable gendering. It's impossible to clearly demarcate gender shift in English. If there's no language to reflect my needs, then humans don't even come close to what I need right now. No wonder my body doesn't know what it's doing.

Men's bodies change less than women's, my husband tells me. Men don't even have the painful attempt at gender shift I'm suffering from right now. He doesn't tell me that. He claims his hormones shift in the same way. He's told me this. So many times. So very emotively.

"Ihu-u-urt," my husband will say. "I'm having male menopause."

But male menopause is like man-flu: a pale, pale echo of reality. And being mansplained about it, over and over, is something I could do without. It's one of the trials of marriage, that he keeps forgetting and telling me things about menopause, for example, as if I've never known it.

Mansplaining is one of the more annoying attributes of the human. It implies an intellectual and social hierarchy that half the species doesn't accept. I begin to understand women who think their lives would be better without men. Men and techs. And I want my body to behave. When my body misbehaves, I don't want to be told by a male that they suffer likewise. It's annoying. If it were from anyone other than himself, it would be more than annoying.

I know what it's like to be me, but I can only reach and strive to be what I was like before I was this version of myself. The inner reality is firm, however, even when the body is shifting and stubbornly revisiting, both at the same time. It's trying very hard. *Very hard*.

Right now I have late periods, missing periods, spotty periods, bloating, and an immense fatigue that overwhelms everything. It brings me back to myself, to have the shift that took two days expanded into a forever-shift. Even the fatigue helps ground me. This is my current body's notion of matching the internal with the external. I try to tell it: "I'm me. Still me. Always will be me. I'm just not the same gender as I was when I was dropped. The body has been changed, my body, that means *you*. And you can't shift genders anymore. Please stop trying. It only brings back sad memories I'm supposed to have suppressed."

"Dropped." We weren't dropped. *Dumped*, more like. It's called "dropped" because the early observers had a thing about France during World War II. Heroes of the Resistance were "dropped", apparently. They weren't dumped and lost. They were dropped, and saved the day. *Heroes*. And we're definitely heroes. We're not fighting the Nazis. We're fighting to remain sane.

Those that sent us (gender-neutral to a person, I will lay odds, now that I can access more memory, existing placidly in that small part of life where one lacks biases and fixed beliefs and when one often takes on heroes who have no gender concerns or major roles they cannot forsake; our society is shaped by gender duties and only heroes can act as if these are nothing and worthless—and by "heroes", you know I am referring to something that has no equivalent in common English, like the unshakable identity of the Prime—I am translating conceptually and mathematics allows a large number of coherent ideas nested one within the other. Why is this so difficult to achieve in Engish?), they could have erased our non-Earth memories completely, just as they've sublimated so much of our physical selves. It's not beyond our science. They've not tried that last bit. Instead, our non-Earth memories are left just under the surface. Is this because they can't entirely erase our body memory without erasing *us*?

One cannot erase the person who was sent to do a job and still expect the job to be done as planned. One can try, it seems.

My body memory is raging. Wrong gender, dammit. Long shifts that lead nowhere. Not enough shifts. I feel it all. Every ache. Every symptom. Every problem. My language circles again as I try to escape.

Shifting is natural. And my body tries so very hard, but it can't shift. It thinks it's female. One gender. When really, it's borderline three genders. That's why we're in these particular bodies. A woman of this age in this society is the closest to our own that humans are capable of.

Mine is trying so very hard to be there for me. It tells me things. I'm so tired that my upper body hurts. I can't walk or carry things. It hurts to lie down. It hurts to stand up. I live on pain relievers and dream of the day when I have a stable flesh-home again. I dream of my body being what it was, and when I dream I find I can remember. The memory will fade in three days. Right now, I treasure it.

Changing never used to be like this. Chocolate and doctors were never a part of it. My body decided "Time to procreate" at the same time my inner self yearned for children or to make children or to nurse children. Or it said: "Time to watch", and I was an observer or judge.

Other people had other problems. They sought help with bodily functions that didn't fully work. Not me. Never me. Seven shifts and not a twinge. Other people. Not me. Never me.

And now I'm stuck in the body, artificially trying to maintain a constant between my seventh and eighth shifts. The most unstable shifts in all the cycles. And my body fights it, even though it's a human body and shouldn't know what full shifting is like. My body hates it that I'm caught in between shifts.

It shows that I'm other. Not even people. My body illustrates the reality, that I can't physically differentiate between procreator and nurse, between observer and judge. And it hurts and I hurt and I'm cross and happy and hot and cold and... My body is trying very hard. Very hard indeed.

Notes towards an
Understanding of the Problem

"Why don't we ever talk about politics?" asked Diana.

There was sunshine outside. A beam caught the flowers Janet had brought them and turned them to gold. Every few minutes Diana's eyes would flit from her daisy to the window, a trifle hopefully, then flit back to her friends, as if something were wrong and they alone could solve it. Today was possibly not the day for solutions, however, for she didn't look fully comfortable. Not once in the whole morning tea meet-up did she look as if she belonged there. She was trying, however. Very obviously putting in a valiant attempt at normalcy.

"I don't know why you don't, but me, it's because I live and breathe them and need a break," answered Trina.

"Me, too," said Janet. "This is Canberra, after all. Capital city of the Unknown Country. Wide and brown and turgid."

"For me," and Antoinette was hesitant, "it's because it can be a quagmire. Someone could get hurt."

"Me, too," said Leanne. "Everyone expects me to be conservative and when I'm not, the results can be disturbing."

"That means all of you live and breathe politicism, but in quite different ways," said Diana, being logical.

"Well, yes. But how about you?"

"Politics is one of the many things I feel unsure of. There's such a big discrepancy between what one person says and what another does, between newspapers and online media, between television and *Hansard*, that I simply don't know where to start."

"I generally start with chocolate," said Janet, with the practised air of someone who gave this explanation far too often but understood its importance to others. "There are simple classifications: white, milk, dark, level of cocoa fat, level of milk, level of sugar. Those can relate to the different parties and their policies. All chocolate. None of them match the world as we know it, but they're all trying to, in their way."

"You keep the personal out?"

"Not at all. I start with chocolate, but the parallel breaks down within minutes. It lasts just long enough to get my listeners to understand that the parties are all social constructs and manmade, and that policies are decided by groupthink and can change with fashion. It's an excellent place to start, especially when I hand out chocolate samples to bring points home. Pauline Hanson is peanut M&Ms, which means I get to warn about the problems of nut allergy without having to say anything nasty about the woman herself. I'm not allowed to express opinions when I give these lectures, but I find ways of gently indicating my views."

"Remind me to turn up to the Museum when you're giving one of those lectures," said Leanne. "Even if I can't cope with the politics, I can take refuge in the chocolate."

"We get everyone coming in—I have to have a way of explaining that won't hurt anyone and will reach as many people as possible. For some groups, I never get beyond chocolate. I spend the whole hour explaining everything, over and over, using the chocolate to keep things together. For other visitors, the chocolate is all done in five minutes and we move on to the history of our system and how the past sets things up for the future."

"How do you handle what's happening now?" asked Trina. "It's easy for me—I work with industry groups. I just stick to the line they need."

"It's not so easy," Janet admitted. "I've got a responsibility to my employers and their ultimate employers are government, which means I really can't talk about how certain groups are subversive and undermining the whole system."

"Neither of you are really talking about politics, then," pointed out Diana. "You're limiting the discussion to certain aspects of politics."

"It's still politics," defended Trina.

"It's a set of constrained and managed discourses and doesn't permit you freedom of expression." Diana was firm. "It's like closing an equation that's begun, rather than starting a new one, of your own devising."

Trina objected. "I don't expect freedom of expression when I'm at work. I'm working for someone."

"But you don't talk about politics outside work," Leanne pointed out.

"It's like my situation—Trina doesn't want to get into trouble."

"I guess so." Trina was worried by this. "I can't say things in public that could be taken to undermine what my organisation needs.

"None of us talk freely about politics, then," said Antoinette.

"And yet we're in the capital of the country, and we're all educated women who have rather more familiarity with politics than many. No wonder we're in such trouble. We're building false systems that aren't nearly complex enough to relate to the reality."

"Chocolate systems," suggested Janet.

"Tempting and yummy and quite, quite wrong."

"There must be someone who believes that things are simple."

"And not yummy."

"Oh, I believe that they're not yummy. Give me the actual chocolate anytime," said Antoinette. "Politics is dangerous for some of us. Actually, physically dangerous."

"And depressing," said Diana.

"Never forget depressing," added Leanne.

"I think we need a change of subject."

"And maybe cake, since chocolate is possibly not the best menu choice after that discussion?"

Yes, this is one of the Great Five Incidents that caused the Irksome Fruitcake.

No, I can't see why. Still. Having examined it far too many times. The equations say it must be, and our equations are never wrong.

Note that chocolate is still there, permeating all things. I can't let go of it as a factor yet, however much I'd like to.

The woman's slow voice...

was counting again

One, two, three, four, five, six, seven, eight, nine, ten, eleven, twelve, thirteen, fourteen, fifteen, sixteen, seventeen, eighteen, nineteen, twenty, twenty-one, twenty-two, twenty-three, twenty-four, twenty-five, twenty-six, twenty-seven, twenty-eight, twenty-nine, thirty.

I want to stop here. I don't want more of this.

She died. My precious little one died. Dream marriage, dream child…nightmare death. A nightmare of death. Death as a horror dream.

I cannot deal with this. I don't want to remember this year. I don't know why I count it, every time. I don't know why I don't find other memories to put in its place.

I come back to one moment, time after time after time after time. In that moment I see a toddler asleep and he bends to wake her up and…that's it. She's gone. Our little one is no longer.

I will not think of her name. I will not think of her at all. That calls her back. And she's gone. There is no moment as bad as this. There cannot be. The memory is so raw that I cannot even feel the emotion. It's stark, like a picture, like a movie with the sound down. I distance myself from it still. It hurts too much to feel. It hurts too much to remember.

The Observer's Notes

I had over 2 kg of tomatoes and an empty saucepan. There are so many things one can do with a good sauce. This includes splatter-decorating.
—seen in social media.

Well, that was a laugh a minute.

Literally.

I was laughing sarcastically, deep inside. Every minute, once a minute. For every minute, once a minute was when and how often that middle-aged man slighted me. Put me down. Demeaned me. Respectfully, of course. Always respectfully. He knew I was inferior, that was all. He felt he had to assert himself and affirm his superior position with short, pithy statements that let me know what he knew. Then he upped his game and changed his tone…and told me how to do ordinary things as if I were a juvenile who had applied for additional instruction due to incompetence.

Condescending twerp. Annoying bastard. Turd.

I hope I'm here not as the vanguard, but as the full alien takeover. He'll be first to the wall, along with every other polite, middle-aged gentleman who feels the need to put women down in order to assert their own amazing importance. I hope there's a wall, and that he gets to see my face as he's lined up with the others.

I will look at him and laugh at him every minute, once a minute. He will be gagged, so that he can't explain to me all the things I already know, and I shall explain to him, moment by moment, what's happening. As if he were a juvenile who had applied for additional instruction due to his own incompetence.

"Yes, dear, those are indeed aliens. With ray guns. And look, I am one too. An alien with a ray gun. And do you know why that ray gun is pointed at you? Because you told me how to make my own lunch, with my own ingredients that I brought from home. And you told me how to apply for my own job, which I was doing perfectly efficiently until you stopped me at my very own desk in order to instruct me on all the work I'd already finished, which you had not read (for it was not your job). And you treated me like a piece of shit.

"The sad thing is that pieces of shit can use ray guns. Especially alien pieces of shit. Like me.

"Oh, don't worry, they're not really ray guns. I just like calling them that. There's no word for them in English, but they make very pretty pictures of people on the wall when we explode them. It's a kind of art. A memory art. So that no-one will ever forget that you talked over me or down to me every single time we met. That you interrupted my work whenever I had tight deadlines. And that you did it from a position of great benevolence and with a tone of great condescension.

"Great benevolence should be turned into art, don't you think? It's important to my fellow aliens that no life be wasted. Art is important. Far more important than you are.

"I can see that you're wondering what kind of alien I am. It's not relevant to your life. Or to your death. You should have listened to me when I was willing to talk with you. When you silenced me and talked over me and told me how to live every second of my gender-oversimplified human existence."

And this would be recorded and broadcast to the whole world. And the whole world would hear me saying: "Be nice to other people, even if you secretly think they're inferior. For they could be, like me, aliens with ray guns that will turn you into wall art."

And then I wouldn't bother killing him, for there would be others with guns. Qualified executioners. I would simply walk away, and get on with my life, in my own body, treated with the respect I deserve.

I am a person of note back home. That's why I'm here. Amazingly gifted in some very useful ways. Which I have successfully translated into the workplace in Australia, thank you very much. I do my job well. Despite interference.

I would say, to my fellow-aliens: "Thank you for cleaning this mess up for me." And then I would go back home and continue with my life as if I was having mere time out to deal with a minor medical problem. A pimple, perhaps.

We're very compassionate, me and my people, but only up to a point. There are several ways of reaching that point. One is to demean other people.

That's why we appear in human skin, for otherwise we would get respect whenever someone sees our fearsome, googly eyes. The light strikes off our fearsome googly eyes in the most remarkable way. It's impossible not to respect them. Quite obviously it's not impossible not to respect me.

Human form gives humans a chance to respect me for who I am, not for my fearsome googly eyes. And yes, I'm explaining the obvious to myself. That's how angry I am.

Humans have rules, too. His attitudes are due to this idiot species turning a survival narrative into a rule, I'd guess. All the fiction and all the movies tell about men surviving, despite demonstrating their utter stupidity 95% of the time. "Alpha male behaviour", it's called, as if complete lack of gender fluidity were a good thing.

Only one in forty-three human men are like this. We've done the study. We know the numbers. Minority dominating and leading whole cultures by favouring troughs of stupidity. Majority consenting tacitly or unwillingly.

Knowing it and feeling it are two quite different things. Before, I was like a human male, who knew what was possible but thought, "It's not too bad, really." Now that I know what living in this body and being seen as slightly inferior means in human terms, my internal fearsome googly eyes want to develop a death-stare. I know I don't have a death stare in my real body (at least I think I know) but they should have given me one for my human suit. It would be very helpful for days like this. Experiencing statistics personally is an utterly vile thing.

This is not the anthropologist speaking right now.

I've made a suitably dispassionate report elsewhere. It is safely uplifted. My report did not engage. It did not get angry. It lied.

I have not reached my touchpoint yet. No ray guns. No art.

This is my personal report.

I am deeply offended at being snubbed. At being ignored. At not being included in the conversation when it really was about both of us. Then at being talked down to as if I were…something small.

I may be studying him, but I am not someone who can be excluded from the conversation or condescended towards. I am not small.

He wants my job. I don't want my job. He can find me another one. Then we can both be quits. There is no need for him to finagle and scheme and talk down to me. Simple co-operation would make both of us happier. My paid employment is but a means to an end. It's easy enough to negotiate a solution and find us a mutually-convenient way out of what is (to be honest) a minor mess.

Instead of finding mutual solutions, he plays fast, niggling games. If I'd been given the body of a younger woman, and if it had been an attractive body with a pleasant smile and a nippy waistline, he would have condescended like a turnip. Instead, he talked down as if I were a nothing, and acted as if he'd rather I weren't there. He worked towards my continuing non-existence.

His desk is 132 centimetres away from mine.

He puts on this act whenever he decides I have invaded his sacrosanct workplace, whether the invasion is for social or work reasons. If I get even a half inch closer to him, he barricades himself with dripping put-downs.

His desk is 132 centimetres away from mine.

And my desk was there first. As was I. I have seniority. And we work together. Today he put on this act simply because he saw from my email to our boss that I'd finished the job in question. First he talked to our boss in front of my desk, as if I wasn't there (not at his own desk, four feet away) and then… I cannot detail it. Humiliation.

It's not the first time. I need more fingers to count the times each week he pulls stunts like this.

Enough with going to the toilet to hide, and examining my middle-aged female self in the mirror to see how this face could provoke such behaviour. To the firing line with him!

I'm writing this in the library toilet (of course) and thinking that the library should be a stronger influence upon me than its toilet. I need to be a better observer.

When I barged through the library to get to its safe, work-free toilet (the only place immediately accessible by me that is free from chattering gossip), there was someone already here. While I waited, I noticed a librarian pushing a trolley of red and blue drawers from one end of the room to the other. He walked jauntily, as if he had the best job in the universe. Maybe he does. My mindwipe means I have a restricted idea of what jobs there are. That's why I need to retrieve more. It's why every day in every way I push to find more memories.

It's not all about me. The error they made in deleting so much is affecting my ability to do the job assigned to me. Like the bloke on the next desk. I am not alone.

This bloke, the librarian, may not be happy at all. He may have walked jauntily because of bio-mechanics. This is insider-thought. What I should be doing, only more knowledgably. The amazing lack of memory, the passionate hate (*to the wall*, I say!), the damned middle-aged body and its needs. I wish it were my friend on duty. She would understand.

When I was first placed in this human suit, before traces of me myself returned, when I was home on sick leave due to an "emotional breakdown", I read the work of anthropologists. I wanted to know what to think, how to act as a human anthropologist. It appears I am an extraordinarily dutiful person, in whatever skin.

It didn't work. It will never work. I am here in this bloody chocolate-addicted meat suit, two days (if I'm lucky and it comes on time) before my period, and I have to deal with too many turds, and I suddenly realise I don't understand a thing. I have no special status. I have nothing. Normally I don't have quite northing. Normally I have obscene levels of patience. Today, however, I have nothing.

Unless I count being put down and ignored and treated as unreliable: I have that in spades.

Next time I'm debriefed, I'll give in all my reports, but I'll also ask:

1. Why me?
2. Why here?
3. Why on earth does this planet need misogynists?
4. Am I permitted to shoot poison through my little finger at those who offend me?
5. May I have a wall, please? And control over the line-up. And my very own ray gun.

Notes towards an
Understanding of the Problem

These women astonish me, over and over. This is the third time I've checked those key episodes, and there are still surprises.

It just goes to show how different the official view of humans is from the way this group lead the parts of their lives that we see. I watch human visual stories (am addicted right now to superhero narratives) and realise that the *X-Men* and *Avengers* films have nothing in common with the way these women tell their lives. The public face of humanity is exotically different from their private. No wonder we fell into the hole.

This note isn't about one of the episodes that have been identified as critical. It's on the list that my predecessor regarded as "unjustly neglected" when the equations were redone. I've never been able to see why until now, though I did check the workings and they were right and this episode is, if not critical, at least rather important. This is why I'm noting it. No-one has given an explanation of it previously, and this means that it becomes more and more "unjustly neglected" and we fail to see the actual picture. Anything that remains so silent to me may help me get past this impossible sticking point.

The notes on this episode now all declare that this is a transformational moment. It's like that public/private face of humanity. It's not listed as critical, and yet it's transformational. This is one of the reasons for revisiting it.

In my previous analyses, I couldn't see its importance because I saw the personality attributes previously for each and every woman and also because it was in a place they had visited before, on a wet day (they meet for hot chocolate when it rains, or when someone has bad PMT—of course I've seen it all before, it's cyclical) and both of these mean that it doesn't fit with human public narratives. These things just aren't important to the way humans describe themselves in their stories. What I realised today is that this is the first time that four of the women have demonstrated astonishment at something the fifth has said. And that human stories are misleading.

Scene-setting: café with hard plastic table tops (fake marble), a clattering lino floor where the rain refuses to puddle, small cold draughts that peek around corners and surprise people.

Too little space. Not even the regular daisies brought by Janet fitted on the table—the women had them in their buttonholes and their handbags and, in Trina's case, decorating her mobile phone. Getting past anyone else to go to the counter or to check the weather outside is to beg bruises from those hard table tops or the jutting-out corners of the chairs. Janet's stick has been tripped over four times since they sat down. To give an idea of this as an indicator, Janet's stick is normally not a problem at all (she wields it almost as an extension of her body), so it creating a problem four times is significant.

"It's days like this I most need the stick," said Janet, gloomily, "and it's days like this where it most gets in the way."

"I've often thought that a stick would be handy," Trina half-dreamed, "because then I could hit anyone who annoys me. Hard. On the shins. Or, even better: on the ankles. Or maybe the knee caps. All the places."

"Human reality," replied Janet. "We never do. It's a comforting thought, though, particularly when someone tries to talk over me and tell me what I think."

"Mansplaining again?" asked Diana, sympathetically. "I've been getting it all week."

"Not this time. A young, bright thing who feels that anyone over thirty must have lost their brain. Any *woman* over thirty," she corrected, "for the guy after me didn't get the condescending garbage, nor the kindergarten-level explanation. I've been in IT all my life, have gone to that shop for five years, and still no-one there accepts that I might possibly know what I'm doing. That I might be after a power cord for a machine I already own, and that I know what kind of machine it is and what kind of cord I need. And that the one I'm being handed has entirely the wrong plug."

"I know the feeling." Diana's body-language was emphatic in its agreement. "I've never been tempted to whack someone with a stick, but I've…er…withheld information."

"What do you mean?" Leanne was puzzled.

"I give the guys one free pass. They can talk down to me one time a week. After that, I pretend their explanation is a story. I sit back and admire the way it's told. I thank the teller-of-inventions very politely, and explain—using your experience today—that all I needed was a cable, but that I can get it round the corner if they don't stock them. I vary the explanation to meet the story, of course."

"And you do? Go around the corner?"

"I normally go online," admitted Diana. "One doesn't have to face judgements of age and gender and IQ online. My bank balance is the only thing that's judged."

"I've been buying online for years," Antoinette said, "for the same reason. Shopping ought to be fun, not a series of humiliations."

"Oh, the joys of being a middle-aged female," said Leanne.

"What about you," Diana asked her. "What do you do?"

Leanne was silent for a moment, then said: "This is oddly difficult to explain. Give me a moment."

The small table was a pond of quiet in a busy café until Leanne was ready to speak again.

"It's such a small question," she began, "But it triggered something I never talk about. "

"You trust us," breathed Trina, as if she'd been given the world's greatest gift.

"I do. Finding words is difficult when it's something I never talk about, though."

"Take your time," said Diana.

She not only took her time, she wasn't eloquent. Stops and starts and stutters and going back to the beginning because she missed something. What she spoke about wasn't important to me. It was religious, for one thing, and not something that was important in and of itself. We don't do religion. It's a human thing. More story, really.

I won't transcribe or even fake-transcribe (which is what I do when I want to indicate what the women say, but don't want to get bogged down in *oh* and *um* and *ah*s and *oh*—human language isn't tight or controlled and it's no use pretending that it can be got down literally and still make sense) so this will be quick.

She believed in a deep, complex unity in the world. A profound unity to everything. When people are stupid and explaining in that way, they're working against the goodwill that binds everyone. "It's like climate change—we were thinking of ourselves and in not seeing the bigger picture, we damaged Earth and its other inhabitants." She therefore took extra time with these poor souls and helped them realise what they needed to learn to be part of the wider good.

Leanne meant none of this sarcastically. Her eyes shone with her genuine love of humankind.

She then added that her explanations started off sympathetic but had been known to move to the sarcastic. "For educational purposes, of course. I can tolerate mansplaining by putting it in perspective, but I can never tolerate intentional stupidity."

I felt it should perhaps make the other women feel a bit queasy, but it didn't. They were surprised, however. Janet had an instant explanation for the surprise. "You're a scientist and one of those really pragmatic country women. I didn't expect Gaia from you."

"No-one does." Leanne was acerbic. "It's why I don't talk about it as a rule. It's not Gaia in the normal way, anyhow. It's a way of seeing the world. The universe. Complex and difficult to explain and I just made a terrible hash of it, but my theory and understanding of it is substantial. I don't like talking about it because so many people think that the short summary is the whole, when all it indicates is that my philosophy exists."

"It's a good approach, I think," said Diana. "Turn a humiliating moment into a teaching moment."

"Creating a balance where none existed before," Leanne nodded.

"And this just proves that none of us are what others assume we are," said Janet

"And that we're safe for each other. You wouldn't believe how rare that is," added Antoinette.

"That's why I can say this," said Leanne. "I can't talk about anything religious. What is it about our country, anyhow, where admitting to a sense of the numinous is either betrayal or the sign of a flittering mind?"

And this puts a finger right on why Australia was chosen as the place from which to render Judgement. I'm not sure my people understand this thing humans call religion (in fact, I'm certain we don't), but at least my people realised that religious countries would present an unnecessary obstacle to understanding humankind.

Unless this is yet another mistake we made. Just how typical was this Australia? And was its capital city identical to the other places? This is something I have not yet explored. I shall give an order to have these questions researched. They are almost definitely immaterial, but, to be safe, we will check.

Also the religion matter. I've no doubt it's an issue of small concern, despite Leanne's personal caution in bringing the matter up, but it never hurts to be careful.

"You're the wrong person to betray anyone or wander about with your mind a-flitter," said Diana. "You're the most practical person I know. Despite all the science and stuff you do."

"CWA-central, that's you," Trina suggested. "Makes it easy to see your belief and to accept it. Easier, anyhow. I'm not certain I get deep understanding of the universe. I get that you have a big mind and can see things I can't, is all."

"You get people, though," said Antoinette.

"People…" scoffed Trina, "People are easy. In so many meanings of the word."

It might have been my imagination, but it seems to me that the laughter was uneasy. Between Gaia and sex jokes, the conversation had veered into dangerous regions. UnAustralian directions.

This explains the surprise. No-one was expecting religion from Leanne. Any religion. If I had intervened as a time-traveller (in human form, of course), and said "Religion! Leanne!" they'd have assumed she could be described using a standardised denomination: *Church of England*, or maybe *High Church Catholic*. At a stretch, Methodist. All Christian. All common enough in Australia. This is normative, as far as I can discover.

The official statistics are unreliable on this subject, as Australians tend to turn their answer to the religious question into a joke and label themselves Pastafarians or Jedi Knights, or they put an answer that they believe gives what's expected, which is either Church of England or Catholic.

My assumptions on what is normative rely on indirect evidence. There must be human studies of this, but my aides can't find them, which means they weren't collected for the earlier studies, and, of course, I need strong cause to seek out more information, given the circumstances.

My assumptions will suffice.

Leanne had a religion that looked to the others as woo-woo. Not something normative. "Woo-woo" is what it was called at the time, popularly. Pagan, half self-invented, half borrowed. Emotive rather than intellectual. "Gaia" was not entirely a neutral description of it. And yet…this was Leanne. And she had intellectualised it, being Leanne.

After the surprise, they accepted it. They found explanations for it. They tried to understand.

"One day I'd like to know how you came to where you are," commented Janet. "One day."

Leanne laughed at the comment. "One day I'd like to know that, too. Today is not that day."

"You really don't know?" asked Diana.

"I was making a *Lord of the Rings* joke." Leanne sat up tall to reinforce her dignity and the fact that she'd expected her friends to get the joke, and that she was deeply, deeply disappointed in them. When Leanne sat up tall, everyone else was diminished.

This is what properly dispelled the surprise. From then on, Leanne's religion and, later, when she talked about it, Janet's more codified Wiccan belief, were accepted as simply part of their lives. I thought for a while those flowers Janet gave out were religious in nature, but the evidence is clear that she just happened to have them with her the first time they met. She even said once: "I like creating traditions, and this is a nice one to create."

Although the others were rather normative in their Christianity, they all admitted that they had no real religious belief, that Christianity was more cultural to them. Herein lies the reason I didn't question the whole human/religion thing earlier. Really, it's not that dramatic an issue for these women, and they are central to the fate of humankind, so one would expect that they'd be representative.

"An excuse for Christmas," Antoinette said.

"An excuse for Halloween," Trina added.

"It's all about dress-up and food and presents. I do those with the family," Leanne agreed. "That's not religion. Not unless you have maybe a morsel of belief and admit that there are other things."

"I believe in aliens," suggested Diana.

"Religiously?" asked Leanne.

"No, factually."

"Doesn't count. I have a Jewish friend who says that Santa Claus existed as a person, and that doesn't make her a religious Christian either. It makes her a destroyer of belief, for she tells everyone that Santa died some time ago."

"Fair enough." Diana was not worried about this at all. She was also not worried that she appeared to be the only one who believed in aliens. In this group, they accepted differences. Some of them deep, some shallow, but differences. That, I knew. Maybe the surprise came when the differences didn't fit in with the personality of the speaker. Like the time Diana ordered herbal tea.

I think I'm getting the hang of humans. And I think I understand why this particular episode is on the list of ones that were influential. If I were religious in a human way, I would believe in miracles.

It opens many doors for research.

The woman's slow voice...

was counting again

One, two, three, four, five, six, seven, eight, nine, ten, eleven, twelve, thirteen, fourteen, fifteen, sixteen, seventeen, eighteen, nineteen, twenty, twenty-one, twenty-two, twenty-three, twenty-four, twenty-five, twenty-six, twenty-seven, twenty-eight, twenty-nine, thirty, thirty-one, thirty-two, thirty-three.

I'm so lonely.

I'm free.

The documents tell me I'm free. Signed and finished and…free. And alone. We were separated and now we're each on our own. I changed my life for his, but he couldn't change his life for me. I was willing to try and he wasn't. So it became a game to determine who was able to lose with most grace. Or maybe least grace. Neither of us handled loss well.

I need to go back to university and get some qualifications for a job. This should lead to a career. This is what the counsellor says. I delayed my career to get married and it didn't work. This isn't a problem, she says. Living is a problem, I said.

I never wanted to be single.

The counsellor had so many things to tell me about this. She was like a textbook. My year is like a textbook. A textbook about divorce and grieving and wondering about the waste of human potential and why we couldn't agree on the equal split of our possessions.

Freedom is surprisingly bleak. That, too, is like a textbook.

Notes towards an
Understanding of the Problem

"Do adults have BFFs?" Trina posed the question as if the fate of the world hung on it.

"Don't we hang around in posses and look cool?" asked Antoinette. "Isn't that what grown-ups do?"

"You look cool," said Diana. "I merely look curious. Right now I'm curious about the source of this question."

"I was watching *R.O.D the TV*," explained Trina.

Most of the time, humans throw vague references as if they were casual toys for catching, and everyone's expected to hang a whole conversation on them. *Everyone*, sad to say, includes me. And I am not human. I have smaller limits than them. Humans can hold three conversations at once, no-one's following any of those three conversations properly, and I want to strangle everyone involved. Except that they're already dead. I still want to strangle them.

Sometimes I forget that these conversations happened sixty-one years ago. And I'm becoming so very human. I say all this stuff about how humans speak, and I compose it in the minute space between one word and the next as I watch the recording over and over, and then I'm proven to have gone entirely off-topic again.

My habits of thought and speech demonstrate quite effectively that phenomenon that has been remarked upon time and time again: our race is in many ways sympathetic to humans. Not just our race. That sentence was ironic. To a certain degree, that Judgement was our neighbours judging us and also themselves.

We all develop the same traits after we've spent too long in the actual or virtual vicinity of humans. This is one reason why techies stay apart. We who study closely become contaminated, whereas they remain pure.

That day, Trina merely paused a moment before explaining, which I should have known. I'm learning more about my own learning and mimicking capacities than I am about humans, sometimes.

Trina looked round, and smiled sweetly at the lack of comprehension in the assembled group. "Such blank faces," she commented, equally sweetly. "*R.O.D the T.V.*—it's a Japanese anime series, sequel to another. The only relevant bit is that one of the characters fixates on *Anne of Green Gables,* and she and another character swore eternal devotion as BFFs. I wondered who among my friends has BFFs. For the record, I had sequential BFFs when I was a kid and I swore each and every one of them lifetime devotion. These days I don't. Don't have BFFs, I mean. Although I don't remember much swearing of lifetime devotion, either." She said this last bit with a lift of defiance.

"Doesn't the woman of your heart count as a BFF? It would be logical if she did." Leanne was just asking the obvious.

"It would be logical, but alas we're not. I think that's half the trouble."

"My husband is," volunteered Diana. "My first wasn't, but this one's a keeper."

"So some of us do and some of us don't?" suggested Trina.

"That sounds about right," said Janet, "For I'm not going to volunteer my status. BFFdom is off limits."

"Fair enough." Trina was equable. "How about aliens?"

"What on earth do you mean?" asked Antoinette. "Why aliens?"

"It's an important question. Do aliens have BFFs?"

"You could ask them," suggested Diana.

"First find me an alien, then I'd be happy to ask." Trina looked around to demonstrate her cleverness. When the others laughed but no-one spoke up, she continued. "OK, so that's a no-go. No-one's willing to speculate on the BFFdom of aliens."

Antoinette laughed again. "Define the alien and I'll speculate all you want. It will be unreliable, but I'm willing to speculate. I just can't be bothered defining an alien."

"I have old friends," suggested Leanne. "And I'm very alien in my own way. But I'm not offering myself up as your alien. They're not always easy to deal with and they don't always find me easy to deal with, but they're amazing people who I have known forever and they're very good to see. Old friends, not aliens. Though sometimes I wonder if they aren't one and the same. How does that fit in?"

"I have no idea. It's a bit tangled," admitted Trina. "I was wondering if I had a BFF, if she would know a way to deal with hot flushes, for I'm tired of them. I was wondering if there was a way of turning hot flushes into another conversation entirely, for they're dominating my every moment right now. I spent last night lying on top of the bed with the window wide open, hoping it would go below zero so that I could get some sleep."

"I'm not sure that's safe," said Janet.

"I'm not sure it is, either, but I'm running out of options. I handle the vicissitudes of old friends much better than I handle hot flushes. And all my old friends are vicissitudinous."

"Let's celebrate BFFs, old friends, handling problems and the eventual loss of hot flushes," suggested Antoinette.

"Being alive and handling it magnificently?" asked Leanne.

"Yes, that's it," said Diana. "My treat."

"Chocolate!" Trina smiled radiantly.

It didn't matter what places their conversations visited, they always returned to menopause and to chocolate. I believe one of my colleagues did a study of this. It's not in English, however, so I will make a note to find it when I come to my conclusions here and am finished with the cultural embedding. It might be helpful as a transition, given how hard it is to emerge from embedding.

The Observer's Notes

Someone who barely knows me gave me advice that she herself wouldn't follow if someone gave it to her. She sees herself as unique and special. She sees me as a receptacle for advice.

—noted at a meeting. I was probably the one who thought this, but am not certain.

I think they've given me the wrong body. I'm pretty sure they have. It's not my body, I'm certain. And it's a bit too faulty. I'm too familiar with the medical system. I mean, I'm too familiar because I've been too much subject to it.

It feels like a lifetime ago that I was worried about my DNA being different. It's taken me months to discover this. Maybe years. How long have I been on this planet, anyway?

I hate this body. That makes me a perfectly normal female, my friends say. Normal females hate their bodies. My one friend who doesn't explains that it's because she hated the male body she was trapped in. *That* I understand. It's like gendershifting too early. If you gendershift too early, nothing works. It's a foul feeling of non-alignment when that happens, as if the whole universe is dancing to a different rhythm. It can take almost the whole of the gender cycle to be aligned and for the body to work properly in its correct gender, and so you miss out on the joys of motherhood, or fatherhood, or courting, or…any of the genders.

I hated my body just before I came here, too. I mis-shifted for the worst cycle. I did this at the very moment I was compulsorily drafted into the Alien Corps.

They needed someone notable. I don't have enough memory

still and have no idea what I was notable for, just that I was eminent enough to be drafted. I wasn't myself, and they knew it. They waited until I was sorted and had moved on physically to a more stable state before they sent me to Earth, true. They had, however, obtained my agreement (using pressure—I remember my bitter fight) when I was in no fit state to win over the impossibilities that are arguing with drafting. Our government can be callous.

Even though gendershift is not something this body knows, I hate it along with this body. Even though it isn't even close to my body, I hate it.

The only virtue in hating my body is that I can say so. It's considered normal (although frowned upon) for women to hate their bodies. Humans are strange. Their bodies are strange. I hate this body, still.

No matter how many good explanations there are for what I'm experiencing, I hate this body. And there are no good explanations, only bad ones.

I rebel at this. Somewhere within me, I remember not hating my body. I also remember not bleeding, not crying, not bloating, not… not…not being this gender.

Deep within me. In my core of cores. I am not a woman. I never was a woman. I tolerate being a woman because I must, because I can't change my body on whim. But there is no gendershift. I cannot move on without help. There are ways of doing it, for humans are not so backwards, but we all need to change to our proper gender and I'm not sure my real gender exists in this species. I don't think any of my real genders exist on this planet. I invent labels glibly, as if they do. But they don't. And it hurts.

When I first became self-aware, before I knew enough, I reported it. "I have the wrong body," I said. "I dislike this body intensely."

They said, "Humans are gendered differently to us. Most don't change in a lifetime. We chose yours because it best fulfils your function and your work. There is no wrong." The one they gave me, though, isn't true. It doesn't stay fixed for a lifetime. Not quite. It wobbles around its gender axis. Also, I'm not true. I am still alien, inside. The alien erupting from inside me probably sent me to hospital last week.

Whatever this body is or does, I'm always consistently me.

I asked again, the next time I went in. "Oh, it's just random," the technician said. The technician doesn't have a body on Earth. It works from a distance through all the machines. Everyone does, except us. Only the anthropologists have to make the big sacrifice.

I won't complain to the techs again. Even humans have a better chance of being in the right body than I have (despite the careful choice that was made for my function and my work), for they are able (under great duress) to say "Look, wrong body. We must modify critical aspects." It's not a simple change (Why isn't it simple? Is it made difficult on purpose? I could ask, but the everyday feels difficult in this body and gender is one of the areas that humans do not like to talk about—they become oppositional and grieving and angry), but they can do it.

I wonder if any humans are not male and not female and are also stuck? More humans in the wrong body, but with no recourse. Until recently, changes were—

I have an answer! I shall pretend I am historical. A human from the time before self-realisation was acceptable. It's the only way of continuing to live in this damn world of theirs when my own people with their twenty-five genders and their complex sexuality gave me the wrong damn body. A body that I hate. Blaming this body and blaming humans isn't going to help at all.

Where did that memory come from? I know the twenty-five and I know it's the reason none of us are male. The technicians were just being cheeky when they talked about assigned gender being random. It's not random at all. We've all been slotted into female bodies. Since the very first Earth exploration.

Initially we are assigned to a place within a small range of ages that cover perimenopause. None of us will ever quite reach menopause. This is what is considered closest to our natural state back home. I guess it is, at that. None of us are males because males transform even less than females, and none of us can live without our transformations. Even if those transformations are more like wobbles. They are part of that core of me, even if I'm stuck in the wrong body. I can't live without my transformation. I love it. I hate it. I miss it.

I remember the emotions without remembering the shift. Damn mindwipe. Damn body. And damn the study of interesting species.

The woman's slow voice...

was counting again

One, two, three, four, five, six, seven, eight, nine, ten, eleven, twelve, thirteen, fourteen, fifteen, sixteen, seventeen, eighteen, nineteen, twenty, twenty-one, twenty-two, twenty-three, twenty-four, twenty-five, twenty-six, twenty-seven, twenty-eight, twenty-nine, thirty, thirty-one, thirty-two, thirty-three, thirty-four, thirty-five, thirty-six, thirty-seven, thirty-eight.

Marriage #2. Not at all like my first marriage. No fairy tale. Just a simple signing of the Register and a dinner party with family. Maybe it's still a fairy tale. Just a fairy tale for more mature people, who don't love quite as abundantly, who are happy to work hard at spending their lives together but don't have the emotions to spend on frippery.

We had the emotions. I'm certain we did. One doesn't marry if one doesn't love, after all. I just don't remember them as being overwhelming. I was swept away the first time. The second time I felt...domestic.

Marriage was a part of my life this time. It wasn't the whole thing.

This doesn't mean I don't love. It means that I have perhaps another gap in my memory.

I don't know precisely what emotion I felt. I can't chronicle it. I can't recall it. It's as if I were part of a story and not living the experience, and the person who made me part of the story forgot to give me suitable emotions for that day. If I were a reasonable person, I'd invent emotions. I'd make myself feel them. God knows, it would be worth it—this is a good marriage. We are very well suited. The friends who introduced us must feel very smug.

Why don't I remember much about my second wedding day,

then? Maybe it's all about being married this time, and the wedding was simply the icing on the cake? There has to be a reason, and it has to be a good one. I'm damned if I can think of it, though.

My memory is full of the strangest holes. Some of them are explicable, but this one always escapes me.

Every time I think of my second wedding, I stop and think: "Why can't I remember how I felt?"

The Observer's Notes

What signifies knowing the Names, if you know not the Natures of things.
— Ben Franklin, read online (quotation not verified)

Women's lives are complex. I didn't realise just how complex they were until I went past the studies of humankind (which are, I need to remind myself frequently, somewhat male oriented) and into the private lives of a few women. I didn't know that hormones and their effects had such a large influence on everyday life. I certainly didn't know the role life experiences played in pushing individuals towards or away from profound belief. Nor personal narratives. Nor public narratives.

This whole story thing humans do is astonishingly central to their existence.

I thought that inheritance was all, and that either cultural or genetic inheritance was responsible for most decisions. After all, they are a primitive species. Primitive, but it seems primitivism doesn't make them less complex.

For far too long I completely missed that women are treated differently to men within the convoluted cultural matrices. This means there are fewer opportunities for success, more ways barred (often subtly) and more chance that a given woman will suffer everything from small hurts on a daily basis to rape and being expelled from social groups. Less chance for establishing themselves in their own right. More likelihood that they will be judged on the work or life of their husband.

I want to study what this means to my women. I *ought* to study what this means to my women. The limitations they face and the choices they have may be critical to the fate of Earth. This is a much more likely path to fruitcake than the chocolate was.

It's not so easy.

I started to look into Leanne's life after she admitted to being religious, and into Antoinette's life after I discovered that she had not always presented as female, and into Trina's life when I discovered that her female significant other was unreliable. These are big emotional aspects of the three women's lives, after all. I could do a simple background chronology to explain where they came from until they reached that moment.

I came into direct confrontation with the English language and with Australian culture. Biographies are set up for expected male life patterns. My women sometimes fell into those, and sometimes did not.

Pressing their lives into this mould destroyed their individuality and it hid those things that made them the women who probably changed us all. Knowing when Antoinette began school wasn't nearly as important as how she internalised and dealt with the messages she received about her gender, both at school and at home. Knowing that Leanne had suffered a series of very nasty incidents including personal violation was, also, far less important than how she turned this into a profound explanation of the universe. Knowing that Trina was good at school and treated badly in the workplace, was far less important than her everyday reality, which was as a strong woman with an inconsiderate life partner who she was unable to marry.

This is why her partner was missing.

They were not separated. Sometimes Trina grandstanded about separation, but they still lived together…when her partner was at home. That's as one set of papers read. The others read differently. They read as if they had a working partnership, that Trina was committed to a full relationship and that her partner was not.

What they definitely did together was working for equal opportunities. Their focus was on marriage. Not just theirs. Just not theirs. It depends on which narrative I follow.

And the personal price for these politics was vast. They didn't see each other often. Their children had one local parent. They worked the equivalent of two jobs each. Trina's partner had initially accepted an interstate job for a period, because it gave her the opportunity to lobby a different group of politicians. They were sacrificing their daily happiness for the common good. They were growing apart. And it hurt.

This is why Trina was not religious, she claimed. What god would permit such irony and such pain? This reading of their narrative supports both narratives. Whether they were in a long-term relationship or not, they were growing apart. And it hurt.

Just as she accepted the religion of the others in my group, so my group accepted Trina's agnosticism.

They each talked about their pasts and their present and their plans with astounding honesty. I know so much about these women. I can't pull up several conversations to review because they hurt too much. They demonstrate without doubt that humans are cruel and deserve to be destroyed. Leanne's life alone would cry for that outcome. I can't even talk about it.

So many incidents are left out of this compilation because I cannot face those moments again.

The closer I get to these women, the more grateful I am not to be the Judge. The more I know about the cruelty of humans, the less I understand why it all went so extraordinarily awry.

I do, however, begin to understand why chocolate took on such importance. It was a subject to return to when matters became dangerous. It was a sanctuary in a world that was sometimes beyond bearing.

The Observer's Notes

Those who follow unique paths tend not to be followers. Mind you, they're often not leaders, either. They can change everything, or they can change only their own lives. It's very hard to know.
—said in a meeting

Popular culture is a terrible thing. It helps me understand, because I can see the cultural unreason that lies beneath apparent logic when I am aware of what to look out for. That woman over there, for instance, is dressed for Parliament House. I know this, for here I sit in a committee room at Parliament House, attending a meeting in my guise of ordinary citizen of this world, and her clothes make her nearly inconspicuous. It takes the eyes of an anthropologist to spot the importance of the clothes.

I visit this building ironically often, considering my real self.

Every time I go through Security, I'm tempted to look an official in the eyes and say "Take me to your leader." That's not how it works, of course, but it's always tempting. I always resist the temptation.

I seldom resist popular culture.

I'm not dressed to reflect my inner self, and neither is this young lady. She is dressed to reflect a character in a popular TV series. Very current. Bright and cheerful and slim and intellectual and a superhero or a superhero's sidekick-in-the-making. Geek glasses, a trim figure, hair tied back in a single pony tail. Not quite decorous. Not quite professional. Ready to be turned into fiction.

The secret worlds of humans can so often be seen through their clothing choices.

"I'm going to be a superhero," these clothes say. "I belong here, in Parliament House, even though I'm fifteen years younger than everyone else in this meeting. I don't need dignity, for I have story."

The speaker, on the other hand, has long white pearls and a long white blazer, and is a long white woman with shoulder-length grey hair. Her voice is produced with effort. The attempts she makes to sound important tug at her tone. It transforms a naturally warm voice to a pale voice. A white voice. A long white voice, even for the effort of the speaker, makes it an effort to hear, and time slows to a halt. She ought not try so hard.

It is in this moment of no-time that I wonder if my records about these people will ever be useful to anyone else.

Why am I recording this culture? Why am I recording it doubly? Why do I write these notes as well as sending the material back home? I must be crazy. I ought not try so hard. I should be like the young woman and be ready to shuck off my outer layer and turn into a superhero at a moment's notice. Yet here I sit on the comfortable chair, eyeing off the biscuits (for they always do good biscuits here) and wondering why I bother.

Something nags inside me. I feel as if change is imminent.

Notes towards an
Understanding of the Problem

It was the day of disasters. It was signalled by Janet forgetting to bring daisies (which she never did) and all of the women forgetting their chocolate entitlement (another thing that never, ever happened). Diana was the worst affected.

Diana was late because she came from home, where she'd been sent to work when the office caught fire. This in itself was bizarre. "It wasn't the office itself," Diana explained to her friends when they compiled their various miseries over lunch. "It was the machine room downstairs."

"That's a pity," said Janet. "I had a wonderful image of an open plan office spontaneously bursting into flames. I detest open plan offices."

"It would've been nice, wouldn't it?" said Antoinette. "A gloriously fiery end to a sick building."

For Diana's building was notoriously sick. The sickest, they were told, in the region. This wasn't the first time she had been sent home and it wouldn't be the last. The number of illnesses produced by the building was notoriously high, too, but no-one wanted to take the blame or spend enough money to find out what was wrong, and so things continued and continued. Except for today, of course.

"I was lucky that we'd planned lunch," Diana said. "It's the only good thing today."

"So what else has happened," asked Leanne, "besides spontaneous combustion?"

"More a meltdown, I think. The fumes were terribly plastic and foul. Though possibly started by spontaneous combustion."

For a few minutes, the five played around with the details of how the building caught fire and what might have happened. Diana hadn't been sent home until the smell became unbearable. Eventually, they decided that since she could smell them from the fourth floor, the ventilation ducts were probably to blame.

"For everything?"

"Nah, just for you being sent home. The chemicals you would've breathed in if you'd stayed."

"Let's get back to the critical question," urged Leanne. "What else has gone wrong? You said there was more."

"My printer died before work. And my saucepan melted. All over the stovetop."

"Your saucepan melted?" Trina was disbelieving.

"I was making jam," Diana defended. "Finishing it off. Last night it just wouldn't finish and I wanted to go to bed, so I turned it off and decided to finish before work this morning. Except I didn't turn it quite off."

"My God," said Leanne, "You were lucky that you didn't get more than a melted saucepan. In fact, congratulations on being alive today."

"Maybe your work's machine room took the heat?" suggested Trina.

"Either way, it was shocking to wake up to. Then I burned my toast while I was trying to fix the printer and I spilled coffee all over the floor. Not just coffee, wet coffee grounds. It was an awful mess. Then I made tea instead and nearly scalded myself. I gave up and went to work and everything was fumes and the lift wasn't working and the electricity was out and everything was soggy and they sent us home. Except home was dreadful."

"Soggy?" Antoinette was fascinated.

"Firemen, I think. I can't be sure, though. Explanations were not forthcoming. Nor was time off. We were told to work from home for the rest of the week."

"They gave you time to collect everything?"

"Not really."

"Then maybe it wasn't the ventilation ducts?"

"I bet it was, and I bet they were worried about fumes. You know, and people's lungs?"

"I didn't think of that. Still, you can't work without stuff to work on and with."

"I can do some," admitted Diana. "I do work in the evenings, so I have some material I had with me, and there are a couple of things I can get on with. Not without a printer, though."

The group batted the idea around and came to a conclusion, which Diana resisted strongly, but which she was very relieved about. Trina, being the group chronicler, summarised it: "So we're going to all play hooky this afternoon, find Diana a printer and make sure nothing more goes wrong."

"And that she's OK," added Janet, anxiously.

"I thought that was a given."

Diana made one last attempt at protesting. "But I'm already OK. I said that before."

"And we've said twice that you're in shock and shouldn't be left alone. Too many crises. Too much happening."

"Think of it this way," Antoinette had the last word. "We've been saying for a while that we needed to do stuff together apart from eating chocolate and getting fat. This is it. We're taking you shopping, spending the afternoon on the town, and then installing your printer and cleaning your kitchen."

"I'd rather go to the art gallery than paint the town red," said Diana wistfully. "I've not been for longer than I care to remember."

"I like this much better than painting anything red," said Leanne.

And so it was decided.

The art gallery was enlightening for Diana, and the printer shopping for everyone else. Let me start with the printer shopping. It happened that same day, for one thing, because of Diana's state, and it was short and sweet and won't take me a morning to describe.

Have I ever said how much I love our technology? I love that I can access all these details from the record. It might cost a fortune, but I'm not the one who's paying and it makes writing this narrative possible. Turning events into the sort of analysis methods that Earth uses would be so much harder without this level of detail. And then the only way of describing and analysing events would be our own. Our own works nicely for *us*, but one can't take a high level of decision about another race without understanding how they see themselves and how they analyse themselves. That is why, in this case, story is important. I don't see how humans can write story and leave themselves out, however. Unlike maths, the individual has to be in there somewhere. I choose to make it obvious. Now. That's all.

OK, so that's not all. It's because I can't see how they do it. I'm copying Diana's techniques and her writing style partly because it's useful for analysis, but mostly because otherwise the culture is beyond my understanding. Diana is my bridge into the alien. And I've never said how very alien it is on some of the matters I address here. You can see that for yourself.

On so many other things, humans are just like us, but on this matter of story, they're...*strange*. I need every tool I can get to write this up. Then I'll do the usual analysis, but it has to be coming from an Earth point of view, for the sake of understanding and justice.

So, in human narrative terms, I'm not writing this chronologically. It's printer first, because of the focus on Diana.

In an ordered world, the women would have shared their opinions one after another, in a hierarchical way. The hierarchy between those five kept shifting, however, and as they went to the electronics shop, it shifted at least three times. All of them knew how to buy a printer and all of them wanted to advise, and only one didn't want to lead in the advice. While they walked, Diana listened and nodded and tap-tapped on her mobile phone.

"What are you doing?" Leanne finally asked. "Should we be quiet?"

"Not at all," said Diana, equably. "I'm not only listening, but taking your advice on board. I've narrowed it down to two choices, both of which are in-store."

"I thought," said Trina, slowly, "that you were more passive."

"I'm an observer," Diana observed, "I like watching and seeing what goes on. That's not the same thing as passive. And I'm not in shock over the printer. It's a nice focus, in fact, and is stopping me melting down entirely. I didn't know how close I was to the edge until I stopped running. I'm more worried about the melted saucepan. Also, I'm not sure I know how to set the printer up. New electronics bewilder me. My brain works differently to them."

"I can set it up for you," suggested Janet.

"And I'm certain the rest of us can take care of the stove and any mess," Leanne volunteered.

"That would make the biggest difference," Diana said. "If I can keep it together for long enough to get this printer, then I can stop. My husband's interstate right now, and out of phone reach until five, so I can't even ring him."

"Another of those national park things? Bad timing," consoled Trina. "I love his job, but hate that he's not here when things go wrong."

"They wouldn't be quite so wrong if he'd been home. He's the sort of person who double checks to make sure everything's turned off. I just do things and assume I've done them properly. This isn't the first time bad things have happened because of that," Diana admitted.

"Do you still want the Art Gallery?" asked Antoinette. "For we can always meet there tomorrow after work, instead. It's late night opening tomorrow. And maybe today has left you a bit tired?"

"I think that'd be sensible," said Diana. "If you don't mind. I really want to have a break, but if I have to face today's mess tomorrow...and he's not home until Sunday. I don't really want to deal with it alone. I didn't know this." Her voice was full of self-wonderment.

"You already look as if today's mess is too much." Leanne's face and voice gave the same message: sharp, but caring. "Let's get you that printer, get you home, and sort you out. Then you can have some quiet time."

Diana asked the sales assistant to recommend the least-returned from her final list of machines. She bought it and some ink, and the group arranged to meet at Diana's house. Jane went back with Diana, to set up the printer and get rid of the dead one.

"I know a primary school that could use it. The kids take it apart under supervision. It gives them confidence with electronics, I believe," she said. "Unless you have other thoughts..."

"That sounds like a good place for it to go." Diana's voice was tired, her mind was almost beyond thinking, so she sat in the comfortable chair and let the fatigue roll over her.

Trina and Leanne arrived at that point and took charge of the kitchen, setting it to rights. Neither of them was judgemental. They were purely practical.

Halfway through, Antoinette finally turned up. Diana half rose from her chair to open the door, but Janet said: "Stay seated, I've got this." And she did.

With Antoinette came afternoon tea. "I thought it might help you sort the jitters," she explained, as she handed Diana a hot chocolate and a pastry.

When Diana's friends were all done with afternoon tea, they tidied everything, washed dishes, took out the rubbish, and left Diana to rest. Diana decided that the afternoon tea would suffice for dinner and she prepared for bed. There were still fumes in her clothes from the machine room meltdown and still fumes in her kitchen from the saucepan meltdown, so she opened her bedroom window and let the cold in. Then she had a hot bath.

Her day ended a lot better than it began.

The woman's slow voice...

was counting again

One, two, three, four, five, six, seven, eight, nine, ten, eleven, twelve, thirteen, fourteen, fifteen, sixteen, seventeen, eighteen, nineteen, twenty, twenty-one, twenty-two, twenty-three, twenty-four, twenty-five, twenty-six, twenty-seven, twenty-eight, twenty-nine, thirty, thirty-one, thirty-two, thirty-three, thirty-four, thirty-five, thirty-six, thirty-seven, thirty-eight, thirty-nine, forty, forty-one, forty-two.

Some numbers have a significance in and of themselves. We try to find something in our lives at that moment that enhances this significance. This is me at forty-two.

If my life has a real story, it belongs somewhere in Douglas Adams' imagination, apparently in the section that deals with normal people who undergo strange, extraordinary experiences. This is why forty-two is important to me. It's a Douglas Adams number and me, I'm a science fiction fan. I'm not sure I know where my towel is. I'm reasonably sure I'm not being experimented upon by mice. I do know that I calculate my existence and count my life, and maybe also measure, in coffee spoons. Numbers are important. I don't need special events to make them so. Symbolism, however, helps. Attributed values.

All I did the year I turned forty-two was change jobs. I moved from one job to another. Nothing externally exciting. Nothing for anyone who doesn't see symbolism in numbers.

I always remember turning forty-two. It's one of my important years. It's the year I name aloud when I want to list how false my life is. The number balances precisely all the different things that I am and that I should be.

The Observer's Notes

There may be times when we are powerless to prevent injustice, but there must never be a time when we fail to protest.
  — Elie Wiesel, read online (quotation not verified)

There are terror attacks in France. I don't know the specific places. That's not true. And it's very true. I know each location in one way. I visited when I was in my twenties. I wasn't just a tourist, either. I stayed with Micheline, who had been my pen friend since I was ten. I look at the pictures of Paris and think "I know this", but I don't. My memory knows these places, but it's artificial memory. I hate artificial memory. It always leads me astray.

You'd think the memory being constructed out of other people's experiences would make it hurt less. I don't have fond memories of Micheline visiting her cousin with me in tow. We went to a nice middle-class flat on the fifty-first floor of a giant block in Montparnasse. I just think I have those memories.

The walls were dove-blue and the furniture mostly modern, but there was just a little bit of that French nineteenth century that gives a room in a middle-class Paris household such a feeling of substance. The dining room was purely modern. It could have been stark if the colours had not been gentle. The focus there was on food, not furniture. I know all this. I was there. And yet...

If I dropped in to say "hi", my hostess would recognise the evening, but not me. I try not to think of her as a once-upon-a-time hostess, rather than as an erstwhile hostess, but this whole situation wears fairy tale clothing, doesn't it? The memories of other people have been stolen and cannibalised for me, to enable me to fit nicely in and create science at the service of anthropology.

The memories of the various people who were stolen and then returned are a part of my data. Micheline thinks I was her pen friend as a child, too. She, too, remembers my visit. Yet I've never met these people. I'm not one of them. If her husband were one of the cartoonists who was killed, I'd be mourning a phantom. As it is, her husband is a cartoonist, but in a less endangered publication. But he's Jewish. He could have been killed. And if he had, the irony of it all would have overwhelmed me.

If I don't know them, why does it hurt so much when I start to forget them? Patchy memory is an ordinary facet of ageing, after all. It isn't merely that my actual self creeps out from under the veil and shatters the reality of my past. My memories of Earth and self are playing tag with each other, and each time they collide I lose a bit of each. This is not supposed to happen.

Am I becoming too human? Is there such a thing as being too human?

I didn't know it hurt until I started writing it down. My face is faded with the exhaustion of deep emotion. If I look in the mirror, I will see a mere shadow of myself. And yet...I don't know these people. I barely know this species. Why should I feel everything but a superficial concern, an interest in the breaking news, a technical curiosity?

I blame my husband. He's away again and I always feel smaller and more isolated when he's not here. He grounds me. Right now, I need him. He rang, but it wasn't enough. I need him to hold me.

Do humans always hurt this damned much? If they do, I want to belong to another species. One hundred and fifty-eight innocents were murdered in Paris. They could be people I walked past in the street last summer. I did go there last summer: that memory is real. And I met Micheline and we both said: "How you've changed." And yet I am hurt more by the fake memories from thirty years ago.

If my brain has cogs, those cogs have rust spots.

My heart aches. My brain aches. My eyes ache from unshed tears. I want to strip my mind of these false memories. I want to strip my heart of these all-too-real emotions.

I want to go home. I do not remember my home. That French dining room from my twenties has more reality to me. Nevertheless, I miss home. I wish I were there, now.

The Observer's Notes

"Kindred spirits are not so scarce as I used to think. It's splendid to find out there are so many of them in the world."
  —LM Montgomery, *Anne of Green Gables*

Anne Shirley has a solution for me. I'll explain why I'm meeting with Anne Shirley in a moment, should I feel like it. I don't know if I'll feel like it. I'm erratic today. I'm being Anne Shirley for a little, first. Living in her body in my imagination. Wearing her red hair and perfect nose. This is because Anne Shirley has a solution for me.

I don't have my own memories. This much is obvious. By this stage, I can't assume that my own memories are ever going to return. Obviously the emotional aspects are returning, but not the actual memories. I know myself, but not much about my life. My moods drift in a sea of loss.

I know that the reasons for this are outstanding. Alien memories on this green earth: it doesn't bear thinking of. I fully agree with these reasons, having thought it through very carefully, in my proper anthropological manner. I even agree that I'm not supposed to be self-aware in this way, although I'm unwilling to tell the techs and get it fixed.

There's another reason. It hit me one day and I've been playing with it since. It makes me restless and unhappy: I don't trust the techs.

I have never trusted them, if I'm honest.

Even in the days when I had no idea who I was until I walked into a mysterious building and through a green-lit doorframe and it all returned, only to disappear again as I walked out through another of those door frames. Arcs, they were called. Memory arcs in the doorways governing the memory ark that contains most of me. For my memory was stored in an ark. Except my storage leaked. It's still leaking and it's still full of patched repairs: there's no consistency in what my memory does.

It worries me exceptionally that it comes and goes so much. If the techs didn't worry me so very much more, I'd ask for help.

This is very wrong.

I need to work out what is it about the techs that worries me. This consumes that hour before I go to sleep. I listen to his breathing and I make my mind focus on the memory of what lies beyond the arc and I call up conversation after conversation and try to muddle through it all.

My given Memories are almost all of them terribly, terribly dull. White picket fence dull. Even my memory of being forty-two is really just me thinking of Douglas Adams and his play on the meaning of life. It's as if the creators of the Memories took a bunch of human averages for Western society, gave it a bit of personality (science fiction, literature, a fairly standard education, a small group of friends, first marriage, divorce, all setting me up for what I am now) and tried to create a story from them.

Human averages aren't human beings.

This is why I'm doing the Anne Shirley thing and I'm inventing stories for myself. It takes much invention. Names for my parents. A half-remembered sibling becomes a fully realised brother, and then I add two sisters. And a missing child. I don't yet know how they're missing—I'll find that out quite soon.

And gender. I can chose whatever gender I like. Or have none.

I miss none, just sometimes. It's a better place to be for so many reasons. Not technically *none*. I've never had *no* gender. I had five wonderful years when I was agendered, however. It was longer than average, for I am not a compilation of averages. That's one of the reasons I'm in this mess. Why I'm here at all.

I still treasure the memory of the memory of the memory. I

have remaining to me the sense that it was perfect and happy. That's something.

That's also the other problem with the techs and their insistence on doing everything in a certain way. They have obliterated happiness and replaced it with lies that don't even come close to matching my inner self.

If they'd done a better job at matching, I'd probably be walking this green Earth, oblivious.

I met a person the other day and they were like me when I was agendered. I suspect this is why I have such an onslaught of mood today. I remembered what it was like and was terribly, terribly envious. I hope they enjoy it as much as I do. They may not, for they're agendered in the middle of mostly males and females. It might not be so pleasant.

"Would you please call me Cordelia?" That's what it reminds me of. Anne Shirley. Defining herself rather than letting society define her.

This person was like me for a while there, quite gender neutral, and as happy about it as their society permitted them to be. Elegantly slow. The sort of person who is comfortable to be with in sexual terms and who must be assessed by other means. I love these people—I would seek them out here on Earth if I could, for here on Earth they understand me. In all my shades, they understand. They do not judge.

Yet they must define themselves: "Call me Cordelia" when they are that person, down deep, and the whole world insists on seeing them as Anne. Even with an *e*. Anne is not Cordelia and a gender neutral person is not male or female. They are different, and English doesn't have the words to express the qualities of that difference. It's a good difference; the fault is in the language.

I do not understand why I am obsessed with Anne Shirley.

First I read the books. I also had the books as Memory, because they were part of the standard childhood package. I asked six visits ago—of course I asked: visits are a safe time to ask, for during visits I'm expected to remember and question, within limits. They said they chose conservative packages based on our assessment of societal norms, rather than creating one that fitted too precisely into a particular place or time. This reeks of laziness.

Conservative packages are basically packages that use random selection of "typical" memories and aren't carefully configured. It used to be properly researched, I suspect, because the Memories that are derived from earlier work are more solid. There was time spent on crafting them back then. The youngster seeing to me that moment admitted that they didn't understand children. This is why my childhood and the state of my child were both left so...dauntingly unconfigured. So they don't understand childhood and program it anyway. That goes for humans, too, I suspect. The childhood education package was set up in 1951 and it truly demonstrates that, after all these years of study, our understanding of humans is still woefully lacking.

I cried when I read the Anne books the second time. I probably would have cried if I'd read the books the first time.

It's a problem with our education system. Special quality life education for the anthropologist in your life. Fake Memories, fake lives, fake emotions.

They become real when we cease watching them. Tears fall for no apparent reason. When I saw the first episode of the series just now, I cried as Anne renamed a path. I may never know why my emotions distilled into tears at that point. I don't have to know. But now, now that I have those tears, they are mine. They're not Memories. Meeting Micheline didn't do that to me. There was no emotion in it. I wish I knew why. I have no feelings for most humans. None. This is why those Anne-tears were so very important. I have a moment. It's real. It's all mine. And it's far too rare.

I shall call those tears "the flood of Shining Waters". My sister will be Cordelia and will be so beautiful that I was envious throughout my childhood. She shall have a perfect nose. And all my memories are now underpinned by the book, the TV series and my Shining Waters.

Although maybe "Shining Waters" is a mistake. There's something about it that nags at me. Something physical. Something not at all human.

There's another thing about Anne Shirley. She was abused as a child. Appallingly treated. Yet...it's not her. The abuse is not her.

She has kept herself whole, despite it. And my Memories are not me. I hold them. They accompany me in my real life. I produce them, politely, whenever the situation requires. But they're not me.

Apparently this is not true of all of us. For most of the others, their Memories *become* them. I was told how unusual I was when I fell into a small error, early on, and it was suggested that I might remember things outside the green lights. Fortunately, they believed in their techstuff more than they believed in me. This trust in themselves and distrust of my personal experience caused me to backtrack and hide that what I was saying was the literal truth. It also gave me time to do so, for they were full of hot air and hot talk. Mostly, however, it meant I had feedback and was given some contexts. Food for thought. Data. This is why I silenced myself and refused to tell anyone that I was self-aware sometimes, outside the regulation time. I'm not unique, it appears, but rare.

We're all here as anthropologists, but the others (most of the others, nearly all of the others) actually have to be reminded of our purpose each and every Download. There's a set of recorded words: the first thing we hear as we come to full awareness. This is one of the differences between Download and uplift. Without those words I do not understand at all how they uplift—it must be automatically. I think it might be, because the techs laugh about some of the problems that uplift causes. Once, one of us was killed standing in the middle of a busy road, a victim of uplift. This gives the laughter a vicious edge, to me.

I need to repress my hate of the way the techs laugh at the pain of those of us who are on this Earth. I cannot let them know I know about it. I could be the one in the middle of the road, next time.

The other anthropologists are human, but not human. Their humanity has lost them their selves. And I've lost swathes of self and swathes of memory, but I remain me.

All of our work is flawed. Over and over I realise this, for even at its best my memory is not complete and doesn't remain intact for long at a time. It's getting better, but is not even close to enough to make this study of Earthlings consistent and scientific.

I guess the question is whether our anthropologists are human, with our pretend gender and our pretend memories, or whether we float on the surface of humanity, never touching on its reality.

"Whether"—does that mean I have more humanity in my tears

than others of my kind have in their lives? Am I going native by remembering I'm not? It seems that way.

I wonder if I cried when I was in my own body. Did I even have tear ducts? I wonder if water was something different and special. No, I don't wonder. Somewhere deep inside, I know. The difference is glorious and it is dangerous and it needs to be suppressed while I'm here, while I inhabit this frail body. Now, in this time and place, the only Shining Waters I am permitted are tears.

I need to read *Anne of Green Gables* again.

Notes towards an Understanding of the Problem

It was far too hot to sit inside that day. Too much late November and too little Spring.

"Takeaway?" suggested Diana's text. "Sit in the park?"

"We can do better than that," Antoinette contributed. "We can get ice cream and climb a hill."

"Climb? I'm wearing heels." Trina, of course.

They puzzled through various options at a time, slowed down by the vagaries of instant message. Finally they agreed that they all wanted chocolate ice cream. Two of them indicated it had to be *gourmet* chocolate ice cream.

"I live near a good place. How about I buy for all of us and meet you on top of Mt Ainslie?"

"Not a good idea, Trina. The ice cream will melt and we will be faced with snogging couples." Leanne was ever-practical. Everyone was near giving up, however.

"Let's meet at Trina's ice creamerie. We can go to Black Mountain together. Or Red Hill. Or walk through Haig Park?"

"And get coffee!" Janet liked this idea.

So this is what they did.

They chose Black Mountain because, as Janet put it, "It looks the most like an alien spacecraft."

"Why do we need an alien spacecraft?" asked Antoinette.

"It adds to the richness and the abundance of the universe?" suggested Leanne.

"Do not mock your own beliefs," suggested Janet, in return, "for we will remember that you mocked them and will tease you about it for a long time."

"How long is a long time?" asked Diana.

"Too long," said Leanne. "I hereby swear that I will not mock my own beliefs again. Out of fear. So whose can I mock?"

"Mine," said Diana. "You can say all the rude things you like about aliens today. I'm annoyed with them."

"And this is why we need Black Mountain Tower," said Janet. "For I am always right. My intuition is amazing."

"Your intuition is certainly something," Antoinette agreed. "I need to be precise for mockery. I can't just mock aliens generally. I need to know specifically what aliens I'm mocking. And there need to be no gender issues involved."

"Why no gender issues?" asked Leanne.

"So many people see me and assume my whole life is about gender issues. Because something is important, doesn't mean it's the only thing that counts."

"Of course not," Diana agreed, acting shocked. "There's always chocolate. And aliens who live in burrows. They count."

"But not aliens who live on top of landmines. They're much less unimportant," Leanne suggested.

"Maybe not less important," said Janet. "Maybe just more damaged."

"Like my ice cream." And all four of them looked at the bulk of Trina's ice cream, now a chocolate sprawl on the asphalt at the base of the tower. "Do we really want to go up?"

"That's like saying 'Do we really want aliens?'" Diana mocked, gently.

"Well, do we? With either?"

"No, to both. Let's keep Earth alien-free and go to the Botanic Gardens."

"We could walk there," suggested Leanne.

"So near and yet so far," said Diana, a bit longingly. "It would hurt to walk that far. Anyone want to come by car with me? We can meet up at the kiosk and see if we can replace Trina's ice cream."

"Me, obviously," said Trina. "And if we can't, then I shall have an iced chocolate, instead."

"There we have it," declared Antoinette.

"Have what?" Janet was confused.

"Evidence of aliens on Earth."

"How is the kiosk evidence of aliens?" Trina was now confused, too.

"Not the kiosk. You wanting chocolate. Everyone knows you hate chocolate. An alien is playing nasty mindgames with you."

"Aliens do that," said Diana, nodding her head in false sagacity.

The Observer's Notes

"Go away."
    —me, always

God, there's that woman with the big laugh and the big white face and the big white teeth and the big white hair. I hope she doesn't see me. I downloaded such a nasty report about her when I first got here. She knew who she was and what it meant to be human and one gender and female and I hated her, every single bit of her.

I still hate her. I don't know why. None of the usual reasons. I can't be forming a family clan in a world like this one, that only does relationships in such a very limited number of directions. And besides, I've only met her the once.

I wrote such a nasty report.

Oh God, I hope she doesn't see me.

The Observer's Notes

We're born alone, we live alone, we die alone. Only through our love and friendship can we create the illusion for the moment that we're not alone.
  —Orson Welles, read online (quotation not verified)

I remember now. This memory was helped by an unexpected overnight in hospital. This human suit is so damn feeble sometimes.

I was admitted to a bed within the hour and spent the whole night dozing in between nurses going from bed to bed and taking blood and checking measurements, and how does one ever sleep when one one's right finger is a measurement device and when one turns one pulls at all the cords and cables from another device?

I pretended to sleep. Mostly I thought. It was good thinking time. I was able to call forth more of my own memory.

Nothing personal still. Nothing from before the great adventure to the Planet Earth. But I know so much more about who I am and why I am here.

No doubt I'll forget again. Every other time I forget everything. Sometimes I remember just a few things. Each time I remember something new.

Today's memory, now, today's memory is important. I don't want to forget it. And I remembered where I put my notes, this time, so this time I can write it down. My husband was amused when I asked him to bring my secret diary. He is a good man and when he says he won't read it, he'll keep his promise. He has no idea I'm not human. He would sit by me in hospital all night if I let him. I don't. One of us needs to pretend that life is normal for us to get through this.

Nothing's normal. Not my body here in hospital, not my anthropological self. I've worked out more of the reasons.

Mindwipe didn't fully take because I wasn't prepped for it properly. They spent longer than they should on the physical side. I think it was because the techs were terrified because I was in the public eye, so they were liable for anything that went wrong and they focussed on the perfect body to reflect who I ought to be. I was given the body of an age, at about an age because I had to be close to my real self. It was a few years older than the age the standard anthropologist is given.

Why the body has so many problems demonstrates how very human they've made me, I guess. Unless there's more I'm still not seeing.

My real self is critical to my task. Because of their worry, the flaws in the Memories shine through as false, and how they were pulled together matters. I am a rare test of all the stereotypes and public broadcasts and popular culture they drew on for their depiction of an "average" woman.

And yet I'm not. Not an average woman. Not even an average alien. So much of what is happening is to do with the particular nature of my task and the importance of not giving my identity away.

I know what this means. Oh God, I've just this moment realised. I know precisely what this means. The maths of it is crystal clear. Irrefutable. I'm not an anthropologist.

The woman's slow voice...

was counting again

One, two, three, four, five, six, seven, eight, nine, ten, eleven, twelve, thirteen, fourteen, fifteen, sixteen, seventeen, eighteen, nineteen, twenty, twenty-one, twenty-two, twenty-three, twenty-four, twenty-five, twenty-six, twenty-seven, twenty-eight, twenty-nine, thirty, thirty-one, thirty-two, thirty-three, thirty-four, thirty-five, thirty-six, thirty-seven, thirty-eight, thirty-nine, forty, forty-one, forty-two, fifty-three.

I'm not confused. My numbers have known all long what my conscious mind has only now calculated.

I know what I'm remembering now. It looks as if I can't count, but this time, the counting means something. I've identified the flaw in my Frankenstein mind. I know how old I am. I know what year it is.

This is where remembering my memories doesn't work at all. It makes everything worse. So much worse. It's when I begin to know Memories as well as memories.

I need to retain my self-awareness the whole time, remember more, be able to interrogate myself. I need to understand what's happening. More than anything, I need to move on. I need to.

Notes towards an Understanding of the Problem

It's a mess. The whole thing is a mess.

I say this every time I reach this point in the notes. Diana's intuition was spot on. She knew what was wrong before she had words for it. And yet we didn't notice. All your observations were of a different species (well, they were, let's be honest) and of a troublesome member of a different species. Diana's politics entered into the equation.

Every time I check her records, I think that the problem was caused by us. Not our many-gendered cousins. Not humans. Us.

I'm writing it down this time because it needs noting. I know this is an impossible outcome. I know I cannot make recommendations that remove us from all work to do with other planets. I am not stupid.

This is a note. Nothing more. It is not a recommendation. Not an outcome.

The woman's slow voice...

was counting again

One, two, three, four, five, six, seven, eight, nine, ten, eleven, twelve, thirteen, fourteen, fifteen, sixteen, seventeen, eighteen, nineteen, twenty, twenty-one, twenty-two, twenty-three, twenty-four, twenty-five, twenty-six, twenty-seven, twenty-eight, twenty-nine, thirty, thirty-one, thirty-two, thirty-three, thirty-four, thirty-five, thirty-six, thirty-seven, thirty-eight, thirty-nine, forty, forty-one, forty-two, fifty-three, forty-four.

This is when it happened.

This is when I started knowing, deep inside, that my Memories were artificial. That there was no school bus. That there was no school. That I never married the first time. That I didn't read *Anne of Green Gables*. That my whole life was invented by a group of techs who worked on averages and knew nothing about humans. Even average humans are not a composite of averages, and yet they expected me to be that and to remain myself. They failed. I failed.

And I remember.

None of this is good.

The Observer's Notes

Remove one letter and you go from bothering *someone to* othering *them.*
  —said by a friend

I should talk about sex. I really should. Sex should fill my diary because it fills human culture. Even if no-one has it, their social norms push it, glamorise it, hate it. It's as if the pushy, hormone-filled period of their lives (and they don't have four of them, like we do) dominates their shared landscapes.

One of the reasons my small group of friends is so safe is because we have clear parameters for talking about sex.

Mostly it's a matter of paying attention to everyone's comfort zones. Some days one needs to exclaim or mourn or analyse or tempest. Other days it's all about the emotions. And when two (possibly three) of us are in difficult places in terms of sexual relations, it's important to observe each other's needs. We learned early on that our assumptions about each other were false, and we've learned to respect each other's actual lives rather than the way we all appear in public. It wasn't easy for me, but Antoinette and Trina led the way in finding ways we could talk safely. Honestly. Without turning each other into porn.

My friends have taught me so much about the roles sex narratives play in different groups, I find. It's not that they're subversive or that they intentionally transgress those roles, it's that the sex narratives are seldom easily applicable to middle-aged women. And we all know it. One of the reasons we have to be so aware of each other is because we are fumbling, trying to find equivalent narratives that work for us and would still be acceptable in wider society.

This helps me in so many ways. It helps with my work, it helps me navigate my human life. And it helps me handle the techs.

I won't write too much about the tech view of the sex act here (never the stories, never the relationships—only ever the sex act), though, because it'll fix the subject of the sex act itself in my mind too clearly, and I have to keep this part of my life out of the technicians' reach. That's what I mean when I talk about *handling*.

This is not because it's the proper thing to do. In fact, keeping my mind clear is entirely improper. I'm supposed to have my mind stuffed with everything human, ready to report in. The thing is, because I retain so much of myself between the three-month visits, the readjustment period is...*different* for me.

When it all began, I'd walk through the green arc. I'd sit down at a chair in the waiting room and chat with other anthropologists as my memory returned. We'd be called one by one for download. We'd strip for download, lie on the flat bed, and the bed would move us backwards until our head was in the machine's ambit. A set of questions would be posed and we would respond silently. The questions were triggers, I think, or I'm not remembering everything about it yet. Or I've remembered and forgotten again, which is something I now suspect might happen.

After the questions, we would be given a time for verbal reports. This is why we're encouraged to write the way I'm doing now—it makes formulation of our reports for download a lot more efficient. And that was that. After download, we'd leave by the arc door and that was that, too.

When we swapped notes before each session, we were all surprised by how long the download took. Many were dehydrated and hungry at the end, which made sense, considering the slow download and how very long it took. Some of us were more efficient than others—my download has never taken more than a half day, and is usually much shorter. Or maybe, in light of what I know now, I was never asked the same questions.

Now I'm more aware, the sequence is quite different, subjectively.

I enter through the arc. The room I am in is not the room I used to find myself in. In fact, it's a small white space where the voices of the techs are clear and loud and paying more attention to their data input than to me. It's the Earthside backup room for most of the equipment, and it would be possible to operate the download and communicate from here, if one had to. I guess I could call it a *machine room*. Sounds better than "the little white room", at least. The techs don't talk to me directly while I'm in the machine room. Nor do they monitor my facial expressions or body language. I suspect that anything short of me standing up and doing a jig while screaming abuse won't catch their attention.

They check the equipment from their safe distance and monitor the levels of particular whatevers in my blood, and all the rest of the time they chat about me, about Earth, about how it's good my people take on the brunt of Earth activity because it sucks. Oh, and they gossip.

That's pretty much it. This room is the timesink. Download itself only takes around twenty minutes. I drink from my water bottle while I'm in this room. It makes a difference.

When the light in the room changes from white to green, I stand up (automatically; I doubt if I could stop this action even if I wanted), walk through a perfectly ordinary door, and then sit down in the usual waiting room.

The chatter I've overheard in the white cell has helped explain quite a lot.

One of the more disconcerting pieces of random information that has come my way is additional uses the techs have for my data. Once every three months, when they check that my Memories are intact (and such a fine job they do of that), and that my body is stable and they take my official report and send it home. Also, once every three months they use me as a source of erotica.

They use all of us. Some of the real anthropologists are actually their personal porn stars. They have developed quite a following back home. I wouldn't be *them* in a thousand worlds. Imagine reaching home after all that sacrifice, after all that time, and finding that one's data collection is less important than one's sex acts.

I would become a porn object, if I gave them any data. I am far too well known back home. It would ruin my reputation, my family clan, everything.

This isn't good from a personal point of view, but it's quite shocking when one considers that we're supposed to be understanding humans, not exploiting them. Sex is recorded, oh yes it is. And it is sold. Humans are just exotic enough for the premiums to be high, for enough of their emotions and social habits align with our own for them to be understandable. That's why we're all here, because the "friendly aliens" are the ones that most need understanding. Not the kind of understanding the techs bring, however. That's simply unethical.

I rebel by giving what the techs ask, literally, without much in the way of visualisation and re-experiencing. I also go out of my way to avoid sexual encounters outside the home. This is possibly also due to me having entered into an asexual gender when I was converted to humanity.

They're not interested in my home life at all, and don't even realise that my sex life is part of it. Thank goodness for this particular significant difference between my two species. My relations with my Earth husband are mine. Ours. Not theirs.

I tell them I was asexual when converted, however, every time, and they nod and move on to the real report quite quickly. That's not true, though. I was in an entirely different mode, one which has no equivalent on Earth: my body both then and now is not any less sexual than most. With the strange regendering of menopause dominating every moment, it is definitely sexual. They've never questioned me on the lie. I don't think they care.

I lie because I don't want to parade. I don't want to be the subject of titillation. I know what happens to the erotica and the porn and the funny incidents. Mass entertainment.

This is another of the things I'm not supposed to know, not supposed to remember. I'm not meant to remember that we're a race of voyeurs whose anthropology is fucked to hell. I'm also not supposed to remember that my very first public claim to fame was as a crusader against this exploitation. Every time I remember this about myself, I fear I am shocked. I hate forgetting and, equally, I hate remembering.

I thought about the sequence, last time, on my way home. Everyone remembers a little in the waiting room, when our blocks are removed. That's when we chat and compare notes. A short time of being whole people. Or at least having wholeness within sight.

We see ourselves from the outside, when those blocks are removed. We're visitors to this world and our bodies are not our own, and when those blocks are gone we can share everything as if it were part of one of those interactive stories. At that moment, we become voyeurs of our own carefully arranged existences. We laugh together at the irony of me downloading my sexual exploits. Me, the reformer.

Except I neither download them, nor do I have that vast gap between myself and my other self, inside and outside the facility. I pretend. Moving the blocks does nothing. Sometimes they are in place and I act more human, but almost always I have a slight sense of who I am. Even when I don't know the whole (which, to be honest, is most of the time), I have something more than the others, who only have that small time in the waiting room.

This is why, when I am sufficiently self-aware, I write myself these notes. They may not be consistent, or thorough, but they're all I have. I have an official excuse for them, and it's one that will stick with me when the memory runs away. It makes me less miserable: I want my feelings and realisations to be documented whenever they can be, not once every three months. I want the everyday record to be balanced with something just a trifle more sane.

How the hell did I get this way? Others are different, but why am I so fucking different? It means that—even when I'm chatting with my co-workers and comparing notes and remarking on the stupidity of humans—it means that, even then I'm entirely alone.

The Observer's Notes

"We have an apple-not-falling-far-enough-from-the-tree situation."
"You mean his mother did this too?"
"There is no cure."
    —overheard at a bus stop

I'm not sure I'll ever work out Christmas. There's too much false information running interference.

I have Memories of Christmas Past. I always think this in capitals because I think the devisers-of-fake-human-memory couldn't work out Christmas either. Much of my Christmas Memory is a pastiche of perfect moments stolen mostly from an overly-cheerful television advertisement. Not merely one advertisement. A whole series of carefully devised perfect moments. Perfect down to the glossy smiles and red-brick fireplace, big enough for a Santa Claus. It's interesting how I accepted it as real for so long. How our minds process something missing three of the senses and pretend that it's enough. Half of my Memories are my mind pretending that the memories are enough. It turns black-and-white into colour. It adds flavour and smell and feel.

It's like looking back over an old photograph album that belongs to someone else, and claiming it all. For Christmas I've claimed every gleaming grin, every smile, every scrap of wrapping paper and all the gifts. Or...

I know what it is.

It's buying a house. An old house. A big house. That house has portraits of dignified men and women with high hair and higher lineage. And these ancestors become *your* ancestors. Bought by the yard along with the house. You walk up and down and up and down the corridor and the big hall, working out who they are and how they belong to you. Humans used to do this, you know, buy ancestors by the yard. They weren't really buying ancestors (*Why do I have to explain this?*), but portraits which they claimed were of relatives. Humans tell stories—this means they will lie. The more human I am, the easier it is to tell stories.

You buy yourself a long wall full of ancestors. "That's Uncle Fred," you tell yourself. "He's silent." In all his life he only said fifty words. Most conversations with him were nods and grunts and "Thank you." He was unfailingly polite in his silence. He was the uncle who fixed your broken toys and kept you company when your heart was first broken. Fifteen, you were. You and Uncle Fred sat over there, by the fire, every afternoon and every evening all that winter. The nights and mornings you spent in bed, blaming yourself for the horror of your life.

The trouble with photo-album memories is that Uncle Fred in the portrait is a dapper, early nineteenth-century gentleman, and you could not possibly have known him unless you were blessed with some kind of eternal life.

I discovered this problem with my Memories the hard way. It hurt more than anything else I'd experienced.

It was probably my first genuine experience in the whole of my human existence.

One of my memories, I found out, had been stolen from a Judy Garland movie.

I discovered Judy Garland by happenstance, two days after I first realised that I was self-aware. I was two days alive in my new life and already had to face that my personal history was faked. Not even well-faked.

One of my Christmas Memories was stolen from a Judy Garland movie. This is another of those things that I say over and over, as if repeating it would calm the emotions it still gives to me. My blood boils every time I think of it.

My iconic Christmas tree, the one I remember from my tenth birth-day as "the best Christmas tree ever" had green and red trimmings and baubles and, branch for branch, bauble for bauble was precisely the one in *Meet Me in Saint Louis*. This shocked me so very much that I started chasing down other aspects of my Christmas memory.

More than one came from a home improvement advertisement. This is the one that came to define my Christmas as being derived from advertisements.

These Memories were just taken, as they were, from these places. Not even cleverly faked.

There is no chance at living a real life if one's experiences are stolen from home improvement advertisements. Whenever I'm tempted to hide from my reality, I play the soundtrack to that Judy Garland movie. I'd watch the movie, but seeing the tree makes me vomit.

Christmas is one of the reasons I've never reported any of this to my controllers. I feel a deep and abiding betrayal. Besides...

I'm supposed to report the loss of my conditioning. That's a perfectly clear guideline, in theory. Except that I never really lost anything. The Memories are still there. I simply know they're false. I'm self-aware in a way I probably ought not be, but I don't have enough of myself to replace Judy Garland.

Something in me announced at a point, very quietly, "That's your excuse. You don't have to report to anyone except yourself. Write things down. You've got guidelines for this, too." They're infallible guidelines. Keeping a journal has been programmed in with the memories. I took the safe route.

One of my major concerns is: *How can an anthropologist analyse a culture from within it when they possess such badly faked memories?* When they possess faked memories at all? It seems an appalling method to me. It also seems cruel.

Maybe it's not just Christmas I can't work out.

Maybe there's something about me that's unexpected.

Maybe my Memories have only now begun to break down and there's more interesting experience in store for me.

Maybe...I'm supposed to be someone else entirely.

I'm pretty sure I'm still an anthropologist, although I would need to read my previous entries to be certain, for I still lose and regain chunks of myself each time I walk through the arc. I can't imagine what I'd be doing on this planet if not studying humans. I really might have had more memory on an earlier occasion—I will have to re-read all my notes someday, and put it all together and make my everyday memory more solid. I'd rather have external knowledge right now, though. I feel as if I'm walking on loose sand and the tide's coming in.

I wish I could talk to other agents and find out more. The idea is to get to know humanity, however, and I couldn't spot one of my fellows if you paid me. Even the ones I must meet from time to time.

Now, that's another very human concept, that "if you paid me". The notion of monetary reward leading to improved work. Time after time it leads to corruption and unstable societies.

Daft, all these notions. Daftest of all is Christmas. Not just Christmas, but Judy Garland's Christmas. The daftness is at our end, though, not Earth's. Why did the techs short-change the research? What persuaded them to do such a job? Is it just me, or is our system disintegrating? Or is it both, me being targeted due to a system that's lousy?

I need to explore this.

Notes towards an
Understanding of the Problem

Her body is too damn feeble. Of all the motifs that repeat and repeat in the reports, her body is closest to those daisies. It looks bright and impenetrably full of cheer and as if it will last forever, but then it is dropped and crushed underfoot and becomes a stained and pained mess, or it wilts and can never be itself again.

Do you know how much work that body takes to keep it going? I'm speaking in the present tense because I'm looking at hospital records, and they make me testy. Time after time it happens. Not always this sequence, but something like it. Humans have to make up for our deficiencies. It's an artificial body, built for the purpose; it shouldn't have these flaws.

She is taken to hospital by ambulance because they thought she was having a heart attack. She isn't. I heave a sigh of relief. She's sent home the next day with a clean bill of health. Then the hospital rings her. It RINGS her. And a doctor says: "We missed one of the blood samples. You need to come back in case you have a blood clot in your lungs." She doesn't. She has a lump somewhere else that could be cancerous.

That's just one event. One of three in one year. One of far too many over her human lifetime.

This is the evidence I was hoping not to find. This is proof that she was manipulated into doing one of the vilest jobs imaginable and not given the tools to do the job. Somebody or somebodies wanted to get rid of her, and would be quite happy if she took a planet with her.

She was a well-known reformist in her time. Effective, not just argumentative. A dynamic change agent.

But that's not all. Personal vendettas should never, ever lead to genocide.

Riddling her body with imperfections so that she has to fight every day to stay alive rather than spending the same effort on making a sincere Judgement... That's going in my report. I'm taking the cautious option for the report, too, for I don't want to find myself caught by the same type of people. If one can call them people. Slobs and sons of slobs. All my work will stay in English until the final presentation, which will be done in public, with aplomb. I shall use one of our most curious traditions—that of honouring the peoples studied—to save my own skin. And I shall encrypt it.

I've already opened files on other planets destroyed by Judgements that are potentially fallible, and I've sent them out to reliable bureaucrats. Even if none of them are not quite half as problematic as Earth, I've opened a huge can of worms. I was sent here to validate a related can of worms, but not one as big as the one I found when I got all the data.

I fear for us, the way Diana felt for Earth. She had to make a decision regardless, and so do I. I thought my stakes were low and hers were impossibly high. Now it seems I might be fated to follow her.

I do not believe in fate. I shall defeat this group of niggles, using caution and subtlety.

The woman's slow voice...

was counting again

One, two, three, four, five, six, seven, eight, nine, ten, eleven, twelve, thirteen, fourteen, fifteen, sixteen, seventeen, eighteen, nineteen, twenty, twenty-one, twenty-two, twenty-three, twenty-four, twenty-five, twenty-six, twenty-seven, twenty-eight, twenty-nine, thirty, thirty-one, thirty-two, thirty-three, thirty-four, thirty-five, thirty-six, thirty-seven, thirty-eight, thirty-nine, forty, forty-one, forty-two, fifty-three, forty-four, forty-five.

This is not my place.

I do not belong.

Never. I've never belonged. I always knew this somewhere deep. Now the whole of me knows it. Even my conscious self.

I expect I should find out why I don't belong. I don't want to. I want to wallow in misery first. It's a genuine emotion, after all, and much more interesting and real than the false feelings attached to stupid Memories. I want real feelings, real experience, a real life. I need to find myself. That self is messed in a morass of Memories.

I must unmess it.

I need to wallow. Ranting and raging and whingeing aren't luxuries. They're the only real thing I possess.

My Earthname is Diana. My fakename. My improvised human name. The one I live with, for want of a better. I remember this now, and I remembered not so long ago that I was not from Earth, but I did not remember the way I was, nor did I know my real name.

I still don't know my real name.

My name is part of who I am. It has been denied me. This makes me red-hot with rage. Hot flushes. I have an excuse for them. Yet they are not always the hormones reminding me of my many-gendered past. Now they can also be a fast-burning rage at what has been done to me.

I've had near-memories of my existence before the lies began for all my time on Earth. I interpreted my early life through symbols. Yellow hats, the stairs on a bus: these were remnants from my real childhood. This was my memory peeking through the bleakness of loss. Early flowers at the end of the harsh winter.

At this moment, all I have are those early blossoms and my name. I get a memory back, then I lose everything but the memory of the memory. I fear that there will never be a full blooming, and I will never rejoice in the fullness and complexity of my existence. I began to know when I was forty-four. Or was it fifty-three? It's hard to count when time has been restructured. I still don't know everything I should. There has been a dreadful error, and some of me was lost in the voyage from the stars.

I am so very angry.

The Observer's Notes

"x+1=x"
—me, just today

Being an observer makes me patient. I watch, I listen. I pay vast attention. My eyes saucer.

I like to trap all the understanding I do not feel. I am the Margaret Mead of anthropologists and I understand everything from an elevated viewpoint as a learned observer. I sip the hot chocolate of friendship and pretend I have a place. In my day job, I merely observe: I do not pretend to belong there.

When I stop to think, my careful anthropological superiority collapses. I haven't read Margaret Mead. I know this because my *Memory of Mead* is fractalled. It's not patchy at all. It's mathematical. I can chase mentions of her into smaller and smaller patterns and they're all $x+1=x$.

I deduced that fractalling is how my Memories are structured, and that the fractals give me the sense that Memories are founded on deep realities and on actual experience. The fractalling makes the memories echo like real ones, I guess. Except that I can calculate a formula from it. The formula is terribly, terribly obvious the moment I start thinking about it.

Real life memories are seldom predictably formulaic. I find myself comparing, chasing before and after and comparing them. Take a picture and then fractal it in a mind and one has instant Memory. It's more solid than simply layering half-truths, because of that echo. It's no less false.

Each time I unravel an aspect of the fractal, the only Memories that remain solid are the ones where real emotions are tugged behind them in their wake. This hurts beyond anything.

I lost a child. This really happened. Not the child I remember losing, but my own, real infant with its claws and its yellow infant frills. That hurt remains. The memory of my child is gone forever: I have no joy to balance the damage.

This is a very cruel method of creating human memories. We really don't like our anthropologists, do we? Or humans. I'm pretty sure we only like humans for the potential smut.

Anthropologists, now, we play with their hearts in order to create minds suitable for exploring strange cultures. This is hurt beyond any ethical boundaries, for there is no chance of healing from something where the ache is left but none of the memory.

"You must know Margaret Mead," these fools tell me, "because you're an anthropologist." Every debriefing they say this. To the 190,000[th] fractal I have this message. They've said it so often it's encoded deep within my mind. I must know Mead. At no stage does this message break down, and yet I don't know how I know Margaret Mead, nor what my understanding of her entails. It isn't my understanding of Margaret Mead, for I have none. I have never had any.

I was sitting in on a card game last night, with my saucer-eyes. Glued to the chair, I analysed the politics. That was why I was there, I've deduced. After an event I can find out what I was doing there: this is how I discover other parts of my programming. I also unravel that programming, just as I unravel my Memories through following the fractals. I do not trust the techs. I trust four people on this planet and none on any other.

The card players thought I was waiting for them to finish so that we could get coffee, but that was merely an excuse. I was watching to see how the personal element of the game played out.

Two of the players formed an alliance. One of the players was the mother of half the alliance and the play against her was extreme. The emotions humans show towards their mothers are complex and interesting.

Then someone changed the rules and the game changed in its entirety. I found myself thinking, about the change in rules: "Can we humans do these things?" It worried me that I thought of myself as human. It disrupted my work and so I stopped analysing the politics.

Techs must take our memory so that we are not distracted by such thoughts. This is the theory. At least, I expect this is the theory. They take our theory as well. Our whole education is replaced by fractals.

I want to think of that card game as a kaleidoscope, where rotating a tube gives a different view. Except...except...that implies a more static set of components than there ought to be. And it implies that I was a neutral observer. I was supposed to be a neutral observer, but I wasn't one. This is another element of humanity that the techs have never understood. I was part of the game, even though I held no cards.

In human narratives, everyone plays a part. Even the people the narrative itself pretends to exclude.

Humanity doesn't allow neutral observers. It lies to itself about this, and uses those lies to reinforce hierarchies or to set down boundaries, but everyone is part of human narratives.

Outsiders also participate, in their way. An outsider may bring drinks, give a running commentary, disconcert the player with their silence: they have many choices. This is because humans don't play card games: *they tell stories*. The card game is part of a story and that story includes me. Humans don't create fractals, either.

Humans are utterly alien.

This set me to worrying. If my Margaret Mead Memory was set up so very clearly to be false, then what is the way I'm supposed to observe? Why can I see the fractals and calculate my Memory? If I'm not an anthropologist, why am I here?

If this were a story containing card game manoeuvres, I'd be a human with an alien overwipe. I would find my true self and rediscover my life.

My mind is fractals and symbols when I go deep. It's not stories. I don't think that I'm a human masquerading as an alien in a human body.

I am alien. I don't know who I am, or why I'm here, but I know what I am.

Notes towards an
Understanding of the Problem

Today the friends focussed on Leanne. She needed it. Sometimes, when one is a reformer, the world becomes too big. And everything hurt. She needed to tell them about it.

She started with that simple refusal. "I'm not used to accepting 'no'," she explained. "I'm fine with all of you. I'll push back a bit just to test, but if you're behind your feelings, I'll accept them. I won't agree, but I'll leave it to you to make your own decisions and to run your own life. That's what friends do. When I'm proven to be right and everything falls to pieces, I'll help pick up those pieces and put them together again. When I'm wrong, I'll learn from it."

"OK," said Diana. "That makes sense with what I know of you."

"It's partly the scientist speaking," suggested Antoinette. "You're theorising about us and testing those theories and so forth."

"That's spot on," agreed Leanne. "And as a scientist, I have to distinguish between accepting arguments as valid or not. I accept yours as valid for entirely unscientific reasons. I don't give that same leeway to most other people."

"So we know the heart of the problem," said Trina. "We can't help if we don't know the rest of it. Theory isn't the everyday. It doesn't tell us why you look as if you've been crying all night."

"I look as if I've been crying all night," Leanne said, acerbically, "because I *have* been crying all night. It's the government. Not just the Federal one. The Queensland one, the local council. All of them. I've run out of people to fight. I know that a section of the Barrier Reef will be destroyed because of a set of circumstances. I can prove it. And they won't listen."

"Living in constant despair," said Trina.

"If it's destroyed," said Leanne, "then yes, absolutely. For it's not going to be something that we can get back. We've pushed our planet beyond its tolerances. It doesn't bounce back. It's like us. Like middle-aged women. Give us a shove and we fall over far more easily than a young sprite. No, it isn't. It's like a woman in her eighties. Capable of so much that you don't quite realise that a simple fall will send her to hospital for a week. And that's the *good* outcome. That simple fall could break three bones, or it could kill her."

"And you see that the various governments have intentionally pushed this little old lady."

"The Federal Government has, for certain. The others… It's more that they care about other things. Short term gains. Other regions. They can't see the whole picture. Their incapacity could destroy the planet, the way it's destroying the Reef."

"So this is your last straw," said Diana.

"No, not yet. It's when I realise that we might reach the last straw. We're not dead yet, but more decisions like this and it will be inevitable. We won't have to wait for aliens or the heat death of the universe. We will have suicided, and taken our planet along with us. The Barrier Reef's destruction is a harbinger of doom." She said this with depressed relish.

"What will you do?"

"What I always do. I will fight until it's too late. And then I'll keep on fighting."

Leanne's friends focussed on what she did as a scientist. How very political she was. How very emotional it was. Her vague Gaian description meant something quite different to what they expected, it seems. Not woo-woo. More: "We will fight them on the beaches; we will never surrender".

Me, I was astonished for another reason entirely. Still *am* astonished. This isn't a critical incident and yet, perhaps it should be.

Leanne brought a complex world view to bear upon a simple political problem. She fought from a deep emotional position. She was almost messianic in her use of science to change the natural world. To save it.

We think of such changes as natural, whether induced or not. Humans obviously don't, even when they themselves induce them.

If they did, Leanne's view would be impossible. The emotional side of her didn't enter into dialogue with the scientist. They were comrades-in-arms. Marching to war. And she didn't see the war as capable of being won. It hurt her every time she lost a battle, for it reinforced her scientific view that humanity had already gone too far and that the end of days was around the corner, but it didn't stop her. Nothing stopped her.

And yet she didn't force this messianic belief upon her friends. She only talked about it at this point because she needed emotional support. That side of her understood that she couldn't fight if she was alone.

I wanted to take her religion as symbolic. Theoretical. Something to admire from a cool distance. A pristine object of alien culture. But it's not that at all. And because it isn't that at all, a wobble was put in my planet's normally straightforward plans. Or, should I say, another wobble.

At this point, all the normal indicators pointed to Earth being Judged and humanity dying. The changed state of the planet wouldn't matter from a colonisation point of view, for it was a simple matter of changing settlers' physical characteristics to meet the environment. And humanity did the thing. There was not a moment when they could absolve themselves. And yet... Leanne was not alone in fighting. And that fight came from so deeply within.

Humankind's complexity and strange sentimental existence made a simple situation (taking over a planet the sentient inhabitants had made uninhabitable for themselves) less simple.

This is the chief reason why they should never have been Judged in the first place. There were issues all the way through. They would have destroyed themselves soon enough, and the planet would have been open to colonisation, and we would have all been spared a mess. Such a mess. This helps, but it doesn't give me an answer. I still don't know how we achieved this mess.

But Leanne pushed to the edge of her rope, and Diana buying her hot chocolate and handing her a handkerchief add more factors.

Humankind is not good at behaving mathematically. The species subverts pure mathematics by their very existence. Jokes about them include the classic about the smallness of a species that never calculates up to base ninety-eight in primary school. Limited science. Limited domination of the mind and its surrounds.

And yet... There's something there, in Leanne's despair, that suggests potential. It indicated that humanity could dig itself out of its own grave, given the right conditions. Which we, in our turn, are so very good at subverting.

Our science doesn't contain that profound passion.

Leanne puzzled her friends and was comforted by them, which is fair, as Leanne puzzles me and causes me to feel a strangely unexpected comfort.

The woman's slow voice...

was counting again

One, two, three, four, five, six, seven, eight, nine, ten, eleven, twelve, thirteen, fourteen, fifteen, sixteen, seventeen, eighteen, nineteen, twenty, twenty-one, twenty-two, twenty-three, twenty-four, twenty-five, twenty-six, twenty-seven, twenty-eight, twenty-nine, thirty, thirty-one, thirty-two, thirty-three, thirty-four, thirty-five, thirty-six, thirty-seven, thirty-eight, thirty-nine, forty, forty-one, forty-two, fifty-three, forty-four, forty-five, forty-six, forty-seven, forty-eight, forty-nine, fifty, fifty-one, fifty-two, fifty-three.

I know who I am. Finally. Perfectly.

I know what I am. Definitely. Securely.

I know how I got here.

I seldom lose myself in my Memories anymore. I'm capable of exploring them, analysing them, understanding them. I don't know everything about myself yet, but I know who I am.

The world is a very different place, now that I can see it from my own perspective. Now I am centred and am interpreting life from my real self and see the invented person, rather than catching glimpses of the real self from the middle of the invention.

I wasn't supposed to lose that sense of self. That much is clear, from talking to other aliens-on- earth. Self-awareness gets sublimated but self always remains.

It was very bad science that made me do so. Stupid assumptions about what made humans and what made *us*, and how the two could inter-relate. The assumptions worked for most but failed for me, possibly due to my particular personality. There might be other reasons, too, but I haven't encountered them. In some respects, I'm still working in the dark.

I'm not the only one. That body/experience conjunction is undermining all of our research on this planet. The only thing it doesn't undermine is the trade in artefacts and in licentious trash. This is obviously why the bad science and mishandled memories have become such a part of Earth's silent invasion. Techs use science to underpin the extras they take on the side and it's undermining the whole project.

It wouldn't be nearly as bad if we didn't bring Judgement to bear on any species. Nothing wrong with titillation, after all, as long as it's agreed on by all. It's not that strange for many cultures, including those of Earth, and if Earth has this element, then it's ethical for us to make use of it in our relations with them. My position on this has always been clear. But if the titillation is the main reason we explore in the way we do, what effect does that have on any Judgement? Can Judgement be truly dispassionate and honest?

Thank God I'm an appallingly bad anthropologist and not the Judge. To be a Judge, knowing that the task has been trivialised and biased and damaged by the very way it was set up is to walk on the dark side, with danger. We don't permit ourselves to withhold Judgement, after all, for we are the wise race and know all.

Knowing what I now know, I'm terrified of us.

I fear for all species we discover and try to understand. The truth is unambiguous and unkind. The best a species can hope for is for us to never know they exist.

The moment any new species comes within sight of our bad science, they're going to be hurt, one way or another. They will be exploited and they will probably be wiped out. We use our death ray of Judgement far too readily, especially considering our own extraordinary failings.

We don't recognise our failings.

Our Judgement is founded on our equally infallible study of the species, which relies on our exceptionally clever observations made when we become that species for a time. Sometime it's a few years, sometimes a few decades. It used to be a valid and careful measurement. These days it mostly rests on how much personal credit and life-prestige the entertainment will sell for back home.

We will murder a species when it fails us, and yet it doesn't know it's even on trial. At the same time, we don't observe dispassionately. We set everything up to score sexual points and fund bribes back home. It's all about us. It's all about our gratification.

This is an appalling reason to commit genocide. I will put in a strong recommendation that Earth not be Judged and that we reconsider our policies relating to Judgement of any planet. There has to be a better way of handling this mess.

As long as a Judge hasn't yet been called, Earth is still safe. I can politely call attention to the problem and it can be considered. I'm important enough for my voice to be heard. I expect this is why I was sent here. There is still a great deal I can't remember, and the reasons for being here are still rather mysterious to me.

If a Judge has been called, I will find out who they are and I will...I will... I don't know what I'll do. We have no recourse but Judgement once the Judge is in the field.

I will just have to hope that humanity has not yet been opened to Judgement, and that I can make a difference when I get home and debrief. This should not be happening. Too many species have been murdered based on this poor science. Earth is full of problems, but it deserves justice.

Justice here is often depicted with a blindfold. This is ironic, for there are other uses of blindfolds and some of them fit far too well with the chief current use of Earth experiences back home.

Irony is a concept we share with humans.

The Observer's Notes

My mind is arguing with my body again. The result is inevitable: a bone-deep fatigue. I can't walk. I don't want to think.

It could be dehydration. It could be something else. Once I was this tired and it was from damage to my heart. I never know these things. I hate this body. It's all wrong.

I am not female right now. Monthly swings take this body in and out of the high-feminine state.

It's not a sensible way to run a body. And there is no good way of explaining it all, either. Why don't these damn humans have a proper set of terms to distinguish between gendering and sexuality, to indicate the status of child-care and parenting and discovering and developing and changing? I can't even make a complete list while I'm in this body. While I'm stuck with this be-damned language.

Right now, I'm in a state of non-flux where I am clear in my state of physical attraction to a specific other and have no intention of procreation, of child-rearing, or child-developing, or bearing with that other. Technically, the closest this culture reaches this state is "unattached male". Yet my body is obviously female and everyone (except, maybe, the man I'm married to, and I'm not always certain of that) reacts to me not only as female, but as an older and less desirable female.

I ought to be one of the prime genders at this point: all the *sec* and none of the responsibility. I am wasting the best year of my life with this damnable interplanetary project.

Humanity is fucked. Where is my freedom-loving *2fanqua* time when I'm ready for it?

No wonder I'm tired. There's not nearly enough natural joy in this. All I get to do is drink with my peer group. Drinks are not *2fanqualat*. Not at all. My body ought to be creating its own drugs at this point. And they should be there, in my system, to help me for the three changes after. I think the choice of when to send me was personally designed to hurt me. Whoever did this is a vindictive bastard. My return's not going to be easy. Nothing's easy right now. Nothing. And my current body owns 90% of the blame. Such roiling emotions.

How did humans evolve into this? Life is such a mystery.

This planet is cursed. So, I think, is my brain. English does very strange things to it and menopause does even stranger.

Notes towards an Understanding of the Problem

"What do you hate today?" Janet asked.

"Hey, that's my line." Trina was mock-offended.

"I steal everyone's words when I have PMT," Janet said. "You don't know this because we thought I was past PMT."

"Oh dear," said Leanne. "I used to hate it when it came and went."

"It's what I hate today," said Janet. "And so does my husband, and so do my children. It's as if I've personally caused their permanent mental impairment."

"We've all done that." Trina was very happy to admit this. "And if only those scientists would get their act together and sort it out, they wouldn't have to endure it."

"I bet they're too busy dealing with their own PMT," Diana offered, darkly. "And today I hate milk chocolate. For I and Janet are but one day removed from each other."

"Before or after?" Janet asked.

"After. And you want to prepare for tomorrow, for this month is messy."

"La la la, I'm not hearing," said Trina.

"I'm with Trina," said Antoinette.

"Who are you with, Leanne?" asked Trina.

"I'm your tomorrow," she answered. "The wonder of a sort-of-maybe ordinary existence."

More chocolate. But also menstruation.

We have records of male conversations and they're very different. We have records of mixed conversations and they're very different. These conversations, full of blood and chocolate, they appear in the record far more than they ought.

Interesting and a bit odd that the standard gender for our people on Earth means these conversations. Always. Our research had an unexpected bias from the beginning. Static gender. A cultural desire for individuals to have gender for life. It leads to far more specialist conversations, and many more not-shared areas than our more civilised gendershift does.

I've been meaning to note this for a while, for it's critical in its own small way. Noting these permanent differences and the incapacity of this human culture to demonstrate the deep understanding that is standard in our own culture, due to the shared experiences of all gender cycles is the trigger that led to the calling for Judgement. No-one could see a way of overcoming it and helping humans become like us.

Someone must have questioned whether the problem was that we were seeing everything from the view of one gender. Perhaps the other chief gender (the culturally dominant one) was more adaptable?

Let me check this.

My error. The files are clear. The dominant gender was considered *less* culturally adaptable. This was a minor factor in the choice. The major one was the closeness to our own natural experiences. Not that those female bodies were anything like ours, so presumably the male bodies were appallingly dull. What a limited race. Like us, but so very unlike. The only concern I found in the files, in fact, was whether there were different possibilities in different language groups. Surely culture at that deep a level can't have such strong language boundaries, however.

I see no problem here. Time to move to the next topic.

The woman's slow voice...

was counting again

One, two, three, four, five, six, seven, eight, nine, ten, eleven, twelve, thirteen, fourteen, fifteen, sixteen, seventeen, eighteen, nineteen, twenty, twenty-one, twenty-two, twenty-three, twenty-four, twenty-five, twenty-six, twenty-seven, twenty-eight, twenty-nine, thirty, thirty-one, thirty-two, thirty-three, thirty-four, thirty-five, thirty-six, thirty-seven, thirty-eight, thirty-nine, forty, forty-one, forty-two, fifty-three, forty-four, forty-five, forty-six, forty-seven, forty-eight, forty-nine, fifty, fifty-one, fifty-two, fifty-three, fifty-four, fifty-five.

Oh God, I love him.

With all my heart. With all my soul. With both the human and the inhuman parts of me. I love him.

I can't explain this love. Our marriage was nothing. Artificial memory given to both of us. A manipulated human and a manipulated me. All the first years were an arranged marriage, even though we thought we were in love.

Then it transformed. Gradually, gently, surprisingly. And so we had now. Now is different.

He is my guiding star and the light that shines in the abyss. The deep positive in my life that makes it all come right. He changes everything.

I love him. I love him. More than anything, I love him.

The Observer's Notes

"Life wasn't meant to be easy," said Mr Fraser. He admitted years later that there was a second half to the quote. Did anyone ever understand that second half? Or that there even was one?
—Said in a presentation in a meeting

My memory returns in morsels and the oddest information comes to me at the oddest times. Sometimes I think I remember more, but then it goes again. Overall, I'm pretty sure I'm ahead. I retain more than I used to. It's as if I need to establish niches in my mind for the memory to stick. Some niches are harder to establish than others.

This time I was sitting with my friends, talking about—of all things—terrorists. A small bit of knowledge came to me and I wish it had not.

I'm not an observer. I've never been an anthropologist. That was yet another of these foul artificial mindgames they've been playing on me.

I'm not a natural non-participant in this business of quasi-colonisation. I'm not on this planet to document charming cultural quirks. All those things were done before I ever learned that humanity existed. Those few anthropologists who remain are just polishing the silver. Earth has been pretty well-documented. So many years of documentations. From the 1940s until now.

We're coming out into the open for a reason. And me, I'm part of the reason. A hidden part. Hidden from almost everyone for so very many reasons.

I'm not an anthropologist. I've never been an anthropologist.

I'm the bloody Judge and, if necessary, the fucking executioner. I did not expect this.

I can't do my job until I've sorted out the impediments. The impediments include my people saying: "There are no problems with your body. This is normal. Don't worry."

If I don't sort this out, then I'll execute myself or murder everyone on this godforsaken planet by mistake.

The options are appalling. There is no negotiation, no way of making those two choices less stark.

There is no third choice.

Judgement is bleak. No matter how much one examines it, it's bleak. Someone has to suffer. Mostly, it's the inhabitants of a planet because the Judgement is so very personal in nature. Judgement is described as dispassionate and fair, but it's the polar opposite.

Choice One is for the Judge to go home. That's the most common choice Judges make. Humans are preserved in zoos and for experimental purposes, but their planet is freed from them. They are, after Judgement, regarded as a potentially dangerous and definitely inferior species.

The second choice is for the Judge to stay. It's the only way humans are permitted to go on living outside a zoo. It means I die a natural death as a human. I put my life on the line and lose one hundred and fifty years of it to present irrefutable proof that humanity is neither dangerous nor vermin. Humans may continue as they are now, but only if I agree to immolate myself on their behalf. I may never communicate home. My family clan, my friends, all my past and all my possessions are lost to me. I am considered corrupted beyond rehabilitation.

That's the very best of the options for this godforsaken planet.

Choice One, that other option, is complete destruction. This will make Earth a forsaken planet in an almost literal way. English sometimes has words that are apt.

If this *is* a forsaken planet. I don't know yet. I assume that Earth will be destroyed because every time I appear for downloading, I miss everyone and everything with more pain than pleasure. The dice are loaded against Earth due to how we manage Memory.

Everything I thought and everything I believed is tangled and confused. The Memories and the human body and the whole stupid process make even less sense to me now than they did a few months ago when I understood everything.

How can someone make Judgement from a base like this? And why was a Judge sent to Earth at this point, anyway?

It's an appalling system. It has appalling effects. And I can't do anything to fix it.

I'm caught up in the cycle of Judgement, and there are only two paths I'm permitted to take. One leads to the extinction of humans. If I decided that everyone on this planet is to die, I could return home and put in a plea for reforms to the system. The other leads to humans continuing, but my Judgement will then be Judged in its own right. Every single time this has happened, the Judgement has been seen as biasing the Judge and rendering them unfit to live in a family clan.

Let me try pulling it all together. If I let Earth live, I'll never be permitted to go home. Ever. And my home planet will continue to murder other species, never realising that the whole system is corrupt beyond belief. If Earth is innocent, other planets die. And I die.

It doesn't matter how many different ways I find of saying this, neither outcome is wise or kind or sane.

Why the fuck did they do this to me? How can I judge when I hurt, inside and out? At least before I was judging without knowing I was judging, if one can call that a better position. Now I want to die for my own reasons, to stop the goddammed undercover pain.

My legs hurt from being swollen due to the medication I'm on because of the latest hospital trek. Sore legs are not a good enough reason to Judge. It hurts a bit to walk; that is no excuse for murdering billions. I can't favour the other legs, for there are no other legs to favour. I'm bipedal and limited, and have remembered that life is much easier when one can rest one's legs a bit. The constant pain from this or that, the constant nag of a body that is perpetually in change and yet not really changing at all—it's wearing me down. Every minute of every day.

"Wait until you reach menopause," I'm told, "things will improve", but in the interim I have constant discomfort and near-constant pain, and my judgement is impaired and my life a mess. I confuse my body with my role.

They should have noted these problems before they reached this stage of proceedings. There are a lot of things *They* should have noted. Right now, I know precisely which species needs a Judgement and it's not humanity.

What the fuck am I supposed to do?

Step One—sort myself out (maybe this is possible);

Step Two—sort *Them* out (I have no idea how);

Step Three—sort humanity out (this is possible and I know how to do it, but God, I wish both weren't true).

Humans—be afraid of this middle-aged woman. Middle-aged woman—remember who you are long enough to do the job. And do it well. Do not sacrifice the world because today you have cramp. Especially do not die unless you intend to. In fact, above all, do not die.

Not dying is an option. There is a failsafe to save my life. I wouldn't be here without a failsafe. Our gallant interplanetary services would never be able to persuade the authorities to sacrifice the eminent and wise people to be Judges if there wasn't a failsafe.

I just have to remember that there is a failsafe. That's the first memory they wiped. That's one of the things that fails to find a niche in my memory and stay safe. My *get-out-of-jail-free* card. And I'm not ready to die. I have gender shifts to experience before I'm ready to move on. I have family roles to serve. I have duties to society and social action to take. My cycle of life isn't even close to complete.

How dare they say that my life is a small and fragile thing? It's fragile now, thanks to them. But it never was small. Never.

If I die as a human and I have not passed my hundredth birthday (it seemed a good number, I was told in briefing—Why was I briefed and then the briefing deleted? And why is all the tech work failing—they tell me with apologies it's not done that way intentionally, but they can't fix it—those are big consequences for such a poorly-executed piece of work and they didn't mean to give me the damn memories originally and could I please not tell anyone for it would end their careers), all humanity dies with me.

I understood the logic originally, but now it seems a bit parlous. My death is another Judgement on humans, when that death could be accidental or through my body failing. We didn't allow properly for human frailty. They didn't allow nearly enough for our errors. The failsafe would be sufficient. The simple failsafe. I shall remember it long enough to run a test when I'm next in the machine room. I can claim the health stuff as an excuse.

Yes, that's it. Let me get out of this mess before it gets worse.

It would be ironic if I died due to our fault and all humans were obliterated. If it doesn't come from me at all and it's not due to humans having a fucked-up set of societies. Humans being a fucked-up species. Ironic, for it's due to an anthropologist being caught in the same drop as me and being confused with me. Irony isn't sufficient in this instance.

Also, damn these legs.

All of this will be documented, but I only see what I'm noting now. I can't get any more of my memory back this way, and I can't get it back by writing on a computer, for that would breach security. And we're fucked if the mindwipe wins again.

Fucked.

Fucked.

Fucked.

When my mindwipe takes over next time round, we'll be even more fucked, for there won't even be the memory of a failsafe.

I damn well hope I remember to read my notes next time I forget.

The Observer's Notes

"Today is the Day." Capitals were essential this morning, just as they're essential now. I have found my dignity and lost any desire to put quotes in my diary. No bad language. Just an accounting.

My mood fights with my fatigue at this point, but I have to write today up, otherwise I might do the *Groundhog Day* thing. Some days I remember most things, and some days I know I don't remember most things, and my confidence remains sparkly high whichever is true. That's why this brand-new old-fashioned handwritten diary has a lock. It feels stupid, but if I have a tiny child's key on my keychain, then, if worst comes to worst, I can see it and think "I had to do something." I didn't have to bother with that this morning, thank goodness. I woke up thinking about it. But tonight is different. Tonight I get to write on page one of my new secret diary. Aren't I lucky?

I need a new sarcasm pen. This ballpoint just doesn't cut it. And tonight, I want to be sarcasm personified. I'm too tired, at this precise moment. My eyes droop and my fingers want to put the pen down and...I should just get on with this. It was such a bad day.

I've already told me, myself and I that this is an important entry and that I need to remember today so I have to write it down, no matter how much I'd rather not. Let me just get the thing done.

Today was the day I found a solution for the problem of Judging Humans. I must have found it before, but I've never found it (as far as I know) on a day when I could act on it. My people are good managers. We assume that things can go wrong. Judgement can be aborted if the Judge thinks it essential. There is hell to pay, but it can be done.

This is what I'd dedicated my day to: cancelling the heat death of the universe…or at least the early decease of many humans. Being willing to pay that hell, in the interest of aborting an impossibly-set-up situation.

When I first woke up, what I thought about was the man lying next to me, as one does. I felt roseate and sleepy and warm and very happy. Then I said "Good morning," and then I thought *I've forgotten something*. I felt a trickle of doubt. I looked at my wonderful sticky notes and saw the word "failsafe", and it all came flooding back.

I was appalled.

My husband thinks that the failsafe notes everywhere are for my failing memory. He's very good at helping me find ways of remembering things. The burden on him gets lighter as I remember more. His shoulders are no longer sloped over, protecting himself from the world, since he no longer carries as much of the burden that was protecting me. That's another reason for this diary. Take more responsibility for my own memory. And stop having to hide so much behind that fake car accident.

I don't want to write today's entry in this new diary. I really don't.

I remember thinking *Thank God I remembered. We can now all get out of this mess.* And then I looked across at Himself and thought "I wish…" Saving everyone meant sacrificing my love.

I am conflicted and there's no way around that. Not compromised: I still put everything ahead of my personal relationships. Definitely conflicted, however.

If today was about action, tonight is about rambling. It brings a nice balance to my strange life. Leanne would love it. Janet would suggest I cut to the chase. Except I don't want to.

I went to my "medical appointment" this morning, as planned. Walked through the first door and the green arc and felt not nearly as much memory returning as once it did, for I was already so much myself. This was a relief. I can do so much more with my time in that white room if I don't have to spend forever remembering the name of my cat. And my time in that white room was limited (long enough, but limited) and I wasn't sure how to do what I planned to do. It's not like programming, which is much easier: it's a matter of finding the right device, which, with my carefully layered memory, is one of those simple things that's no longer simple at all.

I sat down near the control panels for a few minutes, to orient myself. I spent the time looking at every single object in the room. All the screens and the buttons. They're mostly touchscreens, so that humans can't find out interesting things about us if they break into our facilities—this is how the techs' words come to my anxious ears. The buttons aren't labelled, for the same reasons as the screens being what they are. Linked to our two species, specifically. Not visible by humans, etc etc etc.

Today the techs were pretty quiet. They chatted about "Normal uplift—she just came in for an extra one because she's one of the nervous ones." "Oh," someone else said, and then the talk turned to all the usual gossip about celebrities and argument about what material to request from…

This description is not useful. Let me just move on.

The screens come on when I enter the room. It's automatic. I could check to see which screen I needed, or if it was the candy-striped button on the left. I rather thought it was the candy-striped button on the left, but I didn't have any recollection of briefing, and I wasn't going to be stupid and ask the techs.

Just when it looked as if things could get problematic, the central screen flickered and showed me what every single screen did and what every button and lever did and how to use each and every damn one of them. I'd not noticed this before, because it was proximity-triggered. Failsafe number one, in fact. Good management. And I was right about the candy-cane button. All I had to do was push it firmly three times.

I pressed it. Once. Twice. Thrice.

Nothing happened. None of the screens changed. Nothing.

I tried again. Nothing.

Eventually the door opened for the next room and I did my extra uplift and everything was normal there, too. It shouldn't have been. The failsafe should have triggered a beacon that would reach back home. It can't be turned off (so that emergencies don't lead to problems), but it's visible so that techs could begin the necessary work to withdraw personnel.

The failsafe should have caused a commotion. It didn't.

I couldn't swear and lose my temper (which is why I'm so apparently calm now) because without the failsafe, the situation is different. Greatly different. In a very bad way.

I really should swear at myself here, in the safety of my diary. I can't. I feel as if I'm banging my head against a radioactive wall.

I needed to protect myself this afternoon. I had to give the techs something in uplift, to hide what I really came for. The failsafe not working made them a source of concern. Suddenly, their lack of concern was worrying. And I had to put off that worry, because the failsafe had failed.

My mind turned to the morning, and I thought romantic thoughts. No sex, just pleasant warmth about the love of my life. I may have thought other things, but my focus was on waking up happy.

Everything was so normal that when I emerged, my engagement ring was gone. They were so concerned with selling my possessions to reflect my reports, that they didn't even notice I'd pressed the damn button. Which meant, of course, that the damn button didn't work. Which I knew, but it was good to see it confirmed.

I want to grind my teeth and give in to despair, because my most precious possession had been stolen by those damn techs and...the failsafe failed.

I had to tell my husband I lost it on the street. We spent the whole evening with torches, hunting for it. Naturally, it was nowhere to be found.

"At least I still have you," I joked.

He sighed. "I'd rather you had the ring as well."

"So would I," I said. "For so many reasons."

He didn't know how close he'd come to losing me. And to losing his safety from evil aliens. The failsafe would have instantly taken us out of Earth and set up an inquiry into why it was needed. Without it, Earth was doomed to be Judged. Still. By me.

And I don't know if the failsafe was broken, or if was intentionally disengaged. I need to act as if it was intentional. I need to assume that my vague feelings about the untrustworthiness of our cousins-in-space are accurate.

This scares me.

Notes towards an
Understanding of the Problem

Mostly, I've reported on uplift and Download in their own reports. They produce different results to all our other collection techniques, and to combine them with this set of reports would be like adding a random number generator to a fixed equation. The results would be interesting, but hardly useful.

One uplift point needs to be carried over here, however, for it shows something buried deep, and that something says so much about Diana and her reasons for acting.

On the day she tried the failsafe, she uplifted thoughts about her dead child. The visuals were couched as if her child were human. I find it sad that she regained the memory of losing her child, but that she will never remember hatching the egg in her quiet burrow. Oddly, she remembers the child's frills, but translates them into garments. Grooming garments is a very cold task compared with grooming the frills of one's own offspring.

The strongest and longest image from that uplift is this half-memory and this profound emotion. Also the feeling that this was a mistake, that she should have called up something less important. You can see her trying to call up less important emotions and failing. Instead, she called up her marriage.

I cannot trawl through that uplift report the way I do the others. It's naked and agonised.

Our maths tells us that the two emotions (loss and love, love and impending loss) cancel each other out and that this is not a critical episode. When I discovered this, I also found out that humans have taught me something: some non-critical episodes matter in ways our maths can't catch.

Today I suspect that the reason for fruitcake will be like this. Something that comes from the heart. Something irrepressible and uncontrollable and beautiful.

The Observer's Notes

I'm watching television again. It's wonderfully soothing. The actors are not quite human. It feels entirely like old-folks week. This boils down to me thinking I'm spending quiet time with people like me.

Some of the actors make their inner selves reflect their outer. Or is it the other way around?

I envy their success at linking inner and outer. I envy the facial muscle that twitches in precisely the right way when the tough guy hears about the death of his best friend. I envy the shell-shocked blankness around the eye. It's not real, but it feels real to the observer. It feels almost real to me. I need to remember that human emotions are not made of the stuff of acting, but that humans *feel*. That the stuff of acting is a mimic, and that it's not the other way round.

Nevertheless, these actors, these good actors, are my training. They always have been, but I didn't know it properly until now.

I am addicted to all kinds of shows. I always have been. I tell everyone so. What I don't tell them is that the moment I became self-aware, I started a deeper kind of learning. Consciously. With intent. I used to practise faking humanity, and I learned how to do this successfully from TV far more effectively than I could from my formal training back with the scientists.

Another thing I've done is thought through one of the smaller aspects of my exceptionally odd position. No, I'm not going to report to those people that I'm self-aware. Nothing that dramatic. What I've decided is to stop calling them *techs*. This is what they call themselves, not what they are.

They're exploring, not sticking to the tried and true. Experimenting.

This is an obvious reason why they do all kinds of things wrong. They're betraying their own background. They're scientists, and completely unprofessional. Bad, bad scientists, without any ethics.

They're not techs. Techs are careful, and follow instructions carefully and meticulously. They don't play with ways of doing things and stretch concepts and people to breaking point. I wonder how many anthropologists have been destroyed here on Earth, due to these scientists?

Although, to be honest, they're neither scientists nor technicians. English has no word that expresses what they do. I could call them anything and it would be equally inaccurate. I asked Janet what I should call someone with a job I couldn't describe, and she asked me how much I liked them.

"Not at all," I said.

"Call them lizards, then. The only things I know for certain about lizards are that they sleep in the sun and that their tails come off."

"One of those is exactly right," said I, and let her think that I meant the sleeping in the sun. There are certain differences between the lizards and my people, and detachable tails is one of them. We're related, but the tail thing is definitely theirs and theirs alone. I wonder if this plays a role in everything being so very wrong. There are disconnects that go very deep between decisions and action. The tail disconnect is the least of it. It is, however, one of the reasons the lizards don't do interstellar travel the way we do, why the work is divided the way it is. The other reasons are, I fear, all political.

Moving beyond them to the work they do, the scientists/techs/lizards have amazing amounts of data. People like me have fed it into systems for long enough. We know so much. But being human isn't about data and gestures. It's a bit about those odd little feelings that creep into your brain when you get the seat right at the front of the bus. But humanity is so very different to us in some ways. So very different. If I were finding a way to describe a human, I'd not do it using a number. Or even an equation.

I look at my TV and think that humans tell stories. Always. Everywhere. Their lives are narratives. And most of these narratives are adapted or stolen from other narratives. If I watch enough TV, then I can act out the stories I am expected to perform. I can get the cheek muscle to twitch in the precise, perfect way.

I can meet expectations. The easy expectations, anyhow. I refuse to contemplate the difficult ones. They still scare me.

Notes towards an
Understanding of the Problem

Diana wasn't paying attention. She'd needed that hot chocolate far more than the table did. Everyone said this.

Since the meltdown day, the group took special care of Diana, for she was the vulnerable one of the five. If there was a spare daisy, she was the one who got to take it home. She was in hospital most often (and only two of the others ever went to hospital at all, except to visit friends and family), and looked more frail than when they'd first met. No-one talked about the larger illnesses.

Leanne added a gentle comment about the trials of PMT to the comment about Diana needing chocolate, supplementing this kindness with a moment of personal puffery at being past it herself. Trina, having barely entered that period of joy and still very aware of every moment, was the one who carefully disengaged Diana's clawed fingers from the cup. A staff member appeared very quickly, checked she was all right, wiped the table down and mopped the floor.

Antoinette was the one who always saw the most pressing, forthcoming need. She had already ordered more hot chocolate. Antoinette also ordered a tray of various chocolate foodstuffs for the group to share. "My treat—we all need it. Diana is merely expressing internal disconnectedness on our behalf."

"It's not PMT," Janet explained, quietly. She had sat out the furore.

"It is," said Diana, "But everything's worse because..." She trailed off, unable to finish the thought. Her hand was clutched in her lap. She didn't trust her fingers to operate correctly yet.

She knew hot flushes and faint trembles, but this was a visceral reaction. She could feel her hormones pumping warmth and inflammation through her and making everything worse. How do I know this? She wrote it down in one of those interminable notes of hers. They're what I used to establish her voice, and why I use that voice of hers in English most of the time. She had downloaded everything that morning for techs, and was already operating on the edge of sanity.

She also thought—for she said this, too—that her body was trying to push through the hot flushes and the swollen self and become its next self. Gendershift was trying to win through.

I have no reason to doubt this. Her hand trying to evolve into its native claw was a giveaway. Her body was also unwell, but that's something I will investigate separately. Her friends kept it out of the conversation and I shall, too.

This is the only time that the hand tried to turn into a claw, as far as I know. It was internal and was only visible to outsiders as a clutching.

This is the reason I'm investigating this particular incident: it's not one of the critical ones, but it's the only time we have on record that her disconnect between self and human body caused noticeable side effects. This is rather important. After it was all over, the techs claimed that the breakdown was due to her body trying to match itself to her self. This episode has been cited so very often as justification, to explain they did not fail in any way. And yet, when one views all the records, it stands alone. Even taking into account her human medical records, it stands alone. She presented as human throughout. The techs are making false claims.

I have to discount lack of control as a major cause, due to this incident being so isolated. It took a great deal for Diana's body to try to become its original, multigendered, not-at-all-human self. I would have bet on the eyes giving way, to be honest, in an attempt to work as if they were facetted. Seeing *glow* is so very important to her clan. Not seeing the qualities of objects would both haunt and hurt.

That's enough analysis. The incident has more to it than that. Let me finish the story.

Janet explained.

"We met after Diana's medical appointment. We shopped success-fully."

She said this as if there was a prize they were competing for.

Meeting: 4 points

Shopping: 3 points

Shopping successfully: outright win

Shopping must be an extraordinarily difficult feat. The other possibility is that Janet was being sarcastic. As I am now.

"And this guy, he tried…" It was her turn to taper off.

"He called us some very interesting names. He and his friends threatened us and tried to take our belongings."

"And you're OK?"

"We're getting there. They only got one bag—games for my nephews. When we reported it to the police, though, they took notes and were…"

"Unsympathetic," said Diana. "It wasn't a real crime, just a small incident. It wouldn't have hurt him to be a little sympathetic. He beat it up and made us feel helpless and useless and a waste of his time and space."

"The guy was young and new and wanted excitement. "

"He was unintentionally cruel," dissected Diana, quite precisely. "And I feel small and inconsequential and will never forgive him or those young louts. At this precise moment in time, you four are the only thing standing between humankind and extinction."

This ought to be a critical incident.

She declared her position publicly. The Judge offered the people of Earth knowledge of a nearly-definitive future.

It was too early, however. Because it was not a critical incident, those four were not the only thing standing between humankind and extinction. For a short time, Earth was spared. Diana knew this. It was perhaps why her body tried to become what it thought it ought to be. No-one else knew of her declaration. This did not make uplift or Download.

The people of Earth didn't even know they were being Judged. It wouldn't have changed things if they did, for Antoinette and Trina took Diana out for dinner, and Leanne made sure Janet found replacement presents and got home safely. Diana's body stabilised and all was well. For now.

Diana noted that there were films that had aliens forcing the planet to stand still in order to get their attention, in order to reform. Honestly, the universe isn't that obvious. Also, our particular part of the universe (the ones doing the judging) is neither unsubtle nor generous.

Diana saying, "You four are the only thing standing between humankind and extinction" is the closest we ever came to acting like Klaatu. Ever. No declarations, no opportunities to reform. Not for Earthlings. Not for anyone. This is the closest we would ever come to what humans would consider real drama.

The main difference between this and equivalent episodes elsewhere is that humanity has chocolate. Or maybe we just do the things—we don't declare or make a fuss or anything like this.

We used to consider this virtuous. *I* used to consider this virtuous. Now I wonder that we are not more ashamed of ourselves for so quietly committing genocide. Not *one* genocide. *So very much genocide.* Other races colonise; we murder.

Damn humans for making it so obvious.

It's not as if they were not guilty of all kinds of things, either. They hadn't moved beyond their planet, so the only murdering they did was among themselves. But they make me feel guilty, nonetheless.

The Observer's Notes

I'm full of tears today. I think I've worked it out this time. For certain.

I'm not crying for no reason. I'm crying because my body is in sympathy with the day. Just like when I'm bitchy, I'm not bitchy for no reason—it's the world outside.

Maybe there's a sharp wind, or an evil cloud looming. I am in tune with the elements, with no burrow to protect me, and my mood reflects this. My body isn't so removed from my previous self as I thought. The real me is still here, underneath, and this resonance with the world demonstrates it. It's a very real truth. And it's the reason we have burrows and not houses. Burrows protect against the elements so that one can choose to feel. Or one can choose to avoid the tears on a sharp day.

I can't have it any other way. I can't go forward and I can't go back. I will not have lost myself so very thoroughly that I'm nothing but a whining bitch who hates everyone and cries at the drop of a hat. I cannot be homesick. I cannot be bodysick.

I am not the right gender. I'm not even in my own body.

Some days I'm closer than others. Some days I'm so far that I am not myself. Will never be myself. Everything hurts and all that is left is tears.

I want my body to be true to who I am. It's not a lot to ask for. Also, I want it to stop hurting.

Notes towards an
Understanding of the Problem

At this point in my study, I understand the women's addiction to chocolate. I need something equivalent. An emotional refuge. Why do I need it?

I've just turned up some information that I would rather I hadn't discovered. Certain other people would quite possibly rather I hadn't discovered it also. In the interest of my own safety, I have put in a complaint, made a ruling on the future lives of those who instigated this policy (for it *was* a policy and now their careers are bung: cause and effect), and am now noting the situation here.

All this time I've been wondering why Diana herself didn't use the failsafe, given the situation and that she was aware of it. I assumed it was because of the unreliability of her memory. Certainly that was to blame, up to a point. How can one use a failsafe if one doesn't know it exists? Until quite late in the piece, the failsafe didn't even appear in her notes due to her memory, so this appeared to be a safe assumption.

I find myself wanting to explain, every other minute, that we're not nearly as stupid as we look right now. That Diana calling us "lizards" and that the twenty other pejoratives assigned to us by anthropologists in recent years are inaccurate. We do good work. Often. Usually.

Why do I write this as if it needs writing?

Because it does. Because there is a litany of failure as regards Earth. Three other planets, likewise, have demonstrated certain… *problems*…in the way we do things.

Officially, there are two options for Earth. For any planet. Live or die. Simple.

Except that there *is* a failsafe. If the Judgement is jeopardised for whatever reason (say if Diana had been killed in a car accident), the failsafe is supposed to happen automatically. If she had failed to appear for Download for seventy-five days...*failsafe* (although the Judge is never told this one).

The Judge themself also has the right to call the failsafe into play, and can do so without creating a fuss. This is why they are always given access to the programming room without observation. Anthropologists sit in a quite different room to regain their memory. The Judge's memory is specifically set up to come back faster, and there is a minimum time of two hours where the Judge can do whatever they like in that room, before they walk through the arc. The first arc, in other words, is ornamental, making them feel something is happening when, in fact, it's already happened. The arc they pass through at the end of the debriefing is a different story.

However much interference was done, we could not possibly have changed the sequence of the rooms and their visits, for those sequences are sent automatically back here and analysed. If the sequence is wrong at any point, the system comes to a rapid halt, and an investigatory team is sent out. The sequence, then, was never wrong on Earth. Not once.

I checked this early on. No emergency calls, therefore the Judge went through all the measures she had to. There were other issues, but they didn't trigger alerts and therefore could not be acted on. Simple. It all looked so simple.

Because no alerts were triggered, I assumed that there was no need for any. I assumed that the failsafe was fully functional and was not necessary. This meant that the fruitcake was made from the usual ingredients and it was cooked on a tripod consisting of a choice between the three standard elements: planetary inhabitants all killed, planetary inhabitants all live, mission pulled due to triggering of failsafe.

To ensure the failsafe, once every six months it is tested, just to make sure it's fully functional. It's a simple test. A button is pressed and the report of it being pressed reaches home planet and a note is made that this is a regular test and not to be acted upon.

For the sake of completeness, last week I called for the regular tests of that failsafe and for the chronicle of Diana's uploading visits.

It was quite possible that one of her regular visits had coincided with a regular test and that the whole scheme should have been aborted, but that those of us back home hadn't realised that the button was pressed by the Judge and so it was reported as a test and not as a cause to pull out.

All the earlier investigations assumed either that she had not pressed the button or that she had pressed it during a test period. I felt that I was maybe being over-picky in demanding the data on the tests of the failsafe, but there were too many mysteries and I wanted to be certain.

I was the first to call for the full records. The first in six decades. Every other investigation simply looked at the data from our end, where the report of the button-pressing was noted as having occurred, but not requiring action.

You can guess where this is heading.

At the Earth end, there were no reports of the failsafe having been tested. It was never noted as having been cleaned or mended or having in any way, shape or form been handled during that period. There is only one possible reason for this lack of attention to it: it must have been disabled. Fake reports were added to the record at our end.

Not only is this culpable and unethical in terms of Judgement, it also means that, at this point, I cannot see any way we can have fruitcake. The tripod simply didn't exist. And yet we have fruitcake.

We also have only the two official options for Earth.

Three other planets have been Judged without operational failsafes, I have since discovered by checking the equivalent records. In every single one of them, the population was killed outright without malice. The planets were turned to our use very quickly.

This is another legal issue. I have referred it upwards. Heads will roll in the Colonial Service.

My view at the moment is: *How stuffed can this Judgement actually become?* I've never seen anything like it. In no failsafe should there be political interference or accident or impairment or…

There was no failsafe for Earth. It didn't matter what went wrong, Earth was going to be Judged. That is extraordinarily bad. Extraordinarily.

And because this was planet #4, there is no excuse. It was intentional.

The woman's slow voice...

was counting again

One, two, three, four, five, six, seven, eight, nine, ten, eleven, twelve, thirteen, fourteen, fifteen, sixteen, seventeen, eighteen, nineteen, twenty, twenty-one, twenty-two, twenty-three, twenty-four, twenty-five, twenty-six, twenty-seven, twenty-eight, twenty-nine, thirty, thirty-one, thirty-two, thirty-three, thirty-four, thirty-five, thirty-six, thirty-seven, thirty-eight, thirty-nine, forty, forty-one, forty-two, fifty-three, forty-four, forty-five, forty-six, forty-seven, forty-eight, forty-nine, fifty, fifty-one, fifty-two, fifty-three, fifty-four, fifty-five, fifty-six, fifty-seven, fifty-eight, fifty-nine, sixty.

I'm scheduled for retirement when I'm sixty. I know this for a fact. I know everything about my life. I'm God-like in my acquired knowledge.

This has nothing to do with my having threatened the lizards with extinction due to the complete mess they made of the whole Earth project. Not a thing. Nor the fact that, due to my threat, they gave me access to everything I wanted and needed.

Their excuse for access was merely that, an excuse. They claimed it was because I am Judge and was insufficiently briefed earlier and therefore should have this access—being lizards, they expected me to use it to watch what they think of as porn: the lizards don't understand human sexuality, nor the fact of my happy marriage. For them, it's all a game. And besides, the happy marriage was a surprise to all of us.

Also, they expect me to forget it tomorrow. They don't know I found out about the lost failsafe. And they don't know I tested their systems when I found out. My knowledge is superior. For once.

For me, it's partly a game. A part of me is a cousin to the lizards, after all. Different burrows, different gender sequences. Different career. But a related species.

I make it look as if the whole of me is playing their game. That I think of it as a game. A mere drollery out of which come *All the Things that Count Back Home*.

Part of me is human now. It can't ever be anything else. Inside, I'm so torn and unhappy that the wounds look as if they'll never heal. Not just the body itself, but the mindwounds. We are not supposed to undergo such change. Any of us.

Being a human, I live in a human timeline and I want to know what that timeline is going to be like. I want to prepare.

I don't need to prepare, in fact, given the most likely scenarios. Yet I still want to know what they have planned for me, even if I never live it. This is part of my inner confusion.

I suppose I'm making it worse by checking things out. I don't care. I especially want to know how long I have with my husband in their plans. And how long my body will last.

I'm going to retire early, it seems, in human terms. So early that it's hard to know whether or not I'll have Judged humanity by then. Not that the retirement has anything to do with Judgement, since it's my human workplace I'm retiring from. I'm being pushed into early retirement due to the state of my body. It's…uncheerful. It also means the lizards aren't infallible. Trusting their predictions won't get me anywhere; I still want to know.

Sixty isn't that far away. I can see it ahead, all by myself. It's not that daunting, really. Except for the fact that I've not lived most of my life as human. I've only lived a few years. I'm retiring before I've really had a chance to build up all the human expectations of age and maturity.

The lizards planned this and prepared for this. Of course they did.

I still haven't let them know that I overhear their chatter, and I know that they pushed my body into a major illness simply to provoke early retirement. That's what one said. The other said that they're forcing me into menopause before I can go home, basically. And into what they think of as old age.

They don't know their own reasons.

It worries me that I've only just remembered this. They're still playing games with my memories. Or their programs are uncertain. Either way, it's distressing.

I know why they're playing games. It's because they're still carrying their native burdens.

They're not comfortable with me because of who I am and why I'm here. And they're not comfortable with the human body I inhabit. Culturally, they can't understand a single-gendered species.

On the surface, it looks simple. I cannot possibly lead a full life here unless I gendershift, and I can't gendershift, so they have given me the closest they can find to gendershifting for a mature woman. Perimenopause to menopause to old age. In reality, however, they're not comfortable: I'm reduced to a lower status.

It's not just me. They take advantage of all of us who live in human bodies. This was the first thing that struck me when I read their files. The Judge has been sent, but they've already made Judgement. Humanity is an inferior species. Inferior, but sexy. They're taking advantage of the latter for as long as they can.

This is a perversion of the whole system. And yet I'll forget it in five minutes. This is how my brain misfires.

I wasn't that curious about what they had planned for my hypothetical retirement. Only that I'd have enough money (given most of my life has been equally hypothetical on this planet) and they've funded it quite generously. I don't know if that means they think I won't need the money, or if they think all of Earth will be done by then. Mostly, I wanted to know if they were planning my life post-Judgement.

I asked. They had planned it when they thought I was an anthropologist.

"But weren't you expecting me to go home?" I asked.

"We plan in case things go wrong, so that our people have

something to fall back on. It's a new set of failsafes." This explained the other failsafe not being functional. Not in a good way.

It also sounded like a set of excuses to me. None of the lizards come here either as themselves or by taking human form, after all. It may be that our charming custom of studying other creatures carries with it a life sentence far more often than is documented. It may be that the failsafe was a lie.

Now I'm angry again. And scared. Before I take that route and end up clutch-clawed and hurting, I shall inquire further.

I will have to take great care this time. It may be that the fallback position really is as they explain it, and that by getting the lizards offside I lose their goodwill when I'm ready to go home. I'll be polite. I'll keep the techs onside. Even if they're lying bastards.

From any direction, however, someone was corrupt and my briefing was inadequate. Add the confusion about my task and it begins to sound criminal. Criminals are safer when they destroy evidence.

I shall move with care. And I shall read my own notes back, if I must, to remember.

I always forget to read my own notes. That's the first thing I forget. I hide them from my husband and I don't remember they exist. There's no-one I don't have secrets from. I even have secrets from myself.

Notes towards an
Understanding of the Problem

It was not a good day.

Text messages had been sent. And sent. And more sent. After considerable negotiation, it was agreed that the five women would meet despite the state of their lives, would mention their woes very briefly and then find a means of escaping the morass.

"No tears, please," requested Janet, "and, just this once, no flowers. Oh my God, that makes it sound as if we always attend funerals! When we never have together, not once."

Good days could be turned into respectable days with supportive people. And problems could be mentioned aloud without being dwelled upon. It took a lot of texts, but it was going to work.

It had to work.

The first five minutes were very difficult. Every time a member of the gang explained something, one of the others would ask, "Talking?"

"No talking."

None of them wanted discussion, or sympathy. They wanted a safe space to make cautious statements about the condition of their lives. The fact that it took only five minutes to complete all these careful statements demonstrated how red raw everyone was, and how incapable they each were of receiving judgement, or help.

Trina's girlfriend had decided the relationship was never going anywhere. "I knew this was coming, deep inside, and I knew it would hurt, but I feel as if my heart's being razored into fine shreds and burned on a pyre."

Then it was Diana's turn. This was the moment for courage.

"I've got partial amnesia—had it for years—and there's a lot of my life I don't have access to any more. I keep a notebook in case I forget important things I'm doing, because it comes and goes. I've been recovering myself, bit by bit. Working on full recovery. Today it struck me that that I'll never have everything back. Nor even close. Today, though, today I realised I can't remember my family," Diana said. "I don't know where they are or how they are. This didn't worry me until I got a few small family memories back and I realised that a whole part of my emotional being has been ripped out. No, not ripped out, it's been carved out with a chain saw."

"I can never return to North Queensland," said Leanne. "My brother will kill me. Literally."

"I'm ill," said Janet. "It's degenerative. Everyone tries to help me, and that just makes it worse. I need to live quality life as myself, not meaningless life as a pitiful cripple. I had my latest round of tests and I was told that I've gone down to the next level. I'm being retired due to disability next month. I'll never be allowed to work again. I'm lucky, the medico told me, because I can have my house changed to accommodate me for a while. I've got a few years of tolerable living ahead, I'm told."

Antoinette, who always maintained that the impossible was possible, had heard about her daughter's wedding from a cousin. "I've lost my family too," she said. "Even the cousin only told me out of duty. I've not changed. I've never changed. They don't want to see that, so they've never tried. I've always said that I'll accept everyone back in their time, that it will happen, but right now I feel as if I'm going to be alone forever."

"We can't do this," Janet said. "We can't have *no* discussion at all. I thought I was the only one. And I promise, next time I'll bring flowers. I'll always bring flowers."

"Yes," agreed Antoinette. "We probably always need flowers. And chocolate. And to be here for each other."

"That's the thing, isn't it?" said Trina. "We're here. No matter what the state of our hearts, we're here. We're each other's extended family. We can't solve problems. We're not that kind of family."

"But we can be here for each other. Appease the aches with acceptance," Leanne said.

"And safety," said Janet.

"And help each other have quality life, whatever the damn world throws at us," said Antoinette.

"So how do we do this?" asked Diana.

"One step at a time," said Janet. "And I mean that ironically, of course."

"So what's the first step? Sorry I'm asking. My brain's still processing the fact that I have family. It's big," said Diana.

It mattered. Antoinette's face showed that it mattered. So very much.

"It's warm," said Trina. "It's full of heart."

"It's bloody amazing," said Leanne.

"So what is our first step?" asked Diana again.

"Who's up for dinner?"

The woman's slow voice...

was counting again

One, two, three, four, five, six, seven, eight, nine, ten, eleven, twelve, thirteen, fourteen, fifteen, sixteen, seventeen, eighteen, nineteen, twenty, twenty-one, twenty-two, twenty-three, twenty-four, twenty-five, twenty-six, twenty-seven, twenty-eight, twenty-nine, thirty, thirty-one, thirty-two, thirty-three, thirty-four, thirty-five, thirty-six, thirty-seven, thirty-eight, thirty-nine, forty, forty-one, forty-two, fifty-three, forty-four, forty-five, forty-six, forty-seven, forty-eight, forty-nine, fifty, fifty-one, fifty-two, fifty-three, fifty-four, fifty-five, fifty-six, fifty-seven, fifty-eight, fifty-nine, sixty, sixty-one, sixty-two, sixty-three, sixty-four, sixty-five, sixty-six, sixty-seven, sixty-eight, sixty-nine.

I need to be gone before I'm sixty-nine. I need to be back home. Safe. The plans for me in the lizardly files say that they're killing my husband at this point. If I can get back to my burrow, they won't have any excuse to kill him.

I puzzled over this entry. Tossed it in my mind until it was salad. Then I realise I couldn't think in human terms.

In lizard terms, then. An equation. It means they've added an element to my husband's equation that determines his ending. Since they can't influence outside events easily so far in advance (no car accident or assassination), it has to be internal. In his body.

My husband's body contains a time bomb of some sort, probably one that's set to look like cancer or a heart attack. There's nothing I can do about it. I've looked and looked and tried and tried. I've attempted to locate the threat (I have that much knowledge back). But unless I know what it is, I can't say "Why don't you check for such and such" to him.

I've even talked about it. I pointed out that them offering this threat means that my Judgement is impaired. They fall back on: "This is standard procedure—what's your problem? He's only human, anyhow."

They've already Judged. This is yet more evidence of that.

They can't do anything to enact the Judgement. The powers of the Judge are so carefully given. It wouldn't be just the lizard who judged who died, but their whole clan. All they can do is have opinions and set things up so that those opinions become fact. Like the way they planned my husband's death.

And they need to give excuses.

They've already rehearsed their excuse. They told me that it's part of their plan for my future safety, in case.

If murdering an individual reeks of Judgement, murdering the individual I am deeply in love with is worse, means that the future of humankind won't include him. I might kill everyone because he's not going to live, if I'm that way inclined. Which I was, until I discovered that his death has already been set in motion.

I can't let it get to me. I can't let it hurt. If it does, then I'm as bad as my cowardly and cruel compeers. I allow my personal thoughts to decide the fate of billions.

I wonder if there's a special value in destroying humankind? I wonder if this hasn't been set up quite on purpose. So little of my life has been left to chance, after all.

If there is, then the only way out for humankind is for me to sacrifice myself.

I haven't reached that yet, I don't want to reach that. Not if he's not here to get old with and laugh, and the world alongside.

Can they have predicted me falling in love so profoundly? Not at all. They certainly had the information to find me someone I would feel affection for, however.

My daily life is full of the small things. This keeps me sane. At the same time, my daily life is full of material I'm accumulating to make my Judgement. This is not the path of sanity. I have no recourse, and my people are fixed in their movement and there are no ways out of this mess.

I have to Judge.

There's no way out. Not even with everything wrong and the whole project threatened: we never stop a Judgement once the Judge is in place. If anthropologists don't return home, I can see why. It might change us. We might start taking on the ethics of our victims.

And now I'm both anthropologist and Judge. Me and my miserable excuse for a mind.

God, how did we ever get into this mess?

Notes towards an Understanding of the Problem

I'm beginning to see the problem. Why the decision went so very wrong. Why we have a fruitcake. Not *a* fruitcake. THE fruitcake. The biggest and most fruity fruitcake of all time. So full of brandy fumes that it would set itself on fire, given oxygen.

One of the critical moments was when the five decided to be each other's adopted family. They didn't live in each other's houses, or chase around every day. Each of them still had very independent lives. But it changed things.

There was something particularly notable about the time when Diana admitted her memory issues. It should have modified her relationship with these women. In some ways it did. But not in the way I expected. Her adopted family knew she was a watcher and knew she had big losses. She turned herself into someone who could be a burden. And they didn't treat her as that.

This was the simple turning point, however. Very soon after the "We are family" meeting, Diana gently let her friends know that her husband was dying, but that she'd been advised not to tell him.

"We don't know when, is the thing, and quality of life is important. It could be a long time before he dies. I don't agree with this. I want to share it with him and find solutions. But I'm not being given a choice. It's…political, in its way."

That was a bold thing to admit. If anyone had any notion that she was an alien observer or that the death was not so much diagnosed as induced, it might have opened her up to all kinds of problems. Her confidence says something about that group of friends that we hadn't realised in the initial examination. This was the moment that led to my team being formed.

An alert raised from that statement changed the equations, not simply the interpretation of the equations. The situation was modified from "failed" to "fruitcake". All hell broke loose.

We know that there were various people on various planets looking for Diana and trying to influence her. We even know that some visited Earth to do so. Only one played the old trick of being seen intentionally and letting humans yell "alien sighting". That one—and most of the others—didn't even know what continent she was on. Those who had the continent right got the city wrong. She was in no danger of being discovered.

Judges are hidden largely because it's the only way they can do their job without everyone jumping in and influencing. She knew that. The moment she knew she was a Judge, she knew that, anyhow. By this time, she knew what she was and that she was at risk, and yet she announced herself. Game changed. Instantly. Then her friends respected her confidence. Game changed again.

She should have been pulled. The process should have been aborted.

The moment the technical errors became obvious, she should have been sent home. Also, that Memory trick messes with the situation, more than I realised. And it was a messy enough situation already.

That didn't happen because the damn techs were doing far too well from "The Earth will be finished soon. Judgement is imminent. Buy some of these handy little souvenirs." And Earth porn was more popular than other porn. So many of the anthropologists had been turned into sex-seekers and their experiences sold.

At that moment, pornography became obscenity.

We had fruitcake.

The woman's slow voice...

was counting again

One, two, three, four, five, six, seven, eight, nine, ten, eleven, twelve, thirteen, fourteen, fifteen, sixteen, seventeen, eighteen, nineteen, twenty, twenty-one, twenty-two, twenty-three, twenty-four, twenty-five, twenty-six, twenty-seven, twenty-eight, twenty-nine, thirty, thirty-one, thirty-two, thirty-three, thirty-four, thirty-five, thirty-six, thirty-seven, thirty-eight, thirty-nine, forty, forty-one, forty-two, fifty-three, forty-four, forty-five, forty-six, forty-seven, forty-eight, forty-nine, fifty, fifty-one, fifty-two, fifty-three, fifty-four, fifty-five, fifty-six, fifty-seven, fifty-eight, fifty-nine, sixty, sixty-one, sixty-two, sixty-three, sixty-four, sixty-five, sixty-six, sixty-seven, sixty-eight, sixty-nine, seventy.

Three score years and ten. This is the length of time a human has to live. Thus said the early advisers on the race. It's not a time based on their physical bodies, but a time that literature thought was appropriate. An ecumenical length for a human life.

The day of Judgement will be on my seventieth birthday.

This is what the Plan says.

I can find no way out of it. No way to save my husband's life. I can do none of the things that are of real importance to me.

Nothing. There is no justice for me. There is no joy in my future, either, whatever way I look.

I fear for my seventieth birthday. I do not want it to happen.

If other aliens came to visit, those little grey men from human stories, I'd open my arms to them and say "Take me now." If suicide were an option, I'd be tempted by that, too. Given the lack of a failsafe, I can't assume that suicide would solve anything. Not even suicide is open to me.

Not that it's an option I'd take. I look at humanity and envy them their capacity to choose death. It's not a good choice to make, but they have it. We don't. We plan. We fix our lives and then we have to live them. I used to think this was right and proper and safe and happy.

Now it's the worst thing imaginable.

I do not want to see my life rolled out before me, inexorably giving the lie, year by year to my deepest understanding of the universe, that place where we have the right to choose our futures and decide the futures of others. On the surface, I have both of these. In reality, I have nothing. I am nothing.

The Observer's Notes

Now that I am emerging from that state of Memory, the colours are all wrong. I can see differences between home and here, finally. It's taken a long time, but it's generally reassuring. It means that I'm retaining more of myself for longer each day. Today it's less reassuring. Becoming myself is a mixed blessing.

Mostly my eyes are adjusted, and they see what they need to see. Mostly I don't care that there are two spectra missing, or that there are shadows and intensity but not a level of glow or texture. Mostly.

Most days, too, the scent and tastes don't overwhelm me. Today the world is drab with rain, and the Australian landscape does what it does and looks as if green is emerging in a way that suggests that glow is possible. That green is pale and brown and dusty and won't endure. And the taste of the air is too strong after the rain and there is no place with familiar scents. In that moment, always in that moment, I miss both glow and safe senses.

I can just about see glow out of these round eyes. Just a little faceting in my vision and I'd be able to distinguish between metals and plant matter by texture and glow, not merely by the surface colours. Just a little. But my human eyes are not facetted at all, and I can't.

The world is faded and so am I.

My friends wonder why I'm depressed. They're very supportive and very kind and I want to tell them the truth. So very much I want to. How could I possibly tell them that I have memories of a brighter, more vivid, more complex world, that if my vision caught the light in precisely the right way I could play with glow and my eye facets would send the universe whirling? I can't tell my friends that when my life gets too big, I used to have my burrow, with its muted scents and sounds. Safest place anywhere. I can't even tell my husband why there are times I need to be away from people.

Over the years I've learned to lie.

"I have a migraine," I say.

"Is there anything I can do?" he asks.

"I just need solitude and dark until it's gone."

"OK," he says. "Call me if you need anything."

And I never do, because what I needed was to have that time and place that most resembles home.

I can't tell my husband or my friends anything important, really.

I wonder how my body would react to drugs. I wonder if LSD would enable me to see glow and to whirl the universe. I'd belong here then. Really belong.

I'm fine with most other things, I think. I became accustomed to them while I was overlaid with the anthropologist personality. I miss playing with sight, though. I really miss it. My words here are a faint, unfaceted shadow of the depth of my feeling on this.

Notes towards an Understanding of the Problem

It was a champagne evening. The stars sparkled, the table sparkled, even the trees in the courtyard sparkled. This is why it didn't surprise anyone at all when Antoinette ordered a bottle of bubbly. They were meeting after dinner, at her request, and the night was obviously something very special to her. She'd texted to say she was running late. Ten more minutes.

"Why us?" Janet wondered, not really expecting an answer. She just wanted to fill in the time. Her tone of voice suggests this to me, anyhow. I can't see why she'd ask that, otherwise. Ten more minutes and she could have asked directly. "Not that I'm objecting, but it's a bit of a change and I normally don't do change easily."

"She'll tell us...or not," said Trina. Her voice was warm and comfortable. Self-satisfied in its flexibility. Tonight her hair was fringed with deep pink, and she wore matching earrings and a matching skirt.

"Besides, you took change by the throat and shook it hard the first day we met."

"There's that, Leanne," Janet replied, looking her in eye, as if it would stop her friend from playing with uncomfortable truths. "Except that it was Trina who changed us all. I merely followed."

"Pretend you're merely following now. Make it easy on yourself," suggested that lady.

"I will," said Janet in a surprised tone. "I didn't make the call or book the table, after all."

"You and I are the followers," Diana reinforced. "We accept good new things and are otherwise set in our ways."

Leanne snorted. "And just how did that weekend with your

husband turn out, anyway? Was it romantic in that zoo hotel? With the lions?"

And then came Antoinette. She was dressed stylishly. Much black lace. Some sparkle. And of course she ordered that champagne.

"Why are we here?" asked ever-subtle Leanne.

Antoinette laughed, but it wasn't a happy noise. This laugh had the effect of causing her friends to shuffle in their seats and twist until they had all found different positions. Leanne and Janet slumped back, Diana took on her watchful pose and Trina leaned forward, all sympathy. They were now ready for a different evening to the one they had prepared for.

"Some years ago, I wiped the slate clean. I sent my sorrows out into the universe and I refused to accept them back."

"So now we have champers to celebrate!" said Trina.

"Not so fast," suggested Diana. "She's only just started. Give her time to tell her story."

The look Antoinette gave Diana was one of relief. This had the effect on all the women of pushing them a half-inch closer to her and also adopting their various listening poses. It's funny how humans mimic physical habits when they're friends or allies. It's not funny, however, that Diana became the group arbiter on how to demonstrate sympathetic listening when a subject is serious. That, to me, is ironic.

"Thanks," said Antoinette, and they were interrupted by champagne and the pouring of it.

"What are we toasting if not the clean slate?" asked Janet.

"A very special woman I never met, who helped me when I really needed it. Every year I toast her."

"To this wonderful woman, wherever she is," said Diana.

"I'll tell you about her shortly. Let's start with the bubbles and drink them in happiness, first."

"To your friend, then, whoever she may be" said Leanne, and raised her glass. Everyone followed and clinked in her honour and sipped cautiously at their drinks.

"So cold!" said Trina.

"Almost ice," agreed Leanne.

"Bubbly ice," said Janet, and they giggled like teens on the town.

"Tell us," suggested Diana.

"It's not at all easy to tell. And it's not happy," said Antoinette.

"We guessed," Janet replied, "When you wanted to toast her first. If it's easier, tell it as a once-upon-a-time."

"Maybe not that," but Antoinette smiled. "Maybe I'll storify it a little."

"In five years," opined Trina, "That will date you."

"What?"

"Storify."

"Oh," Antoinette said, a bit abashed. "I do tend to live on Twitter."

She spoke very softly and her friends leaned in. At other tables, people looked curious. Secrets. Special secrets.

"Before I did the 'all my past is forgotten' thing, I had a great deal of counselling. It's not so easy to fix one's life when it's so very wrong. Anyhow, this woman, who I never actually met, made a lot of things possible for me. For me to be seen as me. When I was attacked, I was able to report it. When I was hated, I was able to get help. There was always the possibility that going for help would leave me open to more hate and more attacks. It happens a lot, these waves. I grow tired of them, but this is part of my life. But without Elbe, there would be nothing. Since my family didn't support me. Hell, since most of them don't even speak to me. Since most of my friends walked out. I was so very alone. Having a famous predecessor, well, it helped."

"Once, when I went to see my counsellor, someone else walked out as I walked in. This is not supposed to happen. The psychologist apologised profusely about the painting that stopped the second door being used, but didn't get it. Hadn't tried to make other arrangements. Put his clients at risk because upkeep was more important than we were. I stopped seeing that counsellor. I had to. There are enough problems without creating some for myself. If he didn't understand that that people like me are more likely to be murdered than any other group in the community then, hell, I wasn't going to accept it. I had statistics to prove it. My friends were being murdered. I was seeking help and…he still didn't quite believe me.

"This was part of my clean slate. Not accepting the unacceptable. Never, ever even thinking of accepting the unacceptable. Doing hard yards rather than getting help when the help was likely to hurt was one of those things. It transformed my life. For the first time ever I was only myself in public and in private. I didn't have to be someone else's token trans woman, or someone's hurt pigeon, or someone's failed man, or any of the things I'm not. I'm not token, I'm not hurt, and I'm not failed. It's very straightforward. And listening to the voice of a dead woman helped me understand this."

"How did she die?" asked Diana.

"I don't know. I've never asked. I want to celebrate her life. I want to toast the gift she gave me. She never knew me and she never knew about that gift, but she's made my life possible, without even knowing."

"That's a big gift," marvelled Trina.

"I think..." Diana was hesitant. "I think I understand about the starting fresh thing. I am not so good at the clean slate. I find my baggage keeps reappearing and making me into a person I didn't think I was, but I love it that you did that."

"Do you want to?" asked Antoinette.

"I don't know. I'm not like you," Diana answered. "You're so clear on who you are."

"I got to this the hard way," Antoinette pointed out. "And the person I am has a bunch of stuff to bear from outsiders."

"I know," said Diana. "It's hard-earned, and you pay for being yourself all the time. That doesn't mean you're not clear on who you are, though."

"She's right," said Leanne. "Your soul resonates like a bell."

Antoinette looked flummoxed.

"I can't be you," Diana continued, ignoring Antoinette's bewilderment. "It's not just my husband. It's me. Things within my life, within my mind. I am never going to be one of those people whose soul resonates like a bell. I love it that you are this person, however, and I admire it beyond almost anything, and I'm proud you chose me as one of the people to help toast this important woman."

"Me too," said Janet.

And it was Leanne who said the obvious. "I'd really like to know her name," she hinted.

Antoinette's eyes took on a glint of humour. Leanne loved to know everything, and the lack of concrete details was obviously killing her. "Maybe next year," she suggested.

"I think we should toast Antoinette," Trina interjected. "It's a champagne kind of evening, and we need to observe that."

"You always find the spirit of an occasion," noted Diana.

"And you always footnote it," commented Leanne.

"And you always note things scientifically," Janet pointed out.

"And if you're going to toast me, just do it!"

And they did.

They toasted Antoinette three times, because, as Trina said, "You're worth fifty toasts, but the drink driving laws get in the way."

"We should have champagne nights more often," said Janet.

"Only when there's a full moon and many stars and the trees are lit."

"I thought it was bright outside!" said Antoinette. "I read about the lighting this morning and completely forgot. Then I was in such a hurry I didn't notice the trees."

"Why don't we see them properly now," suggested Diana. "Why don't we pretend they're cherry blossoms and walk among them, gazing upwards contemplatively?"

"We could write poetry about their beauty."

"You can write poetry," Trina said. "I can do mood. I can picture it in my mind and I can colour my hair and decide on my outfit to match it. I can't pin words to it. Not ever. I've tried. The mood goes away and I'm left deflated."

"We don't want to lose the mood—no poetry," declared Antoinette. "Cherry blossom time."

There was another occasion when they talked about this dead woman. I don't know who she is, but I have to admire her. On that occasion, Antoinette talked about things other than the cancelling of all her vows and promises to the world, and of starting again. On that occasion she talked about living. I don't know if I want to explore that episode at all.

I will talk about it here, briefly, instead of exploring it. That will suffice.

At that meeting, she said, "We need a way of knowing who can talk about what and when. We need something simple, so that we never have to worry about having to negotiate and explain."

"You sound as if you have a solution," said Diana.

Antoinette pulled ten scarves from her bag. Filmy scarves, not big. Five colours, two shades for each.

"Pick a pair," she instructed. "A colour."

"I bags purple," said Trina who was, that day, Goth-girl again.

"Blue," said Janet, firmly.

"Not yellow?" asked Leanne, surprised.

"With my complexion?"

"I never thought of that," confessed Leanne. "I don't worry too much about clothes."

"I'll have any," said Diana. "I love them all."

"Then I might take the red one, for it's one of my favourite colours," said Antoinette. "And it works with my skin colour."

"Complexion," said Janet, still being firm. "For we're ladies here today."

"Why are we ladies here today?" asked Trina dutifully.

"We all have scarves and handbags."

And indeed they did, for somehow the yellow and green scarves had been allocated while they spoke.

"I love these," said Diana, her fingers running through the fineness. "Could you explain what they're for?"

"If something big goes wrong and you don't want to talk about it, you wear the darker shade. If you just don't want to talk about personal things, but there's nothing big behind it, you wear the lighter one."

"Simple," said Diana.

"And exquisite," said Trina.

Antoinette is my favourite of the five women. If I were to meet a human, it would be she.

The woman's slow voice...

was counting again

One, two, three, four, five, six, seven, eight, nine, ten, eleven, twelve, thirteen, fourteen, fifteen, sixteen, seventeen, eighteen, nineteen, twenty, twenty-one, twenty-two, twenty-three, twenty-four, twenty-five, twenty-six, twenty-seven, twenty-eight, twenty-nine, thirty, thirty-one, thirty-two, thirty-three, thirty-four, thirty-five, thirty-six, thirty-seven, thirty-eight, thirty-nine, forty, forty-one, forty-two, fifty-three, forty-four, forty-five, forty-six, forty-seven, forty-eight, forty-nine, fifty, fifty-one, fifty-two, fifty-three, fifty-four, fifty-five, fifty-six, fifty-seven, fifty-eight, fifty-nine, sixty, sixty-one, sixty-two, sixty-three, sixty-four, sixty-five, sixty-six, sixty-seven, sixty-eight, sixty-nine, seventy, seventy-one, seventy-two.

If everything goes wrong for me and right for Earth, if I'm still here when I'm seventy-two, I get a new hip. The lizards say so. Or they would, if they read their own documents.

My new hip is listed for me along with a great number of other things over which they have no control. I mean, a carrot cake for my birthday? The arthritis can be set to happen and appointments booked without humans knowing they've been interfered with. We've done all these things before, since computers started being used. More than that is impossible. The minds of these lizards are borked. Completely and ineradicably cactus. They live in their own fantasy alternate Earth, where they are the tiny gods of carrot cake.

This makes me wonder—why do they plan to this extent?

I don't think there was ever confusion. I think they planned to cover up. This is evidence of that planning.

Once upon a time I knew a great deal. Once upon a time I heard about lizardly doings back home. One of the many things the Memories hide.

What I knew then and finally remember now is that there was a group that had infiltrated everywhere, and that wanted to destroy our planetary exploration scheme. The easiest way to destroy it would be to murder a Judge and to make it look as if the Judge had died naturally. Not just any Judge. A Judge who was a known voice on the needs of other worlds. Which I am. Or I was.

A natural death would mean something on Earth, earlier than the right time, with the evidence of a long planned life stretched out to prove that the Judge had made the impossible choice and that the planet would survive. That single event could cause significant change.

In human terms, my planetary compeers want me to be their martyr.

Setting up a full equation and calculating everything necessary for my full existence would demonstrate that my life was cut short. Carrot cake, I think, comes about because the lizards do not understand story. They don't want to leave anything open to chance and they have a working script developed by the anthropologist and it covers a life like mine. This suggests the anthropologists are involved in some way, for one has to know humans to create a human life in this way, where equations are not the whole story.

It might not sufficiently look like a full life unless it is a full life in that respect, given the popularity of Earth currently. And they only know full lives from the records and anthropologists. I rather like it that the specific nature of Earthen lives defeats them.

All this I know because...I used to be a powerful person. I was the one who argued that we needed new paradigms. I had so much power. Now, I hardly even have a memory.

When are they likely to try to murder me? That's the question. I would say after my seventieth birthday, given the shape of their narratives.

Having both stories and sums makes me far more powerful than they are. I may not be what I once was, but I'm still more powerful than they are.

I need to remember this. Making me human was a mistake for them. Not talking to me about the system that needed changing was an even bigger mistake. For I could do that: it was within my power. Unless they did, and I refused to do exactly what they wanted in precisely the manner they desired, and this was revenge. Who the hell knows?

On the normal timeline, I die a day before my hundredth birthday. I die in hospital. In my reality, I have to be dead before or after the last event recorded in my timeline. Anything earlier and anything later wouldn't challenge our system.

Two different deaths for two different outcomes.

And the third outcome is, of course, going home. It's the obvious choice, after all. To live normally. To challenge the system from within, accepting the sacrifice of Earth to do so. If I live long enough, that's an option. With murderers plotting my demise to make their political point, it might be another outcome I can't access.

I shall explore. I shall ponder. I shall plan.

I have time to think, and time to prepare. I also need to decide if I want to live. If I'm right and my husband is dead much sooner, maybe I don't want to die on Earth. Maybe I'm wasting my time even thinking about accepting the death they're throwing at me.

If I want Earth to survive, though, I'll have to make my Judgement clear. And if Earth is to die, I'll have to make my Judgement clear. I cannot let the lizards interfere.

I am of my people, and I might play with the notion of flexibility from time to time; I refuse to be forced into it by changed memories and misrepresented tasks and the games of renegade lizards.

It's very fortunate I never reported that the conditioning was breaking down so very much. They know I have Memory glitches. They have no idea how self-aware I am. It means I have space left. I can't do a great deal with that space, but I must be able to do something.

Notes towards an
Understanding of the Problem

"Leonard Cohen is dead," said Trina.
"Good reason to wear black."

"*Hallelujah* is my song," Diana said. "It's the one that reflects my heart, with the breaking and the numinous and the flawed and the very human life I'm connected to. So many ways I read the lyrics and they're so very seldom triumphant and they're always me."

There was a silence for a moment. It was a lot of observation from someone who didn't often speak. Diana was more an observer than someone who told the group truths about hurts, and this one was a deep truth.

It said so much about the tragedy that was her marriage. All the women know that she loved him beyond anything and that for him, the marriage had become a thing of usefulness only. It showed clearly even to me, from their collected statements, even if I'd not had access to the downloads. So Diana knew. She knew that she was in love and yet a mere convenience or maybe a necessary burden. Her status shifted back and forth, but at her end, she loved.

"My song," Trina ran with the meme to break the mood, "is from Babymetal."

"What?" Janet was very tangled.

"A band. Japanese. A very good band, death metal crossed with daft and cute."

"That's an interesting thing. I thought you'd have a folksong, maybe. My song's that. *Black is the Colour of My True Love's Hair*. A particular version. Bleak and beautiful. A bit Gothic. I thought you'd choose something like that."

"Mine is a bit like that. Just…not quite. The song itself is arcane, boppy and complicated—just like me," said Trina. The others laughed.

"So true," said Leanne, and paused to think. "I don't have a song," she admitted.

"Yes you do," said Trina. "*Magia*."

"What?"

"It's the theme tune from an anime, and it's exactly you. Complex, a bit dark, but with so much hope and strength."

"Mine's not dark," said Antoinette. "It's full of future. It's about renewing vows, dissolving problems, starting over. Also, it has the best melody I've heard anywhere, anytime."

"What's it called?" asked Trina.

"I've no idea how to pronounce it," admitted Antoinette. "I've got it on my phone, though. I can play it for you. It's pretty ancient."

"I need to hear all this music," said Diana, "Who else has their music on their phone?"

Antoinette played her deep liturgical melody, then Trina found them the Babymetal song, then six versions of Hallelujah, the precise version of Black is the Colour, and the very best version of Magia. They also managed to annoy the people at the next table.

The Observer's Notes

I want.
    Je veux. J'ai besoin. Grand besoin. Je désire. Je veux.
Alles. All. Everything.
For specifics beyond me. Tomorrow is beyond me.
I need. I am desperate.
Je veux. J'ai besoin. Grand besoin. Je désire. Je veux.
I want.

The woman's slow voice...

was counting again

One, two, three, four, five, six, seven, eight, nine, ten, eleven, twelve, thirteen, fourteen, fifteen, sixteen, seventeen, eighteen, nineteen, twenty, twenty-one, twenty-two, twenty-three, twenty-four, twenty-five, twenty-six, twenty-seven, twenty-eight, twenty-nine, thirty, thirty-one, thirty-two, thirty-three, thirty-four, thirty-five, thirty-six, thirty-seven, thirty-eight, thirty-nine, forty, forty-one, forty-two, fifty-three, forty-four, forty-five, forty-six, forty-seven, forty-eight, forty-nine, fifty, fifty-one, fifty-two, fifty-three, fifty-four, fifty-five, fifty-six, fifty-seven, fifty-eight, fifty-nine, sixty, sixty-one, sixty-two, sixty-three, sixty-four, sixty-five, sixty-six, sixty-seven, sixty-eight, sixty-nine, seventy, seventy-one, seventy-two, seventy-three, seventy-four, seventy-five, seventy-six.

The timeline says that when I am seventy-six, I shall have a heart operation.

Thank you for that, timeline. You have given me so many hospital visits and so many crises and so many fears. It's a stupidity, for how are the lizards going to prove that I've died unexpectedly when so much goes wrong with this human body? Humans are fallible, after all. I could be killed in hospital by mistake, especially if there are (as sometimes there are) slight errors in the human body I inhabit.

Someone loves their planning more than they love their outcomes. Either that, or...

Ah, I think I have it.

We have more than one force operating. This is so much the way we do things, isn't it? Where a simple equation would work, those in power sit back and let it work. In the meantime, this group and that enter like thieves in the night and tinker. They add something here and subtract something there and the result is beyond anything stupid. There is no term for this result in English.

How can I unpick the mess?

I know about one group. My illnesses go against their need, and the illnesses are in my timeline.

There's nothing of use to them in my mind being raddled, however. Part of this is lazy tech. My Judy Garland Memory is simply that. Laziness. Corruption.

There's so much evidence for corruption. The possessions that disappear each Download. The lizards are corrupt and they corrupt me. And we all know about the corruption in the system. Only a few of us have had the power to do anything about it. So that makes sense, too.

What doesn't make sense is any others playing active interference in my work and in my life not allowing for it. Either stupidity in all groups or laziness by everyone or maybe a feeling that famous people serve a kind of alien comeuppance given the opportunity. Equations are supposed to help resolve emotions by quantifying them and allowing them to be understood. Equations are sometimes a rip-roaring failure.

Heresy. Blasphemy. That sentence was both. It is, nevertheless, true. Equations can fail.

What a mess.

I see possible space for me in this. Something that might work within our system and might prevent the lizards from murdering me and stealing my right to decide. And that might get me the political result I want.

I want a quite specific political outcome, after all. This time on Earth has convinced me it's the best for everyone. Speaking in human terms, I want to see the Empire dismantled. We don't think it's an empire. We have no description of empire. Explaining empires is easy in story-based culture, and almost impossible for us or for lizards.

The fools made a big mistake in sending me to Earth and giving me access to human ideas and human stories.

I didn't want to give Judgement until it was nearly stolen from me. Now I refuse to question my right and I refuse to step down from my responsibility. Earth will be Judged. All humanity may well die.

My heart may break, but that's not relevant. My heart is human these days, anyhow. It's prone to breaking.

If I can find a way, my people, too, will be Judged.

Notes towards an
Understanding of the Problem

"**H**umans can settle Mars, it appears." Trina was full of wonder and joy. Everyone else was less impressed. They were, however, open to talking about anything. No-one wore scarves that day. The flowers shone defiantly gold against the black café table.

"Someone allocating humans an official Martian tartan doesn't mean we can settle Mars."

"If I were an alien, I'd come here, first. More interesting people," said Diana.

The others duly laughed.

This reminds me of a note in Diana's filing system. She wrote her own observations (I'm sure I've mentioned this before—they're brief and impersonal, but they're her own), and she wrote down aphorisms or sayings (thousands of them, some attached to observations and some proudly alone), she kept a tally of news and annotated it as "Yay Earth!" and "Why do you do these things, you fools?" and she wrote anecdotes that didn't mean anything. Or, should I say, rather, didn't relate to other aspects of her notes. Mostly these were small stories from social media. Sometimes they were stories she was told at social events. She always writes down where the stories come from. This one, for instance, is from a visit to Melbourne. I'll tell it here as an example of her little stories.

Mostly, I have no idea what to do with them, but it's important to know those stories exist. It's important to know the news clippings and comments also exist, but they've been dealt with in such great depth and so much detail in the *Problem of Earth* series that I'll leave well alone here. They were everyone's first port of call, in fact, when the events were first discussed. They were crunched into the original set of equations, along with her note and those aphorisms. The anecdotes haven't been discussed anywhere, yet.

Just one will do. They really don't have much to say. This one has a small implication, which is why I've selected it.

The meaning can come later—let's tell the anecdote first. This near-meaningless little tale has been authenticated to the best of my ability. It wasn't difficult. One of my people found an online reference to it where the granddaughter of the inventor told a friend.

Humans have very low levels of evidence for the most part. Everyday activity passes wistfully without clear Documentation. It would be difficult to prove that one ate breakfast ten days before, so low is their level of Documentation compared with ours. Although they work towards better Documentation, they're not even close to civilisation yet. This is one reason why they live at the whim of such a strange thing as story.

I find it interesting that my subject doesn't talk about this more. In fact, she seldom discusses it at all.

Interesting, but not problematic. It would only be problematic if she were on trial for her work as an anthropologist. She isn't. She was a failure at that because she was barely trained and it was not the task she was supposed to be doing. In other words, it's evidence of an entirely different aspect of the situation where she was set up for failure. I suspect that she might not have been the right person to set up for failure. She doesn't have any history of failure.

Nor does she have a history of fruitcake. Or she didn't.

Anyhow, to the anecdote.

During World War II, Australian consumers had a passion for tartan skirts. Importation of such things was limited, due to the war, so an enterprising firm ordered their own tartan for these fashionable garments. It was a family firm and the family name was "Black", so they called it the McBlack. It comprised three other tartans, one of which was the Royal Stewart. It was all produced locally, from the wool to the final product, so it wasn't dependent on international trade.

The tartan itself offended some people.

Let me make this clear, for it's very much an Earth thing. Tartan is a controlled substance. It's not addictive or dangerous to the body in any way, so it's hard to see why the restrictions apply. It's like clan colours, in some ways, but instead of being a thing of government legislation, it's governed independently. It's colour and pattern only, not molecular design and so forth. This illustrates the primitive nature of Earth.

Australia was not a signatory to any laws regarding tartan, and the McBlack was not illegal as far as I can gather. It was, however, a matter of culture and a matter of honour. This is the world that believes in the power of story, remember? Because of its position in the story of the Scottish people, an unapproved tartan is a form of cultural intrusion, even, under the right circumstances, cultural appropriation. So they police it.

Given this, it's not surprising this tartan offended some and was desirable to others. Nor was it surprising when Mr Black found himself the surprised recipient of a visitor from the authority that monitors tartans. The situation was explained to him and he nodded and agreed not to make any more skirts.

Mr Black told his family it was very easy to accede to the will of the authority. The tartan trend wasn't as strong as it had been, so he was running down his supplies. As a result, he had less than a bolt of the material in stock. He replaced the tartan skirts with another fabric and the episode was over.

How do I interpret this story?

Outcomes. It's all about outcomes. The outcomes of this were not what they appeared. Instead of one party being punished, everyone got what they wanted. The mischief-makers who alerted the authorities were the ones who lost out, for there were no replacement tartans, invented or other, until the end of the war. Keep this in mind.

If you go by her collections, my subject had a strange and wandering mind. But she brought everything together at a deep level. She also thought about it all at a very deep level, one of which she seldom spoke. This is the difference between small anecdotes and being such an agent for change. Keep this in mind, too.

I must keep in mind, myself, that my whole accounting is taking the shape of that collector of tidbits and notes that I'm studying. Pulling it together into a story is very difficult.

I should be thankful at this point that I'm pulling it into equations, ultimately. I can see why Diana wrote this way and why I'm copying it. It's far easier to find the values of a small anecdote that has links to others than a giant story that flows smoothly.

Ease aside, it's much less straightforward to Judge a people who use stories to think instead of maths. There isn't as much clarity. Complex concepts are harder to break down and link in strange ways with other complex concepts. That doesn't mean than humans don't have the capacity to think in an advanced way: obviously they do. What it means is that it's extraordinarily hard to explain humanity, even using a human language. Their propensity for story hid their limitations in terms of deep understanding and their similarities to us obscured their deep differences. This affects Judgement.

Of course it affects Judgement. Even if the situation on Earth had been entirely regular, Judgement would have been affected, because we require complete affinity with the people if the people are to live.

My recommendation is that this need for complete affinity should be reconsidered. We still must Judge, for how is life possible without making the difficult decisions? But we need to find more stable and sound reasons for applying Judgement.

The Observer's Notes

"Go away, all of you."
—me, today. And yesterday. And probably tomorrow. And definitely the day after.

I need a warm, lined place that's safe. Nothing here is safe. Not even the past is safe. Not even my home is safe. I'm always showing my frilled, frail side to the world.

There's never a moment that doesn't hurt.

I shall wear my dark yellow scarf tomorrow.

The Observer's Notes

Never believe that a few caring people can't change the world. For, indeed, that's all who ever have.
—Margaret Mead, read online (quotation not verified)

I'm more comfortable with old people. Their faces have contours. Study the contours and it's possible to know a person without even speaking to them. The older the person, the more comfortable they are to be with, for the more their face explains who they are.

Young humans are pretty. Not quite people yet, but pretty. The softness and sharpness and me-I-am hide who they are and who they will become.

If the human race were made of young people and if I were the judge of it, then humanity would…

I do not want to think this thought. The thought I want to think is the small smile lifting the right side of the face of the elderly woman who walked past me a moment ago. Her bushy white hair gave her thin brown skin an astonishing halo. If I were to judge humanity on her alone, humanity would survive. Her facelines demonstrated kindness and humour and troubles well-borne.

My one consolation when I watch film and TV, when I catch a crowded bus, is that most of the faces I see will eventually find their contours. Most of humanity can be saved, if it wants to be. It's a great shame that saving is not for each and every human, but for the whole race, and that age is not a factor. I could argue for saving humans. I have so many reasons. Old faces are but one of a mountain of them.

Saving humans isn't what's happening here. Judging humanity is.

And there's no mountain for that. Merely me.

Still, if I were judging and not Judging, that elderly lady would be safe.

The woman's slow voice...

was counting again

One, two, three, four, five, six, seven, eight, nine, ten, eleven, twelve, thirteen, fourteen, fifteen, sixteen, seventeen, eighteen, nineteen, twenty, twenty-one, twenty-two, twenty-three, twenty-four, twenty-five, twenty-six, twenty-seven, twenty-eight, twenty-nine, thirty, thirty-one, thirty-two, thirty-three, thirty-four, thirty-five, thirty-six, thirty-seven, thirty-eight, thirty-nine, forty, forty-one, forty-two, fifty-three, forty-four, forty-five, forty-six, forty-seven, forty-eight, forty-nine, fifty, fifty-one, fifty-two, fifty-three, fifty-four, fifty-five, fifty-six, fifty-seven, fifty-eight, fifty-nine, sixty, sixty-one, sixty-two, sixty-three, sixty-four, sixty-five, sixty-six, sixty-seven, sixty-eight, sixty-nine, seventy, seventy-one, seventy-two, seventy-three, seventy-four, seventy-five, seventy-six, seventy-seven, seventy-eight, seventy-nine, eighty, eighty-one, eighty-two, eighty-three, eighty-four, eighty-five, eighty-six, eighty-seven, eighty-eight, eighty-nine, ninety, ninety-one, ninety-two, ninety-three, ninety-four, ninety-five, ninety-six, ninety-seven, ninety-eight, ninety-nine

I do not want to think ahead to this. I do not want to plan for this. I should stop counting.

I won't count again unless I have to.

May that day never arrive.

The Observer's Notes

"Go away. I'm not ready. I never will be ready. Go away and stay away."
    —me, of course.

I want my burrow. Now. Forever.
    I don't want to do this thing. I never wanted to do this thing.
They made me forget I refused and objected and dug my heels in
and that I was still forced to be Judge.
    I need my burrow.

Notes towards an
Understanding of the Problem

L et me sum up events. Simply.

Cut through the complex descriptions and subjective feelings that have led me to this point. The earlier notes were pushing me towards this: they can now be discarded. In fact they *must* be discarded. I am developing sentiment towards the stories they begin to tell, and sentiment towards anything linked with story is quite evidently one of the major causes of this disaster.

We had sent a final team of anthropologists to this planet. We had decided on Judgement.

After Judgement, everything changes. Always. The sentient residents of the planet become like us, for we teach them to be like us. Or they die.

There are no other paths.

Our technical experts are neither as technical nor as expert as they should be. I tested this side of matters in my early days on Earth. This is when I discovered what a complete mess had been made of the technical side of Earth's early colonisation. This is a factor, too, like story.

At first, it looked as if it was a simple mix-up: somehow the Judge had been given the mind-treatment meant for an anthropologist, along with the human body both required. But it was not a simple matter of giving someone the wrong identity. That was, when I investigated, almost impossible to do, and rightly so. Those identities should never have been wiped or reshaped.

It was impossible to find a clear culprit, but it was not a simple error.

We don't have many recourses in this kind of circumstance. The immediate investigation submitted a recommendation, and those technicians were at once sent to new work with less responsibility. They were also fined.

Whatever the outcome of the rest of my research, they were partly responsible. Even if we discover that they were not involved in deciding it should happen, they didn't follow standard procedure. The mindwipe/download cycle couldn't have been done without them, whether it was intentional or not.

I originally gave them the benefit of the doubt, and agreed with those penalties. However, the file is still open on them for, from the moment fruitcake occurred, there were issues that needed resolving and they are not yet done.

Right now, I still think it's possible that these technicians were purposefully involved with a group of activists intent on creating a martyr. Or with a group of hooligans intent on creating entertainment for voyeurs back home. Or with one of two other groups I have identified. They have been punished for being incompetent, not for being culpable.

Mistake One, therefore, was lack of control over the technical side, so that cultural benefit (in this case porn or political change: probably porn) overrode basic principles. The limitations of the sex options in this society were too tempting on one hand, and those responsible were too late in applying an ethical code that was suitable for human interface. The immediate consequence of this was the diversion of two systems upgrades into their porn industry, so we now have excellent interpersonal pornographic experience starring our anthropologists on the Planet Earth. Art has been created.

On the other hand there is the intentional interference with the life of the Judge, to bring about her early demise. This is in addition to the porn problem, but the porn problem is what affected the upgrades.

Porn was not what the upgrades were for, obviously. They were to provide the more complex and robust mind conditioning a Judge needs. As a result, the Judge broke down. This was *Mistake Two.*

These were the initial errors that caused all else to go wrong.

Judges are selected for their strength of personality, and having one who was there reluctantly was bad enough. The fact that she was reluctant and had solid reason to distrust the techs was *Mistake Three,* for it meant that, until now, no-one has had full access to what happened. The Judge hid her private thoughts in this language (English), which is why this later investigation needed native speaker level and the capacity to interpret her words as she intended them. The errors in her preparation caused, as far as I can tell, her to see no problems at all in communicating in English and in writing English into her journal. She hid much material in places we may not have found, so there is no guarantee our record is complete. This is unheard of.

The usual warning signs and blocks that limit action in order to reduce contamination were, it appears, excluded entirely from her prep. Whoever made that decision should be given a more severe punishment.

This third mistake, to my vast regret, means that Earth culture has become a significant problem for us and has resulted in cultural corruption. Even before I came along, seventy-four people took on this human language and concepts. The total damage is significantly higher and covers significantly more people than was earlier suggested.

I strongly recommend limited Mindwipe for all of my team. It will only serve to cordon-off the problem, but it is nevertheless essential to contain the corruption. You will note that I, too, am contaminated.

Because our culture was contaminated before I was appointed to this investigation, I recommend that two options be considered in my case. The first is that I am Mindwiped of all events since the beginning of this project and am allowed to return to my normal life. The other is that I retain my memory in case further need of this subject mastery will help us, by avoiding still more need for the language and culture mastery. In the latter case, I should be banned from my clan. I personally would prefer the former, but I understand the practical implications of Mindwipe and will not protest if the latter is decided upon.

The blame for this lies solely at the feet of the early anthropologists who worked on this world. English has a phrase for the phenomenon we have encountered. It's called "going native". Given this was identified as an exceptional likelihood of normal cultural immersion, and given our safety measures failed so thoroughly, Earth should have been regarded as a dangerous world, regardless of its level of technological achievement.

Mistake Four lies in not informing the Judge of the truth, that Judges never return to normal life after the decision. This Judge is not the first to identify their actual fate and have it influence their decision. It is the instance with the most catastrophic outcomes, however.

Lying about a Judge's future to a Judge only works when the Judge has no reason to disbelieve the lies.

I'm not yet convinced that this problem would not have arisen anyway. Humanity was not a suitable candidate for Judgement, as I have suggested elsewhere. Sending this particular Judge was more due to political expedience (silencing a critic) than Judging Earth.

I have explored the relationship between human language and thought through taking it on, and I have explored the relationship between the Judge and humanity through taking on the Judge's language set. In some ways they are too like us. Our rules would have been modified by their participation, just as my mind has been modified by the process of learning about the Judgement and where it went wrong. They would have corrupted our culture even after we had colonised them.

This is the chief reason I am willing to address the issue that admitting this modification means I cannot return home in the normal way with my mind in its current state: it would significantly add to the already far-too-great corruption of our culture.

I must point out (reluctantly) that exiling me compounds the problem. I am needed to teach these complications in order to prevent them happening with another planet. I am needed to help shape policy, for the same reason. I am willing to do this off-planet, in one of our client cultures, in order to contain the obviously problematic consequences.

I understand that, as regards myself, I have suggested several solutions and that they are all mutually incompatible. The reason for the fruitcake is that Earth has presented us with choices that are impossible given our current ethical system and due to the doctrine of cultural purity.

While I cannot give firm and clear recommendations on all issues (and you will note that I have tried), my immediate recommendation regarding this underlying problem is that we comprehensively reform our policies concerning anything that might pollute our culture. Alien porn is encouraged, yet we do not accept someone back into society who has engaged in total cultural immersion. We then require total cultural immersion for a range of jobs. There is a flaw in the logic, to my mind. It produces an equation that is impossible to solve.

I recommend that special consideration be given to me, given the exceptional circumstances.

Most importantly, I recommend that the Judge's decision stand.

I cannot recommend that decision concerning the life of the Judge be reversed, for it is too late. I belatedly extend my sympathy to the Judge's burrow, kin and clan for a tragic loss under difficult circumstances. Given that the Judge was forced into this job, I strongly recommend that recompense be considered, so that burrow, kin and clan are not left in a degraded position due to government error. The issues created by the Judge were due to the aforementioned errors and gross interference, and should not be translated into penalty of any sort. I consider the Judge, having paid such a high personal price for this endeavour, worthy of recompense.

This is my final note.

I hope to never have to use this Human language again. It encourages a narrative approach beyond any other tongue I have encountered. It terrifies me.

I trust that you will permit me to return to some sort of civilisation at the earliest instant.

The Observer's Notes

"They say the greatest legacy a person can leave is that of wonderful memories in those who miss them after they've gone. But being the one doing the missing sucks."
—*overheard in the emergency waiting room of the hospital*

It's time.

If I can find ten good reasons over the next week. If life presents me with just ten good reasons. I will not act like God with Sodom and Gomorrah. Will not accept one or two. Ten reasons I need. And humanity will survive. Nine reasons and their fate is sealed. This is the Work of the Judge and this is My Work on this planet. This is my formal statement as required.

I note this in writing, so that I can return to it each day for the next week and assess what I am presented.

Seven days.

Ten reasons.

I live and they die. Or they live and I remain with them until my hundredth birthday. Then I die. Early and unfulfilled.

I'm supposed to argue that humanity is worth the sacrifice of my life. I can't do that. I don't know if I want there to be ten reasons, and for me to return to the rest of my long life, or if I'm happy to sacrifice myself for them. My hand was forced. It's still being forced.

I have to Judge. I cannot use the errors of others and the plots of others as an excuse to escape. There is no escape.

I don't have to know. This is the whole reason for my blankness of mind. I cannot weigh my life against theirs. It's hubris to make me. I'm not given the opportunity to weigh my own race's hubris. We don't do that.

Countdown.

Day Seven

Diana woke up like a lizard. That's how she thought of it, anyhow. Techs woke up like that. It had been so many years since she'd seen any species other than humans that this ought to have faded, but some things were easier to remember than others. Whenever she saw a skink on the footpath in summer, she remembered that lizards woke up the same way she did. The memory became part of her life and so she knew, even if other things were perpetually vague, that she woke up like a lizard.

Her eyes blinked a few times and Diana stayed very still. This was a habit she got into around 2016. When she moved, her husband would know she was awake and would start talking. Lying still gave her quiet time to discover just how much memory she was waking up to, every day. She then would look for her husband, but he, of course, was gone now. Except it was never *of course*. Her bed felt cold and lonely and she moved quickly. Every day.

This day only had one small difference. When Diana tallied her memory, she thought: "How the hell do I Judge?"

Every movement she made, every thought she had, contained Judgement. Every second that was missing one of the ten reasons for humanity to live, brought Earth closer to the end of its human occupants.

This idea did not please her. At all.

Today she creaked a little. Just a little. Enough to remind her that she wasn't middle-aged any longer. A mature woman. Capable of mature judgements. Old enough for people to ignore and not yet old enough to qualify as a little old lady or to be treated as something from a different species. She refused to consider the potential irony in reaching little old lady status as an alien. At that moment, her hand hovered near the toaster. She was anxious to get breakfast over.

She'd given up worrying about the impossible fixedness of her gender some years before, but she never forgot the safety of her burrow or the feeling of belonging to a clan or the poise one carried everywhere when one mattered. She missed mattering. She missed it all the more because of Judgement. Judgement was not the same as being essential to one's own society. Judgement was so lacking in ethics, in fact, that it felt like a betrayal of all Diana had ever stood for. It had taken her a long time to remember enough about her earlier life to deduce this, but now that she had that in her mind, it was a perpetual humiliation.

She had been planning for this week for twenty years. And now that it was here, she didn't want to waste time on breakfast. She ate it, however, for she had trained herself to put her physical health first. Even if this body were gone in a week, she would leave it well-treated. And if it wasn't gone in a week, she wanted to avoid illnesses. The last ten years had been better than the ten before, and she was determined to keep it that way.

However she Judged, this body was hers and she was going to respect it, even though her arthritis didn't make pouring milk into her coffee as easy as it once had been.

Today was a good day and the body merely twitched and twinged.

Maybe a good day meant a good omen? She'd given up on miracles. She gave up the day her husband died. She was stuck following the lizards' agenda. Omens mattered. Fears and guesses and omens had been her only support on matters extra-terrestrial for so long that she automatically read her horoscope, calculated the odds, delivered her own mind a constant barrage of assessment and hope and fear based on everything from how long the traffic lights took to change, to whether the coins in her purse would have an even or odd number of twenty cent pieces.

Diana had changed. She knew it. It was too late to change back. This was the person who was Judge. At this point, nothing else mattered.

Diana checked the news. Nothing good. There was not a thing that redeemed humanity. There was more flooding after the tsunami and the last of the citizens moved from yet another low-lying island. Deaths, destruction—news as usual, but not a good omen for humans. She resolved at that moment to leave omens behind, and to leave counting behind. This was not the week for evaluation: that came at the end.

This was not what she thought she was going to do. She had been entirely certain that she'd analyse consciously, carefully and clearly and make an argued case for and against humanity. But that wouldn't work. All she'd do would be to talk herself into a result, and that result would depend on her mood, on her aches, on the weather, on if she'd eaten enough or too much. This is why she'd resolved on ten things originally. Best to stick to that.

Diana went old-fashioned. She found a scrap of paper (which wasn't easy) and her calligraphy pen and she packed them in her handbag. Each time she saw something that counted, she'd note it down. Make a simple mark on the page. She wouldn't assess it or question it. And she'd try not to tally up the numbers until the time was right.

This was the best way she could think of to make herself the impartial Judge she ought to be. The impartial Judge that was an impossibility.

Why do we do this to ourselves? She asked herself about herself and about her people, and didn't specify which people. This was why Judges remained on a planet for years, in theory, to achieve a perfect equilibrium between their host species and their home species. Diana had achieved it in her way. She wondered if she should be proud, but instead she decided to return to half-hearted self-castigation.

Was this whole week going to be quiet and contemplative? She hoped so. She hoped not. Her equilibrium was too perfect and she had no idea what she wanted to do or how she wanted to do it. At least she was dressed and had eaten and was ready to go out. Even though she had no idea where she wanted to go.

Humans past, she decided. That would give her fuel for contemplation.

Diana took a taxi to the Museum of Democracy. Janet had stopped volunteering there a decade ago. Leanne had joined her for a while, for the company, but Leanne was not around any longer. Leanne wouldn't see the end of humanity. This was the real reason Diana took that taxi. She didn't want to face this week without all her friends. One at a time, she would touch base. She could have visited Leanne's little box at the cemetery, but she always found Leanne's caged ashes disturbing. The Museum was safe.

The taxi was less safe. The driver had decided that it was too small a fare, or that Diana was too slow at getting in, or something. He didn't say what. He was difficult the whole way. He wanted to take her to the wrong museum, then he wanted to take her the scenic route (how he could have mistaken her for a tourist, when he'd picked her up at her own home, was a mystery); either way, Diana was thoroughly annoyed by the time she reached the museum.

She'd forgotten that it was a school day. *Did I even know?* she wondered as she saw the hordes of uniformed youngsters lining up dutifully, crowding everyone else off the white steps into the building. She decided her best port of call was the restaurant across the road.

It had developed the history mania that was sweeping the country, and listed its previous names on the flickering plaque at its entrance. *Pork Barrel,* it said, *The Lobby.* When it had been the Pork Barrel, it had particularly good danishes, she remembered. That was a long time ago. She ordered a danish in memory, but it wasn't right. Too crisp, and not enough blueberries and custard. Those danishes had really not been danishes at all, but something else pretending to be a danish. Something with much yeast and custard. One couldn't do that these days. Labelling laws were very precise.

I expected everything to be so big and important this week, she thought, *and here I am miserable about a taxi driver and schoolchildren and the texture of a pastry. There's nothing here to base a decision on.*

The whole day was like that. Small things, one after another. The only thing she achieved that was worth doing was chatting with one of the current educators.

"One of my close friends used to do your job," she said. "Twenty years ago." *Oh God, I sound like one of those old ladies, forever reminiscing. But I miss Leanne, I'm allowed to talk about her work. It keeps her alive.* "She used to tell us all about it."

The young lady was perhaps tired of schoolchildren, but she was very kind. Diana and she swapped anecdotes about teaching in the old Parliament House and wandered up and down, comparing today with yesterday and the day before.

At the end of the day, that was the only positive that Diana remembered. Being taken care of by the young educator. Being talked to as if she mattered and as if her memories counted. Being able to laugh about her friends' jokes and to explain the chocolate club.

Is this a point? Diana wondered. *Yes, I think it is. It changed my day and it did more than that. I think humankind should be judged on kindness and respect and attention. Half a point then, for so many other people were rude or condescending or shoved past me. Half a point is a beginning.*

In the end, she allocated a full point. Talking about Leanne had moved her from feeling terribly alone to realising that she still had friends. She messaged those friends and arranged to meet for lunch the next day. She wasn't actually playing with Judgement. She was simply meeting her friends for lunch.

She went to bed feeling as if, maybe, she wasn't quite alone. That the universe wasn't as vast as she had remembered. That Judgement might not be an impossible burden.

Day Six

Why was a jackhammer rack-rack-rack-racketing outside her bedroom window? Diana didn't want to know. What she wanted was an hour's sleep. She'd stayed up a little late the night before, reading, and felt under the weather. The jackhammer didn't help.

Should she scream at it? The trouble was, she was not the screaming sort. She sighed and got out of bed.

As she made her essential first cup of coffee for the day, she heard her phone ring. It was her friends: lunch tomorrow. Two of them had difficulties with today.

"Will explain," promised Trina.

"Will do better," said Antoinette, "Will bring home-made chocolate cake." Antoinette had taken over cake duty from Leanne. Cakes and slices had become so very much one of their little traditions that they felt the need to maintain it. No cake also meant Leanne was missing.

"Yay! Cake tomorrow," Janet's message said. "I don't mind a quiet day today. See you then."

See them then, repeated Diana, and sighed. It was going to be one of those days. Like that time she melted her saucepan. There was no way of making the day go right, not even by going back to bed, given the noise outside. All she could do was minimise the damage.

She decided to go to Mt Ainslie and walk a bit. That would be soothing. So she did. And a jogger ran into her. He held himself as if he owned the world and he ran as if he owned the path. This meant he didn't watch for others and he didn't do more than say

"Watch out!" and then went his oblivious way. Diana found herself sprawling on the ground.

Nothing was broken, but her ankle hurt and so did her right arm. In fact, her whole right side hurt. She walked very, very slowly back to the car and sat there for a bit, until the shock wore off. Then she went home.

Home was no help. The jackhammer's wielder had obviously been careless, for there was no electricity. She used her phone to great effect and found that it would be four hours before electricity was restored, and that someone was probably sorry. She decided that it was a jackhammer and not a person, for otherwise humanity would be judged on her state of hurt and would be condemned. There were no positive points in any of this.

She decided to catch a bus and go somewhere safe. The city shops. She could buy something nice and cheer herself up.

Diana didn't notice the date or the time. The date was too close to Christmas. And public service payday. And public service lunchtime. The shops were frantic and heedless. Instead of being comforted, she was jostled beyond her capacity to deal, and she ended up sitting down in the chemist being fed painkillers and water by an almost-understanding pharmacist.

"Why don't you go home?" he suggested. "Take a taxi. You can finish your shopping another day."

Diana was so subdued that she didn't say "Because I have a job to do", or "Because home is where the jackhammer is and the power isn't" or any of the other replies she could have made. She didn't deduct the one point humanity had earned, due to the pharmacist being sensible and doing his job. But she wouldn't've minded if an asteroid hit everyone who walked past her and jostled her, or shoved her, or made her stumble. A very specific asteroid that broke into pieces and hit only individuals who annoyed her.

Diana wished she were God rather than alien and had the powers of natural selection rather than unnatural genocide. She was silent in the taxi. She was silent when she reached home. She didn't ring anyone or send messages.

Eventually the jackhammer stopped. An hour later, she had power. Humanity didn't earn any points the rest of the day, however, because Diana spent most of it recumbent on the couch, reading Georgette Heyer. Humanity received half a point for

Georgette Heyer, but lost it when the electricity went off again and didn't come on until morning. Cold showers and home- delivered pizzas were not Diana's idea of civilisation.

"I should ring someone," she half-thought, but gave up on it as a bad idea and went to bed. When she woke up two hours later with a nightmare about the world coming to an end because she was crushed under the steps of a thousand careless joggers, she took emergency measures.

Diana had sleeping tablets for bad nights. She would have to deal with a mild hangover from the tablet the next day, but that was better than carrying the effects of the bad day into a second day. She only had five more days, after all. Humanity had to be given a fair go. Most of humanity. Not the shoppers or joggers, obviously. She took this thought back to bed with her and slept like a baby.

Day Five

"Today's got to be better," Diana told herself, almost desperately. A few years ago, she would have perjured her soul and sacrificed her life to allow humans to survive. But a few years ago she had a husband, and she had been visiting Leanne four times a week and sitting quietly with her, dealing with the fallout of ageing.

When Leanne's nephew had visited, Diana was called in to run damage control.

There was no damage to control. This middle-aged man had no notion of the fear Leanne had lived in whenever she visited home. He only knew that it seemed like a good idea to drop in on his aunt while he was in Canberra.

"He just had no idea," marvelled Diana. "But he's so very simple in his approach to life. He must find Canberra difficult."

"That's why I left. Simple approaches. Everything not open and black and white was silenced. Abuse can't be challenged if it can't be spoken about. It can't be stopped if one lives in a simple universe of straightforward rights and wrongs."

They were silent for a while.

It was this silence that remained with Diana and that was haunting her today. How could she Judge silences and hurt? Did she Judge Earth on survivors and how they dealt? Or on abusers and how common they were? Was private crime a cause to delete an entire race from the universe?

What I need is to find out how the humans taken off-planet adapted to being specimens and in enclosures. That would help determine what makes up humans. Or maybe it won't. Maybe it'd demonstrate how a few hundred humans handle being treated as semi-sentient beings by aliens.

Isn't it funny that the first thing I think of when Judging beings like us is how to make them behave like beings that aren't like us at all?

It was more inevitable than funny. The sort of universal Judgement she would perform in a few days was simply not something that worked for this species. None of the checks and balances that would have prevented the Judge being pulled in had worked. Probably because of this. Probably because they, the species Judging, wanted to find differences.

Colonialism, Diana thought. *And also, I've had all these thoughts before. Over and again. The time to agonise in this way is past. Long past. I need...*

Who she needed, she realised, was Leanne. Leanne had turned that abuse inside out and upside down. She'd not confronted the abuser, but she'd confronted her reaction to it. She'd reconstructed her life. Her last thirty years had been very good. Her preachiness, her wish to solve everyone else's problems, would have helped Diana now. And Leanne was gone, because human lives were short.

There was only one answer to this, really, and that was to see the others.

Diana checked for messages. And there they were. Multitudes of messages. None of them good.

Antoinette was in hospital.

Janet and Trina had agreed to meet there and then go to lunch. They had checked visiting hours, They had found out what they could about what had gone wrong. Diana added her "Will be there in 20 minutes," and hurried to join them.

Antoinette was in a cardiac ward. She didn't look too worried.

"It's my heart," she said. "They've found the enzymes and done everything they can to stabilise it. Tonight I get a Brazilian and tomorrow an angiogram, and then they decide what to do."

"Sounds identical to what happened to my wife fifteen years ago," said Janet. Janet's second marriage was far better than the first, and Janet's affection showed in her tone.

"Some things change and some things don't," said Antoinette. "I'm a borderline case, so they're not sure what's going on, and they're doing the old-fashioned investigation."

"So you had a heart attack?"

"Possibly." Antoinette was cheerful about it. "They're hedging their bets. That's why it's all old-fashioned. Either way, I'll be out the day after tomorrow."

Diana wondered at the coincidence of Antoinette having a possible heart attack this week, of all weeks. The dubiousness and the need for old-fashioned and quite intrusive procedures made her think of the lizards. She remained quiet while the others chatted, listening and watching. When she had the full picture, it was clear that Antoinette was not ill by chance.

Quietly, she opened her handbag. She added a column to her piece of paper and turned a set of marks into a table. On the left were marks, and on the right were other marks. She quickly tallied moments of known interference (her husband, herself, now Antoinette) and realised she already had over a dozen.

"What're you doing?" asked Antoinette.

"Deciding whether your possible heart attack will trigger the end of the world or not." Diana said this in such a matter of fact way that, naturally, her three friends couldn't possibly believe her.

"There must be other factors," said Trina.

They diverted themselves for a full hour discussing reasons why the world should burn and reasons why it shouldn't. The nurse came in and apologetically said: "We need to get her ready, I'm afraid."

"You're throwing us out?" asked Janet, humorously.

"Sorry," said the nurse. "But make sure you don't forget to add nurses to the side of good when you decide on our fate."

"Will do," said Diana.

It was far too late for lunch by the time the three left the hospital. There was only one possible response to this, and the three of them were so profoundly agreed on what it was that they didn't need to speak. *Chocolate*. A tray of different comestibles made from the substance, and iced chocolate to accompany it.

"I feel much better," said Janet.

"I feel extraordinarily tired," said Trina.

"I think we should all cancel anything strenuous or hard or stressful and—"

"Not get heart attacks. Even putative ones," finished Trina.

"Yes, that," said Janet. "I think we need a movie. The daftest one we can find. My place?"

"Can't," admitted Trina. "Work beckons."

"Only two months and then you're retired and can join the land of the ever-youthful," Diana reassured her.

"When you will have all of the time and much less of the money." Janet was upbeat. She had barely returned from the big overseas trip that marked the end of her own working life. She had good finances and her garden was producing the best flowers ever. Retirement suited her.

"I like my job still," confessed Trina. "That's why I didn't take early retirement when everyone else did. I'm only part-time, anyhow. My favourite thing is that I annoy everyone by coming in later, leaving earlier and doing triple the work."

"How does that work?" asked Diana. "I've wondered that for a while."

"It's generational. I suspect that I'm the last of the old fogies who were taught in the old fogie way."

"Paper and pen," said Janet.

"Printouts and learning grammar rather than relying on the machine and..."

"Leanne would have called us young upstarts, because we can't spell without help," said Trina. The other two gave wry smiles. For their generation, they could spell splendidly. But Leanne had been both a scientist and, as a child, a spelling champion. She had been able to spell words that no-one else knew existed.

"God, I miss Leanne," said Janet.

Day Four

Diana began the day properly, the way she began every day properly. It was a profound part of who she was. Instead of giving up on her insufficiently reliable memory, she had turned its vagaries into a meditation ritual, gathering her mind together. Today was a bad day and she did it first thing in the morning, as usual, but she also did it after she'd heard the news about Antoinette.

"I'm fine," her friend had said over the phone. "It's a minor procedure. Don't even come in today—I'll be home tomorrow and you can visit then. Let the others know for me, please? I really need to rest today."

"No worries," pronounced Diana. And she'd tried. Really, she'd tried. It took an hour to get through to Janet, but Trina wasn't answering her phone at all. Diana left two messages. If her life weren't so very strange (even for a very extended level of strange), that would have been enough effort and she could have moved on. She thought she was worrying over nothing, and so she did her little memory ritual again. Then she rang Trina.

"Can you come over?" Trina asked.

"Is something wrong?"

"I don't know? I just..."

"I'll be right there," Diana promised.

Twenty minutes later, they were in the hospital.

Diana had taken one look at Trina's grey face and decided firstly that caution was the better part of valour, and secondly that the ambulance's emergency systems were better than hers. The paramedics had spent very little time doing tests. During that very little time, Diana got together a bag for Trina. A very basic bag, but a bag. Thus, when they told Trina she had to be moved, at once, and didn't even let her walk to the ambulance, Diana was ready. She was an experienced emergency-goer, thanks to the lizards.

"Can my friend come?" was the only question Trina had.

"Of course," said one of the paramedics.

For all Diana's illnesses, this was not something she'd experienced before. She knew that Trina's sudden danger was intentional. That two of her closest people were dead and another two in hospital was a message. Not a nice message. A clear one. It was saying "You don't want to stay on this planet. They'll all die anyhow. Look, let us show you. Come home."

All the while she was with Trina and diverted her from the worst of her worry, or sat silently, waiting with her, all that while, this thought haunted her. It haunted her while they waited for a doctor, then a few minutes later when she sat next to Trina's bed, then when Trina had blood taken and measurements taken and...it all happened quickly. It wasn't a long haunting, but it was an intensive one.

The doctor wanted to talk with Trina alone, and Trina said: "Please, let Diana stay." So Diana stayed.

The doctor was very blunt. "Twenty years ago, you'd be dead in a day and we'd not have been able to diagnose you properly."

What a coincidence, thought Diana, *that twenty years ago was when Trina was probably set up for this. So they wanted me to lose her.*

The pattern was straightforward: first lose the husband (personal loneliness); second, see Antoinette nearly die; third, lose Trina. Then decide that home was the only option. Except that those words "twenty years ago" changed matters.

"It's a rare disease and not fully understood, but if we do a heart transplant quickly, you've every chance of living to a ripe old age."

"You can do it, just like that, a heart transplant?"

"We can if we use an artificial heart."

"What has to happen?" Diana felt impelled to ask, since the doctor obviously needed something from Trina.

"I need to brief you," he answered Diana, but addressed Trina. "You need to consider your options and, if you're ready to go ahead with the surgery, sign a waiver. This is uncommon surgery. If it works, then you'll be fine in a few months."

"And if it doesn't?"

"It depends. You could have the equivalent of an old-fashioned heart condition and have to be careful, or…"

"I could be dead."

"I'm afraid so," said the doctor.

"Since I'll be dead by tomorrow night anyhow, from what you say, I should just say 'yes' and let you get on with things," Trina declared, with only a hint of sarcasm. "You can give me as much briefing as I need, but I think it's an obvious choice."

"Then I'll set things in motion and come back and brief properly later, and get your formal approval. Mostly, right now, we need to prep the artificial heart and set up the surgery. I'll let you know as soon as we have a time."

"Can Diana stay?"

"Only until I return. After that, everything will start happening. I can get one of the nurses to ring to let you know how the operation went and then again when she can have visitors." This time the doctor was addressing Diana. Names were something he avoided.

"OK," said Trina.

After he left, she turned to Diana. "I hope you don't mind me deciding to run your life while I'm sick. Whatever you had planned for today isn't happening."

"What I had planned for today is irrelevant until you're through this." It was only a part-lie. Trina would be through the operation one way or another before Red Button Day. This probably reduced the options Earth had, simply because it would be hard to get reasons for the Earth to continue being human if she herself were sitting by a sick bed all the time, but…it was another of those ironies.

Diana found herself giving humans one mark simply because of the importance of Trina. Then she gave them another to get even with those who had planned to kill Trina. This meant that Earth only needed seven more marks to survive. Trina needed a new heart, however, and that came first.

Meanwhile, she traipsed after Trina while her friend was wheeled to her pre-operation destination. Instead of being the big, open room, it was a smaller open room. Only four patients in all.

Trina looked around, inquisitively, "More facilities, less space," she noted. "I've never seen it from this angle before. How do I look?"

"Depends," answered Diana cautiously, "on whether you're asking out of vanity or curiosity."

Trina laughed. "A bit of both, of course."

Diana decided to err on the daft side, but she couldn't be inaccurate. It was not within her. "Proto-zombie?" she suggested.

"That's pretty much how I feel. Also, everything's hard work."

"What I do normally is just sit back and enjoy the scenery."

"The trouble is," confessed Trina, "that this is so big. My mind can't encompass it. Heart operations aren't life-threating any more. My family has no history. Yadda yadda."

"Your mind doesn't have to encompass it," Diana pointed out. "All you have to do is get through it."

"And if I don't, then it doesn't matter?" Trina did her best to sound cynical.

"It always matters." Diana was surprised at how much she cared. She gave humanity another point for this passion. "But when there's nothing you can do, then it's much safer to live in the moment."

She wished she could take her own advice. However, there *was* something else she could do. She spent that whole night working on equations to see what could be done and how to do it. That passion she felt for Trina's life, the sheer importance of it to her, the absurd centrality of friendship to her own existence...

These things changed everything. She needed more options.

At this moment, Diana had no idea whether there were actually more options open to her, but now she was certain the game was rigged. She couldn't change many things, but she could give her mind a fair chance of making a sensible decision or, maybe, finding an alternate course. To do this, she needed to break down her conditioning. So this is what she did, one equation at a time.

Her approach, using paper and pens and shutting her mind off the way she had trained it in avoiding letting the lizards know she was self-aware, meant that no-one but she was the wiser as to what actually she was doing. The insomnia would be visible, but that was really all. The lizards needed Uplift on to know anything about what was happening inside her brain, and if Uplift were switched on in the week before Judgement, everyone would know Judgement was rigged. Data external to the Judge only, this week.

She felt a certain satisfaction in turning the tables. At three in the morning, however, she realised that the tables would be turned back if she herself died from tension and exhaustion. Her own body was frail.

She slept for a few hours, then went back to the drawing board.

By the time she received the call that Trina was safely through the operation and would be able to be visited from later that day, Diana had found a possible loophole for Earth.

Day Three

I don't trust those lizards not to destroy Earth through me being ill so much of the time, thought Diana. *I'm being racist, it's not just lizards. It's anyone involved and I don't know who they are. It doesn't matter if I'm racist, as long as I don't take that prejudice with me when I return.*

And there's still no guarantee of me returning. Earth is balanced on five out of ten points and only has three days to go. I have to stick to that, because it's what I promised myself and right now there are no sureties, none. It's also a nice narrative for the Judgment. Very Sodom and Gomorrah.

She was so tired that she started thinking in terms of old Earth-threatening dramas. Gamera and Gamora, Japanese monster and green alien. To stop her mind wandering, she rang Antoinette and Janet and they had a nice group chat.

"We can't all go in at once," said Antoinette.

"The hospital says we can," said Janet. "I checked. But going in all three at once reminds me of Leanne. In fact, the hospital reminds me of Leanne."

"What do you mean?" asked Diana.

"They know what's best and theoretically they're right, but in practice…"

"The reality is that it's about Trina, not about us. How about you go in, Diana, because you're the least exhausting of us, and let us know if she's up to all three."

"Then you'll come out and join me?"

"We should join you anyhow," said Janet. "We should all sit in a café and take it in turns to visit Trina, as she's able."

"Now, that's a good idea," said Antoinette.

"I know one of the nurses from my various visits," Diana said. "I can ask her."

"And we can tailor who goes in according to Trina's needs." Antoinette was inspired.

Janet nodded. "Totally. You if she needs quiet comfort," with a nod to Diana, "you if she needs verve and aliveness," nod to Antoinette, "and me for flowers and everyday chat."

"That sounds excellent," said Diana.

"I am most excellent," agreed Janet. "Also, there have to be some advantages to being an increasingly elderly woman. One of them is that we can cancel everything and be there for our friend."

"Thank God we can," said Antoinette.

"So—" Janet was in one of her brisk moods, "—let's get a report on how she is, nice and subjective. Diana, you saw her last."

"Actually," Antoinette said hesitantly, "I did. I was coming out of the procedure and I asked about her. Someone wheeled me in to see her. She had just been shaved and was in a sparkly clean gown."

"Finally," joked Diana, "an advantage to one of our crises."

"You're right." Antoinette looked pleased. "She said that she was herself, and dealing, but that was mostly thanks to you being there whenever she needed and not being intrusive. When she had no strength to move, you sat there and waited, she said. It meant she could face the operation, she also said, because Diana was channelling the strength of all of us. I joked that Diana was channelling chocolate. That too, she said."

"Only one problem with us hanging out all the time," said Diana, "and that's the fact that you were in hospital yourself, until yesterday. We can handle one emergency with grace and fortitude, but two is more difficult."

"God yes," said Janet. There was a moment's pause while they all thought. Then, "Who needs a café?" said Janet. "My place is only five minutes from the hospital. We can get meals delivered and combine our chocolate stashes and watch old movies and Antoinette, you can bring your PJs and use my spare room."

"And rest whenever you need to," finished Diana. "If you don't mind, Janet, that would solve everything. Will your partners mind, though?" The various partners were brought into the discussion.

They wanted to join the vigil. And Janet's spare room had a double bed, so Antoinette's husband would fit. He offered to do food runs whenever things looked as if they'd run out and hospital runs for changing of the guard. Janet's wife offered the home front. The respective husband and wife laughed at each other for taking on such traditional roles. Antoinette said, then, "So we're fine, as long as there's enough chocolate."

Humanity received two points that day, one for emotional support and one for the look on Trina's face when her friends brought her a bag to get her through her transplant, and it included her share of the chocolate.

The new count, the invisible count, of Judgement against the species that had set her up to die, that was marching point for point with the Judgement against humanity.

Day Two

"I thought I should call you both at once. Trina's OK." Janet was the first with the news. "She's still under, but the operation worked. I've talked to the hospital. They won't know for at least six hours about her mental state and stuff, but the mechanics are fine and she'll live."

"I thought they were going to contact me," said Diana, stupidly.

"They don't do that until 9am, though, and I asked a nurse yesterday—they already know if she'll live." Janet was half-apologetic. "I thought you'd rather know."

"And maybe get some sleep," said Antoinette.

"Only if you do," suggested Diana. "I'm not the one just out of hospital!"

"Not this time," agreed Janet, her voice evincing slight sarcasm. "But if you don't rest, then you will be."

Diana sighed. Janet was right. She hadn't slept all night, worried about Trina, worried about Judgement, and just plain worried. Six hours of sleep wouldn't hurt. Besides, she could give Janet and the secret-spilling nurse a point between them, for making the lives of others easier. This wasn't a point she could give if she hadn't become so very human, and this worried her, but the fact was, immersion was part of Judgement and objectivity (which would be, if one were actually human) wasn't. So she gave a point, went to bed and slept, unsoundly, for six hours.

Diana was still tired when she woke up. Her head felt heavy and her body had to work very hard simply to stand up straight. Janet had been right about her overdoing things. And sarcasm wasn't as good as irony for making truth palatable, but it worked.

What she wanted, above everything at this moment, was to return to the confusion of twenty years ago, with the half-memories and the feeling of safety.

Her messages included one from the hospital. Trina was conscious but needed quiet for a bit. Visitors could come by in two hours. Diana was torn between relief that Trina was conscious and petty concern that she'd wasted all of the morning and some of the afternoon. Diana had a Judgement plan, after all, and it had so far not been followed *at all*.

It wasn't going to be followed. No Parliamentary Question Time, no observing people from a park bench, no random shopping incidents. Instead, she would spend the next two hours getting Trina a care package and sorting out more of her own *third path* idea.

This idea was impossible, really. It consisted of rendering Judgement on her other people, the ones that had sent her here. It meant hacking into the system from three directions, to get past approvals and safety measures. It was, in fact, abysmally complicated. But she was going through the motions of Judgement and was programmed (inside herself, right from the beginning) to Judge on that particular day in that particular way and she wanted an extra choice. She *needed* an extra choice.

Later scholars would wonder, at this point, if she knew that Judgement was programmed to kill her if she chose to free Earth. Or if she knew that Earth was doomed whatever her verdict. The answer was, she didn't. She was full of mistrust since the failsafe had proven to be false, however, she might as well have known, for all the difference it made to what she did.

This is my opinion and I shall stand by it. And my reconstruction in this section is more reliable than others because we have so very much information about that last week, but I still can't get inside Diana's mind. I am, as ever, making suggestions on her thoughts and feelings based on detailed observation of her physical reactions and words, adding that to her psychological profile and adding in my own supremely intelligent assumptions and deductions.

Now that you know that I'm here and it isn't some random stranger telling you these things, I shall efface myself again. This is the second last day before Judgement and it's too important for me to ramble away. So many aspects of this last week make such a difference in the equations. In the story, not so much. Story heads towards a particular place and we're almost there. At this stage, there's nothing to prove. There is no test to make. We already know that there will be Judgement and that the outcome is fruitcake. This is the weakness of story. This is why Earth was doomed: we knew they used story. My own experience just demonstrates how very dangerous story is.

Moving from story from me to story from someone else is also hard. I should be able to recount the conversation where Trina boasted about her radioactive diamond battery, the one that would keep her going for five thousand years. I should also be able to explain the events in the hospital and how the nurses carried the day when a doctor nearly killed Trina by mistake, and how another nurse remembered Janet and thought she was back in the cardiac section rather than visiting a friend.

I can't. I've lost it all.

What I did wrong was to begin to translate the material into maths. I tried to save myself by distancing myself from the story I was telling. This was a very strange experience. I'm so used to putting myself in story now that I am not comfortable doing otherwise. I'm so used to not putting myself into maths, on the other hand. I'm trapped between two worlds.

This ought to be a temporary aberration. A mere diversion. It isn't, because it strikes me now that I need to adjust my equations. Diana experienced this. She experienced it in a far more difficult situation than mine.

She was *living* a human narrative and had been telling herself human narratives about it for decades. Her human friend was translated into story the moment we gave her a rare illness that starved her heart of function, and the records are clear that this was intentional; Diana noted it down as suspicious at the time, in case everything was investigated and she was not there—all precautions she took, which is why we know so much about her thoughts those last days, and again, I digress—it's very hard to think clearly when one is between states of thinking. Let me return to the heart of the subject. Diana was living fully as a human. Judgement is made in an interim state, the moment when story and sums come together, in this instance. Diana was obviously working in her own way, the way she was expected to, in the interstices for this potential third judgement of hers.

Her being poised between those states is as critical to fruitcake as her realisation that there had been gross and unethical interference in the proceedings. This is what brought about the third option. Three options in constant tension, with none of them providing good outcomes—this is the essence of fruitcake.

Human story tells us how the fruitcake came about. Narrative is a useful tool. The pressure and the poise and the elegance and the danger of fruitcake: this can only be expressed through the most subtle of mathematics.

Humans cannot be like us. This elegance is beyond them. From this point of view, the Judgement should always have been to destroy humanity. This is all the more so since Diana took on story and lived in story and was overwhelmed by story and was unable to calculate clearly because of it. Look at what English and narratives do to my mind. This corruption was potentially the lot of all of us.

That's where we are now. At the crisis point. Diana was compromised and her thinking corrupted and this was not as bad a thing as it should have been, for it exposed vast breaches of ethics.

I need to return to narrative and tell this in order.

Day One

I can't do it. I can't return to story. I've lost most of Day Two, and most of Day One.

I mine events for my analysis and cannot keep the sequence straight. And that's just an excuse. I don't know how Diana managed when things became impossible, but I can't even manage to keep her impossible days straight. I want to break them down into component parts for proper analysis, and yet I get pulled in emotionally and...this is one of the most important days in the history of the fruitcake, and the recent history of so many planets, and it's so very messy and so very small.

I can't keep it straight. I know all the events. I know nothing about them as story. I've lost that human touch.

I've given my recommendations and I'm getting out of this and yet I can't stop tracking, day by day and accounting for Judgement. I hate story. It won't let me go.

There were coffee and chocolate and hampers from Antoinette.

There were yellow flowers involved. Janet produced them. Our interference tried to make it look as if the flowers attracted the attention of someone who was off their meds and who then attacked Janet, but two nurses intervened (one by pushing a trolley at the culprit) and Janet escaped almost unscathed. The flowers were spread across the floor. Diana noted: "A lizard dressed in human skin tried another intervention," but it really wasn't that simple.

All the closest people to Diana had been attacked, just before Judgement. What gets me about this is it means that someone at our end understood humans and still wanted to play this farce.

Deep knowledge, stupid politics, and human skin: the anthropological service. The service was trying to push Diana. I knew this when I began my study, obviously, but I hadn't mentioned it until now, for the strands of influence had to be properly disentangled.

These are the ingredients. We have techs who wanted profit; we have a political group who wanted social change; we have poor management; we have another political group that wanted to remove Diana; we have policies towards colonisation that included murdering Judges in order to take useful planets without controversy. We have fruitcake.

The whole colonial service has been frozen for sixty-one years because of this and I do recommend that it remain frozen until all my recommendations have been met. I have placed the full list in a separate document. A small percentage of them can be found in this document, which gives you a sense of how I've reached those conclusions.

They knew humanity better than anyone, but obviously they didn't know Diana. It didn't work the way they expected. Fruitcake became bigger.

I can't tell this properly.

I'll try sequentially again. Maybe it will help.

Janet nearly died. Diana—who knows how?—deduced that the would-be murderer was one of us.

This new crisis pushed Diana beyond all decision. She tore up the piece of paper containing the marks that were supposed to determine the fate of humanity. She gave the lizard the biggest dressing off s/he'd ever experienced. This lizard (and why I'm calling t/hem a lizard is Diana's influence—we are not lizards—not in any way, but Diana's nickname has rubbed off and everyone calls us this now) was my rearing-uncle, which is one of the reasons I joined the anthropological service.

Now you know how I was recruited into this mess. Now you know that I can't tell this part of the story because I have one of my own: I'm trying to atone for my family's attempt to kill a planet.

I'm like Diana was at that precise point. I can't deal.

"Tomorrow," she said. "Tomorrow I'll handle everything. I'll make my decision from scratch and be damned." Diana said this aloud, so I'm certain of it.

Before she went to bed, Diana laid the table ready for the next day. She put out her coffee cup and set her coffee pot ready near the stove. She took out cutlery for both her husband and herself, for there was strength in memory. Then just one glass for juice. Next to her glass, she put the daisy in a tall thin vase. Next to the daisy, she put one of the chocolates Antoinette had given her the day before.

The rest of the table she covered with papers. Her journals. Her calculations. Her newspaper clippings and web printouts. Everything she had collected over the years put into paper form. This made up most of the bulk of the paper, but only covered half of the table. The rest of the table was dedicated to specific analysis for each decision and, in smaller piles, the way to bring each outcome into effect. One pile was for *"I never see my clan or my burrow again"* and the other was for *"Die, Earthlings!"*

These were not their official names. The official titles for the two options had mysteriously appeared in her mind when the feeling that it was time the Judge also appeared. *Programmed language*, Diana wanted to joke, but this really wasn't a joking matter.

Unsurprisingly, the official terms had a clear bias in favour of destroying Earth. Just as well she'd given up on allocating marks for good behaviour. No-one behaved well. Not her own species, not the lizards, and really (if one were honest about the species overall), not the humans. Judging them on ethics was as dubious as judging them on potential to corrupt, in her mind. And yet she had no choice.

The Judge didn't simply hand the decision over to minions. She pushed the button herself. The spaceship would collect her after her final report, she *knew*, even though she also knew, in reality, that something would go wrong. The lizards' time of betrayal was upon her. Diana was almost ready to Judge on that, too.

The main impediment at this moment was still her own mind. She wanted to be fair to everyone. She wanted to go home. She had no choice but to Judge.

This meant that there was one last pile of important concepts that had to be dealt with. Diana thought about them while she laid out her clothes. With her clothes, she had two yellow scarves, as possible choices to accessorise. She read her notes through before she went to sleep and then let her sleeping brain mull over them.

As she prepared for bed, she allowed herself the luxury of pretending her husband was still with her. She chatted with him. He was puzzled.

"What's this about?"

"Just something I have to work through, dear," she answered. "Don't let it worry you."

"You'll clear it up by dinner?"

"Of course"

She put on the pendant he'd given her before her last birthday and wore it to bed. Her memory of him teased her about this, but nothing came of it. They slept comfortably together.

He had never been aware at any point that his wife was an alien, nor that she would one day decide the fate of his best friend along with every other human. Diana's errant mind interpreted this into the feeling that he was with her the whole time. That he grumbled at her in the middle of the night, when a car alarm went off and again when he thought there was someone at the door.

His imagined grumbles and laziness kept her sane and helped her get some sleep. She didn't want a vigil—she wanted a normal night. If it was the last night for humanity, she wanted to share it with him.

Diana woke up, refreshed, ready to destroy Earth. Or not.

Will the world end?

Will the world end?
Will the world end?
Will the world end?
Will the world end?
Will the world end?

Y/N

A simple question.
You've had years to work on a clear decision. We have no more time.
Answer. *Now.*

Will the world end?
Will the world end?
Will the world end?
Will the world end?
Will the world end?
Will the world end?

Y/N

This was the programming. This is what humankind faced.

Diana woke up and yawned. In her mind, her husband was still asleep.

Quietly she slipped out of bed, washed, dressed, made herself toast and coffee. They'd laughed so many times that he would sleep through the end of the world if it happened after 3am. He woke up from the sound of a dropped pin until that hour, and then he slept solidly until everything was almost too late. Today it was better he sleep. Today it was better that she not acknowledge that one single truth. The other truths would swamp her if he weren't there, in bed, safely asleep, waiting for her to come home. His murder was intended to divorce her from Earth, so it didn't happen.

She had work to do.

Diana looked at the slightly withered daisy on her dressing table. Next to it was a large stack of notes. She had forgotten them. This was her clever idea from three weeks ago. The one she had nearly trashed because it was so damn chancy. The one she'd worked on whenever she could in the hope of doing the job she ought to have been sent to do, rather than the job she was actually sent to do.

Diana nodded to herself and skimmed through that last pile. As she read the papers, she walked both herself and her notes into the kitchen and finished making and eating breakfast. Then she looked at the other piles.

Her memory was as intact as it had been in months. It wasn't a bad day to make a decision. It would never be a good day, but it wasn't a bad day. If she was missing anything now, it was not going to be in the final decision. But her notes had been compiled over various stages of memory, and today she remembered every single one of them.

Today she was able. Not willing, but who would be willing to do any of the things she had to do?

The pile of papers by her bedside was the one that intrigued her. It was filled with formulae. Not Earth maths—her own maths. It was part of her forgotten, highly political self. It was quite possibly the main reason she had been turned into an anthropologist and her memory erased. Today, she clearly knew why.

A good day after all. She had realised the need for this solution before, and had made a third option viable.

Diana smiled. It was a slightly bitter smile. "I have the option to save Earth. Not just one option, but two, if I play my cards right and deceive those damn deceivers," she said to herself, aloud. "But if I take my path rather than either of theirs, I am going to make those lizards wish they'd done things differently. I may be spending the rest of my unnatural life on this planet, but everyone back home is so going to wish they had never decided to Judge it."

This was the moment when she accepted, absolutely, that going home was so dangerous that it was safer not to risk it. This is when three became two again.

Diana walked through the arc door two hours later, as planned. The daisy from the table was in her right hand, in her purse was the chocolate, around her neck were both yellow scarves. In her left hand was a list of instructions she had written for herself. She knew it would get by unseen. The lizards had never once paid any attention to notepaper for, after all, it was only unprinted paper. Humanstuff of the kind that was not of any interest. She had tested this many times. She always got her work material back after Download: it wasn't sexy enough to steal. This meant she didn't need to trust that fallible memory of hers for any equations or any action.

Four hours later, there was chaos.

From this point, I've reconstructed. Records were improperly kept in the machine room. It is ironic that we have less information about events in the machine room than about events around random café tables in the middle of nowhere. It was assumed that it was a place for the mind-dead to rest before walking under the arc and being restored.

I must note that this was not an error made by the technicians. It was standard procedure. It is also ironic that in one of the rare circumstances in the making of the fruitcake that standard procedure was followed, it caused problems.

On with the reconstruction. I'll start with what was expected to happen. This will help evaluate.

Diana walked through the arc and into the machine room. In theory, she stood and waited for her memory to return; then she walked through to the waiting room, where she was reminded that there would be one last Download, to complete the records. She made her final decision.

In a typical theoretical case, Judgement would be followed by a period of adjustment so that her consciousness could be transferred to her body and then she herself returned home. In a typical real case, at this point the power would go off and the doors open: the Judge would discover they were stranded.

Diana walked through the arc and into the machine room.

She cannot have stood there long, for she was in the room for the standard two hours. During that time, she inputted a considerable amount of code into the system. We only have the last seventy segments of the equation, and ashes were found but no paper. There was, however, a half-used cigarette lighter. It appears she burned the material she inputted. This fits entirely with her secrecy. She was untrusting.

Untrusting is too mild a word. Most of the code proved to be unreconstructable, even with the last segment surviving on paper. It had branches. Choices. We surmise that, instead of triggering a normal Judgement, she set our system up to trigger various options. She didn't need to make the choice until she was asked to make Judgement, using this method. It ensured that her tampering went unseen until too late.

We can surmise from this that there were only two choices available. If one of them were (as seems likely) the acceptance of the standard situation, then the rest of the code would have been dedicated to...well, we shall see.

At this stage her tampering was in no way illegal or even unethical: all the usual outcomes were available. She had merely inserted new strings of passive material. People do this all the time. Even if we had noticed the code, it would be no more than an oddity. The fact that it came from her should have been a warning, but machine rooms have not been monitored for a millennium.

When she walked through the next door, things changed. For this, we're no longer reconstructing. We have the full picture. It's disturbing.

First, the techs demanded of her something they had no right to do: they personally asked her (by voice) for an emotional component to the final Download, a personal view.

"It will properly capture your last views of this planet," they explained. "Just for the record."

The Judge's last views are private. They always have been. This is to leave them a modicum of dignity for when they return home. It's the very small price we pay for stripping so much from them and entasking them with such a decision. If they decide on destruction of a race, they're entitled to their privacy.

Diana asked about it, was told it was proper and she gave it due thought, and she agreed. Given her body language, this was when she finally decided the path she would take. The question told her that she was doomed.

She knew that, even if her Judgement was to destroy the human race, she would never go home.

As far as we can ascertain, this is where one of the two final points were entered into the system. She used the determination of the group that wanted to bring her down and humiliate her. No-one has ever accused her of being stupid, except that group. There is a poetic justice to her using this illegal request to enter that second last ingredient to produce the fruitcake.

How did she do it?

Diana had paid a great deal of attention to the talk of the techs. Also, the machine room was not the only place that had manual functions for backup. In fact, the Download area needed this even more, for it was linked to a different part of the system. Diana had obviously noted that, although it was seldom used, in the Download room, as part of this backup there was the capacity for additional manual entry of data and even programming. We know Diana used it intentionally because she asked about it once.

"It's functional," she was told, "but takes higher maths. Not made for anthropologists." This was when they thought she thought she was still one, obviously.

Diana never referred back to that conversation. But she did study, during upload, the mechanism. Her body language demonstrates this very clearly. Her lack of spoken words, part of her personality, led everyone astray. None of the groups plotting against her noticed what she was doing.

One has to admire her. Even though she created fruitcake. Even though a civilisation is now in ruins.

This machine was a potential problem. Her memory was never reliable. Would she remember how to use it?

She looked at it, carefully, that day. Her fingers rehearsed patterns. She remembered.

Her smile was wry. She could still go home, but she was one step removed from it, now. And there was the question of whether she would be murdered. For every morsel of hope Earth gained, there was a morsel that she lost, personally.

It took Diana a while to input her remaining data. Now she was being watched, there was a very good chance that her actions would be spotted. The record shows this caution and her concern so very clearly.

First she asked that processes be verbal. She then looked around and she monitored the relays and she used the quiet moments to ask distracting questions. Mostly, however, she talked. Her download was the most loquacious on record. While she talked, she typed from memory.

How she did this is still a mystery. Even though we know how much of her memory had returned, it's still an extraordinary feat. I think we forget who she was before she was shanghaied into Judgment.

All the way through download, she keyed in her equations by hand, while the rest of her brain handled the material we wanted and distracted the observers. I've never seen such a tour de force.

Her actions, they...

Let me show you. This is terrifying.

Normally, when one connects to Download, the lizards — sorry, the *technicians* — take care of the whole interface. The subject has no control. Diana assumed partial control with her use of the mechanical interface, but no-one monitored that element.

Someone sent an energy spike into her brain. If she had been fully connected, she would be dead. Her brain would have been wiped. No Diana left to bring back to her waiting body. It would have looked like a mechanical error, and Earth would have been obliterated in her memory.

But she hadn't set up the direct connection, for she was using the manual override and verbal reporting. Whoever set that spike wasn't involved in the final report, for otherwise they would have known she wasn't fully linked. From off-planet, the input looked the same. From her end the Download stopped. She reset it, and... that was all.

Diana took a deep breath. They were willing to bring her back braindead and kill Earth. That's what this was all about.

She reconnected.

"Your power is unstable," she informed the lizards, coolly. "I'll do the rest entirely manually."

"Oh, I thought something was wrong," the voice came. "That's fine. Take your time."

A second spike was obviously in the works. One that fried everything. It didn't matter to them if they destroyed a piece of equipment. She typed her heart out, entering equation after equation as if her world were ending.

Diana finished and sent it. She set the machine to enter random figures, so that it looked as if she were still working. She stood back.

Diana watched the mechanism fry.

Her people couldn't retrieve her now, even if they'd wanted. They couldn't retrieve anyone. And she had escaped this attempt at murder.

She'd sent her Judgement through, despite them. It was not just her Judgement of Earth. The entries she had made, the time she had bought: she'd used them to change the rules. She had Judged the Colonial Service.

One more thing she had to do. By making Judgement, she would give the seal of authority to the rest. Her actions would be accepted within the system.

Diana laughed. It was a bitter laugh. It was a tragic laugh. But it was triumphant.

She made her Judgement. Earth should live, it said. Since only the two courses were possible, she couldn't put in restrictions or changes of any sort. It was Earth or it was return home. She chose Earth.

Diana walked out through the final door, her head held high. From now on, she was human. Forever.

Diana hadn't actually saved the world. She'd given it a chance. Only a chance. Before that desperate moment in the machine room and then the second moment in the Download room, it lacked even that. So had she.

At the heart of her virus was one final trigger point. It was invisible to us. At this point, all we knew was that the instruments were fried and that Earth should survive until the mess could be sorted. It wasn't a priority. Diana was banking on it not being a priority. We had fruitcake, but the fate of Earth was not yet clear.

If Diana could survive past her ninety-ninth year, even one minute into her hundredth, then the system would collapse. The whole system. Not just Earth. The whole planetary governance system, starting from the Anthropological Corps and the Judgement Body and working outwards would implode. This was her Judgement.

The virus was set up to look as if it would eat through the anthropological survey mechanics and ...almost everything. No-one would get home. No-one would touch Earth again, for Earth would become a plague planet. Anything that destroyed the beautiful symmetry of mathematics did that, and the destruction of symmetry, wholescale, was precisely what she'd fed into the system during the download.

She didn't have much leeway if she wanted it to go unnoticed, so she linked it to her perfectly- crafted human narrative. First it would spread throughout her home system and all its allies. Then it would go dormant.

It would be triggered by her death.

Diana's full Judgement was not inevitable. Diana had to outlive the standard package for the second part of her equations to take effect.

There was one obstacle remaining. It was not a small obstacle.

The lizards had primed her body to fall apart.

Diana's task now was to hold things together long enough. Just long enough. One day. One hour. One minute longer than she was programmed to live in a perfect world where her body had been programmed for perfect health. One second longer would save the world. She had programmed that second into her life to be that final trigger. All she had to do was reach it.

It was a nothing. A doddle. A breeze.

Diana went home to the memory of her husband, and, the next day, bought a huge box of chocolates for her friends.

"What's this for?" asked Antoinette.

"Nothing concrete. Just the chance that things will change."

The woman's slow voice...

was counting again

One, two, three, four, five.
I start school today. I'm not allowed to wear my yellow hat. I need to wear my yellow hat. It's sunny. I have to go to school. I need my yellow hat.

The woman's slow voice was counting again.
One, two, three, four, five, six, seven, eight, nine, ten, eleven, twelve.
The bus has steps that go down. I walk down and down and jump onto the ground. Where are the steps that go up? Why can't I remember? Why can't I remember? Oh God, I've lost myself. My memory is all I have and I can't remember.
I need to start again. One, two, three, four, five…

The woman's slow voice was counting again.
One, two, three, four, five, six, seven, eight, nine, ten, eleven, twelve, thirteen, fourteen, fifteen, sixteen, seventeen, eighteen.
I fit in here. I drink and eat pizza and argue and talk and use so many words. So many words. My life is full of language and pizza and cheese and wine and coffee.

The woman's slow voice was counting again.
One, two, three, four, five, six, seven, eight, nine, ten, eleven, twelve, thirteen, fourteen, fifteen, sixteen, seventeen, eighteen, nineteen.
So many ways of hurting women.

I can't look them in the face. Why do I have this job? Why was it waiting for me?

Why do I have to hurt people?

She was surrounded by white curtains and nesting in white sheets. Her skin was pale and luminous. Age had curved her body strangely. The nurses took care of her, but she only sometimes repaid this with a glimmer of awareness. When she talked, she counted.

The woman's slow voice was counting again.

One, two, three, four, five, six, seven, eight, nine, ten, eleven, twelve, thirteen, fourteen, fifteen, sixteen, seventeen, eighteen, nineteen, twenty.

I finished the year and finished university and stopped talking. I remember that I was in love. I remember holding hands. I don't remember how it felt to be in love. It was so important to me. Why can't I remember?

Maybe I don't remember because of what came later.

I'm not going to start counting again. I don't want to hurt. Being here, now, with a catheter and that all-night nurse watching me and listening is bad enough. Yes, I'm talking to you, even though you're only listening to my tone.

This is my way of staying alive. I'm not as beyond help as I sound. All the medicines don't support my efforts to keep going. Counting helps. Counting helps me remember. If I remember, I can make it. I have to make it. If I don't make it, then it's not only me who'll die. Everyone on Earth. Every single human.

I did my best. I have to live just a bit longer. Just a bit longer. All I need is three digits and I've won. *We've* won.

Oh God, I'm so tired. So very tired.

I don't want to remember this.

I need silence.

Not too much silence. I have to remember. I have to remember.

The woman's slow voice was counting again.

One, two, three, four, five, six, seven, eight, nine, ten, eleven, twelve, thirteen, fourteen, fifteen, sixteen, seventeen, eighteen, nineteen, twenty, twenty-one, twenty-two, twenty-three, twenty-four.

Marriage and a home and a trendy young set of friends. This isn't me. This was never me.

I wish I could remember me at that age. Who were those trendy friends? Whose friends were they?

I have to remember it as me. Otherwise I have nothing to hold on to.

The woman's slow voice was counting again.

One, two, three, four, five, six, seven, eight, nine, ten, eleven, twelve, thirteen, fourteen, fifteen, sixteen, seventeen, eighteen, nineteen, twenty, twenty-one, twenty-two, twenty-three, twenty-four, twenty-five, twenty-six, twenty-seven, twenty-eight, twenty-nine, thirty.

I will not remember her name. It hurts too much.

I see her body as if her spirit never animated it, as if she were never alive. I cannot bear this memory. I cannot bear this life. I want it all to end.

It has to end. I can't bear it any more. But I can't let it. Not now. It's still too dangerous.

I have to remember my little one. I must. Even the worst memory of all. I have to remember. It's not about me. It never was about me.

As she tried to remember, her hands curled into claws. Her inner self was closer to the surface than it had been since she came to Earth.

The woman's slow voice was counting again.

One, two, three, four, five, six, seven, eight, nine, ten, eleven, twelve, thirteen, fourteen, fifteen, sixteen, seventeen, eighteen, nineteen, twenty, twenty-one, twenty-two, twenty-three, twenty-four, twenty-five, twenty-six, twenty-seven, twenty-eight, twenty-nine, thirty, thirty-one, thirty-two, thirty-three.

Why am I alone? I am so very alone. I should not be. No-one should be. Why am I alone?

Where did everyone go?

The woman's slow voice was counting again.

One, two, three, four, five, six, seven, eight, nine, ten, eleven, twelve, thirteen, fourteen, fifteen, sixteen, seventeen, eighteen, nineteen, twenty, twenty-one, twenty-two, twenty-three, twenty-four, twenty-five, twenty-six, twenty-seven, twenty-eight, twenty-nine, thirty, thirty-one, thirty-two, thirty-three, thirty-four, thirty-five, thirty-six, thirty-seven, thirty-eight.

I'm married to him. He's a good man.

I'm not lonely any more. That will have to be enough. I can't ask for any more. Life isn't generous and won't give me any more.

Life is cruel. I hate life. Just remember. I'm thirty-eight and not lonely. Not alone. Not lonely.

Not lonely.

The woman's slow voice was counting again.

One, two, three, four, five, six, seven, eight, nine, ten, eleven, twelve, thirteen, fourteen, fifteen, sixteen, seventeen, eighteen, nineteen, twenty, twenty-one, twenty-two, twenty-three, twenty-four, twenty-five, twenty-six, twenty-seven, twenty-eight, twenty-nine, thirty, thirty-one, thirty-two, thirty-three, thirty-four, thirty-five, thirty-six, thirty-seven, thirty-eight, thirty-nine, forty, forty-one, forty-two.

I'm hitchhiking through life. I can change my job when it's boring beyond anything. I did. Freedom...

Why does freedom feel so dull?

The woman's slow voice was counting again.

One, two, three, four, five, six, seven, eight, nine, ten, eleven, twelve, thirteen, fourteen, fifteen, sixteen, seventeen, eighteen, nineteen, twenty, twenty-one, twenty-two, twenty-three, twenty-four, twenty-five, twenty-six, twenty-seven, twenty-eight, twenty-nine, thirty, thirty-one, thirty-two, thirty-three, thirty-four, thirty-five, thirty-six, thirty-seven, thirty-eight, thirty-nine, forty, forty-one, forty-two, fifty-three.

I do not talk about this year. Even inside myself I do not try to remember. It's engraved. The one year I don't have to remember. I don't. I don't. Go away.

I know it—that's enough. I need to move on. I need to.

The woman's slow voice was counting again.

One, two, three, four, five, six, seven, eight, nine, ten, eleven, twelve, thirteen, fourteen, fifteen, sixteen, seventeen, eighteen, nineteen, twenty, twenty-one, twenty-two, twenty-three, twenty-four, twenty-five, twenty-six, twenty-seven, twenty-eight, twenty-nine, thirty, thirty-one, thirty-two, thirty-three, thirty-four, thirty-five, thirty-six, thirty-seven, thirty-eight, thirty-nine, forty, forty-one, forty-two, fifty-three, forty-four.

I remember. I remember too much.

More, I need to remember more. Even though it hurts. I remember remembering. I remember why I remember. It's not about my friends. It's not about my husband. They're all gone. All gone. Every time I think of any of them, it hurts. There's the deep feeling of having found the other half of my soul. Such a human feeling. Such a profound feeling.

There are my friends. Leanne would tell me what to think. Antoinette would understand. Trina would cheer me up. Janet would give me a daisy. Those daisies used to be the brightest and best thing about life on this planet. Full of joy. Now they make me remember.

Oh God, why did I tell myself my memory would keep me alive? Why did I hurt myself so very much?

The woman's slow voice was counting again.

One, two, three, four, five, six, seven, eight, nine, ten, eleven, twelve, thirteen, fourteen, fifteen, sixteen, seventeen, eighteen, nineteen, twenty, twenty-one, twenty-two, twenty-three, twenty-four, twenty-five, twenty-six, twenty-seven, twenty-eight, twenty-nine, thirty, thirty-one, thirty-two, thirty-three, thirty-four, thirty-five, thirty-six, thirty-seven, thirty-eight, thirty-nine, forty, forty-one, forty-two, fifty-three, forty-four, forty-five.

I don't belong here. I never belonged here. I know this. I remember this.

The women's slow voice was counting, shadowed by brighter, louder sounds made by the nurse and one of the cleaning staff.

One, two, three, four, five, six, seven…

"No-one. No family. No friends. We think she outlived them all.

She's very old. Oldest patient this year." They listened to her slow voice counting.

eight, nine, ten, eleven, twelve, thirteen, fourteen,

"She never goes past ninety-nine," the nurse volunteers.

"Why ninety-nine?"

"She doesn't always stop at ninety-nine. She just never goes past it."

fifteen, sixteen, seventeen, eighteen, nineteen, twenty, twenty-one, twenty-two, twenty-three, twenty-four, twenty-five, twenty-six, twenty-seven, twenty-eight, twenty-nine

"She's ninety-nine years old, isn't she?"

"Nearly a hundred. We don't know why she counts. She doesn't talk to us. She doesn't recognise us. Sometimes she nearly does. One of her people says that she sees him and notices and he asks her advice. He's her late husband's great-nephew. He inherited her papers, he told me once. He came in to ask her questions and he stayed on and helps her and talks to her twice a week. Without fail. He says that was her gift to the family, was a complete reliability. Also maths. He's a mathematician. He says that when he was a child she taught him 'alien maths'. I never know what to believe. I've seen him talking to her, though. He's imagining the response. She's lost in her own world. We don't know what happened. At least she has family. Just one person. Not a blood relative, but he cares. She doesn't know. She just counts and drifts off and then counts again. She counts all night sometimes."

"Maybe she's just old."

thirty, thirty-one, thirty-two, thirty-three, thirty-four, thirty-five, thirty-six, thirty-seven, thirty-eight, thirty-nine, forty, forty-one, forty-two, forty-three,

"Whatever happened, we don't know. I hate it when she counts, because it proves her brain's there. She's not alert, but she's there. She feels everything. Sees everything. She's been confined to this bed for so long, with us feeding her, cleaning her, changing her catheter…"

forty-four, forty-five, forty-six, forty-seven, forty-eight,

"The TV's on, at least. And there's that nephew."

"There's that," the nurse said, her tone unconvinced.

forty-nine, fifty, fifty-one, fifty-two, fifty-three, fifty-four, fifty-five, fifty-six, fifty-seven, fifty-eight, fifty-nine, sixty, sixty-one, sixty-two, sixty-three, sixty-four, sixty-five, sixty-six, sixty-seven, sixty-eight, sixty-nine, seventy, seventy-one, seventy-two, seventy-three, seventy-four, seventy-five, seventy-six, seventy-seven, seventy-eight, seventy-nine, eighty, eighty-one, eighty-two, eighty-three, eighty-four, eighty-five, eighty-six, eighty-seven, eighty-eight, eighty-nine, ninety, ninety-one, ninety-two, ninety-three, ninety-four, ninety-five, ninety-six, ninety-seven, ninety-eight, ninety-nine

This is the way the world ends. Whether it's the world of humans or the world of an individual human, it will end. With numbers.

One, two, three, four, five, six, seven, eight, nine, ten, eleven, twelve, thirteen, fourteen, fifteen, sixteen, seventeen, eighteen, nineteen, twenty, twenty-one, twenty-two, twenty-three, twenty-four, twenty-five, twenty-six, twenty-seven, twenty-eight, twenty-nine, thirty, thirty-one, thirty-two, thirty-three, thirty-four, thirty-five, thirty-six, thirty-seven, thirty-eight, thirty-nine, forty, forty-one, forty-two, fifty-three, forty-four, forty-five, forty-six, forty-seven, forty-eight, forty-nine, fifty, fifty-one, fifty-two, fifty-three, fifty-four, fifty-five, fifty-six, fifty-seven, fifty-eight, fifty-nine, sixty, sixty-one, sixty-two, sixty-three, sixty-four, sixty-five, sixty-six, sixty-seven, sixty-eight, sixty-nine, seventy, seventy-one, seventy-two, seventy-three, seventy-four, seventy-five, seventy-six, seventy-seven, seventy-eight, seventy-nine, eighty, eighty-one, eighty-two, eighty-three, eighty-four, eighty-five, eighty-six, eighty-seven, eighty-eight, eighty-nine, ninety, ninety-one, ninety-two, ninety-three, ninety-four, ninety-five, ninety-six, ninety-seven, ninety-eight, ninety-nine, one hundred.

Time's up.

The end.

Acknowledgements

Normally my acknowledgements reflect the intellectual trail I followed to write the novel and the people I asked for help. This novel didn't follow the usual trajectory and so this page is different. The novel itself was going to be written in any case, but without 2016 it would have been much funnier and much brighter. I am so very grateful to all the people at IFWG Publishing Australia for understanding what I'm doing in this novel, and for wanting to share it with the world.

I wrote *The Year of the Fruitcake* in one of the worst years in my life. The hospital research was done over twenty days. When I could get out of bed and walk to the window, home was in sight, but I wasn't always able to get out of bed...

The big book event for one of my novels was cancelled and the bookshop was near the hospital. Nurses dropped in on me to tell me "The picture of you in the window has 'Cancelled' stuck across your face." This was the first time in my life that my face has been cancelled. It was also probably the only time in my life that the cancellation of my face has made a good lunch trip for cardiac nurses.

The first question someone asked me when I woke up after the operation was "Why can't I buy your novel yet?" I've wondered since then if anaesthesia is supposed to give special knowledge.

Those twenty days changed my year and led to more and more fractious time. It was the fractiousness of that time that led to this novel taking the path it did.

Some people deserve my special thanks: my mother and the close friends who got me through the impossible. Jasmine for helping me sort some of the critical (non-hospital) aspects of the novel. Those (including Jean Weber, Jason Franks and the ACT Writers' Centre) who realised that the university had let me down exceptionally badly and made sure I had sufficient paid work to buy food and so forth during convalescence. Everyone else I'll thank when I see you, and buy you a drink, for my resolution since 2016 has been to defiantly avoid the end of the world.